Back to
Blueberry Pond

Carla Trueheart

World Castle Publishing, LLC
Pensacola, Florida
Copyright © Carla Trueheart 2017
Paperback ISBN: 9781629896632
eBook ISBN: 9781629896649
First Edition World Castle Publishing, LLC, April 10, 2017
http://www.worldcastlepublishing.com

Cover: Karen Fuller
Editor: Maxine Bringenberg

~ Dedications ~

This book is dedicated to my mom, who always reads my stories, to my family for supporting my writing over the years, to World Castle Publishing for giving me my first opportunity in the publishing world,
to Aunt Anne for giving me my first writing lessons at Gotham as a Christmas present,
to all my writing teachers and classmates for their help and patience,
and to my readers. Without you, I could not do what I enjoy the most ~ writing.

Thank you!

Prologue

Blueberry Pond, June 1988

Vanessa Lawrence knelt on the grassy edge of Blueberry Pond, waiting, as she always did in the late evening, for her neighbors Kyle and Brandon to finish up their dinners and meet up with her. It was the last day of eleventh grade, a dazzling early summer night, and the silvery moon and stars reflected off the still blue water of the pond. A light, warm breeze blew through the evergreens behind her, scenting the air with fresh earth and pine. She reached out, dipped five fingers into the cool depths of the pond, and let the starlight scatter, amused with the blurry alteration of the surface.

Blueberry Pond was not a magical place, but Vanessa always thought of it that way. The pond held something even better than magic: the memories of her childhood, ice skating in the winter, and chasing fireflies in the summer. It held the sweetness of her first kiss with Kyle and the intensity of the many talks they'd had there. It held all the details of her three-way friendship with Kyle and Brandon, their hushed discussions of high school crushes, their private conversations about life and love and the future. It held all the sleeping dreams of yesterday and the alluring promises of tomorrow.

5

The pond was a neighborhood hangout, set back off the street, accessible enough for the neighborhood kids to play there during the day but secluded enough for the teenagers to hang out there at night. The water was never murky but blueberry blue, and only in the late summer did any greenery clutter the surface. The rear banks were surrounded by a thin wooded area that Vanessa could navigate with little difficulty.

She sat back on the grass and dried her wet hand down the side of her jeans. The trees behind the pond rustled, followed by the low murmur of male voices. Kyle and Brandon were always together when they came to Blueberry Pond or hung out in the neighborhood, but at school, they pretended not to know each other. They were different entities in high school, sparks in different directions, but at the pond, they had everything in common. They shared every secret at Blueberry Pond, talking for hours with Vanessa, until their mothers' panicked calls rang through the neighborhood at nearly eleven o'clock.

Kyle and Brandon greeted Vanessa with the traditional "What's up?" before dropping down beside her, sandwiching her as they always did. She anticipated the nostalgic end-of-the-school-year talk, the highlights of their junior year: Remember when Brandon drove his new car to school? Remember when Kyle skipped three gym classes and got detention for a week? Remember when Vanessa colored her hair and it turned orange? Remember this, remember that…they had this talk every year. But tonight, leaving junior year behind and going into their last summer before senior year, it had a different, colder feeling. These were no longer lighthearted memories edging their way into new beginnings. This was the last year. The last time.

Kyle tossed a pebble across the pond, and it nearly made it to the other side before gravity took it and dragged it downward. A tiny splash sent ripples through the water, and Kyle watched

6

them until the water stilled. "What do you want, more than anything in the world?" he asked, not specifically addressing Vanessa or Brandon, but leaving the question open for anyone.

"To build big houses," Brandon said, stretching out his arms to demonstrate size and mass. "To design an entire neighborhood, cut right through the woods, built right into the landscape."

"For my mother to get off my case," Vanessa said with a massive eye roll heavenward. She gazed at the silhouette of her ranch-style house, far in the distance. Her parents were recently divorced and her mother had full custody of her and her younger sister, Morgan. Her mother worked long hours to keep up with the bills, so Vanessa got stuck with all the housework and babysitting. "And to not have to watch Morgan all the time."

"I mean in the future," Kyle clarified. "I mean, we sit here all the time and talk about when we were kids, and school stuff, and how much our families suck, but we never talk about what we really want in the future."

Vanessa shrugged. Kyle tended to ask these deep questions, always tried to figure out what made people the way they were, what they longed for that they weren't getting. She was sure he was going to be a psychiatrist or some kind of therapist someday...somebody who helped others search their own souls for answers.

"Vanessa wants Ronald Crane," Brandon said, and laughed.

"No, she doesn't," Kyle replied, and hurled another pebble over the water. This time the pebble made it all the way across the pond.

"I don't know if it's your business who I want or don't want," Vanessa told him. "We're not together right now."

"We'll get back together," Kyle said. "We always do."

Vanessa and Kyle had an on-again, off-again relationship, and even though they were off right now, Vanessa knew the feelings were still there and always would be, fueled by the memories of first kisses and first touches. Vanessa frequently thought about that first touch, sitting at a picnic table in her backyard, just after a neighborhood picnic, when Kyle first slid his hand into hers. His hand was clammy and the clasp was awkward, but it was a moment she would never forget. That was five years ago, and now, at sixteen, their touches were a bit more risky.

"You didn't answer my question," Kyle said and nudged Vanessa's elbow.

"I guess what I want more than anything in the world is to be successful," she replied. "To work in fashion and to design dresses with zebra stripes and big bold colors—all of them with matching hats and handbags."

"That's what I want to do, too," Kyle said. They all laughed until Kyle fell silent. "Really," he said. "What I want is for this moment to last forever. For no time to pass, to just sit here at the pond and not have to worry about school or jobs or any shit like that."

"You need a job to survive," Brandon told him. "If you don't work you'll end up a poor, broke loser. If you don't go to college, you'll end up tossing salt onto french fries and wrapping hamburgers up in paper."

"So you're saying that everyone who doesn't go to college ends up working in the food industry?"

"Ronald Crane's brother works the grill at McDonalds," Vanessa said. "He says it's not that bad." She leaned back on her elbows. The last few kids in the neighborhood were heading home in noisy conversation, and in the distance doors slammed and dogs barked until the silence of night closed in around the pond. The scent of tomato sauce and garlic drifted from the house that neighbored Blueberry Pond, but even that scent was fading as night edged on.

8

The ownership of Blueberry Pond had always been a mystery to Vanessa. She didn't think it belonged to the neighboring house, a tiny white cape, although it seemed likely that if anybody owned the pond, it would be the occupants of the cape. That house was the closest, and *someone* in the neighborhood had to own the pond. It was just strange to her that all the kids used it as a neighborhood hangout, and no one ever complained or told them to get out.

The couple who owned the cape beside the pond were older and rarely came outside. Sometimes, when Vanessa was at the pond in the daytime, she would see the gray-haired man in a rocking chair in the enclosed back sunporch, sipping lemonade, his wrinkled fingers wrapped around a pencil as he figured out a crossword puzzle. The couple kept to themselves, didn't appear to have any children or grandchildren, and never hollered at anyone for trespassing on their property. Either they were too old to notice a disturbance, didn't care, or perhaps even they didn't know who truly owned Blueberry Pond.

"Even if you did end up working in the food industry, that wouldn't automatically make you a loser," Kyle said.

"Uh, yeah, it would," Brandon replied. "Do you have any idea what those people get paid? Even in managerial positions?"

"Why does everything have to be about money with you?" Kyle returned. "There are so many things more important than money."

Vanessa sat up, positioning her body as a human wall between Kyle and Brandon. They sometimes fought like this, and this topic had all the makings of a huge argument. "Let's say that to be successful, you do what you love to do," she said. "Whether it's the food industry, or as an architect, or working in fashion. Let's just forget about all that and agree that we're all good friends. Let's agree to stay in this moment until we're

9

forced out of it. Until we graduate and we go our separate ways. We have one more year, and after that...."

"The talks at the pond are over," Kyle finished. He slid his hand beneath his gray jean jacket and pulled out a can of beer. "Everything we've ever said and done here will just be some stupid memory. Maybe that doesn't matter to you two, going off to college next year, but for me, it may be all I have to hang on to." He pulled the tab off the beer, took a long sip, and tried to pass it to Brandon, who refused with a wave of his hand.

"Of course it will just be a memory," Brandon said. "But that doesn't mean we won't always be friends. It doesn't make the talks less important. I would never have dated Gillian if not for you two telling me to ask her out, and Vanessa never would have gotten through her parents' divorce if we both didn't help her through those nights when she was crying."

"Can't we just talk about our junior year?" Vanessa said. She didn't want to revisit the memories of her parents' divorce. Not here. Not now. Not ever. "Can't we just do what we always do and look back at the year and laugh at all of it?"

"What the hell was so funny about any of it?" Kyle said. He chugged the last of his beer and tossed the can over his shoulder. Vanessa never let him throw garbage into the pond. It was a firm rule of hers. "We all know this is going to be a memory someday, but I think it should be something more. To me, it's always been something more." He stood up and paced. "You guys don't know this, but our talks at the pond — that's what I cherish most. It's the only thing that got me through the nights of my father falling down drunk, and the days of teachers bitching at me. I know I totally look like an asshole for saying what I feel, but I guess you guys should be used to that."

"Calm down," Vanessa said, glancing at Brandon. They never really knew what to do when Kyle went off like this, and

10

it was often.

"What do you guys cherish most?" Kyle asked. "What's the one thing you have that you could never live without?"

"Here we go with another one of his crazy questions," Brandon mumbled.

It was moments like these that Vanessa found herself wanting Kyle again, craving his arms around her, longing for his kiss. He was dark and insistent, and through his strange questions and long talks, he had pulled every hidden emotion out of her. When those emotions were at the surface, she could easily inspect them and solve her problems. A talk with Kyle was a remedy to whatever was bothering her at the time, like a session with a psychiatrist who had peculiar ways of getting at the truth.

But this weirdness and darkness was also what kept her away from him. He overdid it like nobody else she knew, even the messed-up group of kids at school who listened to punk rock music and colored their hair fifteen different shades of green. He always had beer or some kind of alcohol on him, had experimented with drugs, and had even been so messed up one night that he sat on her doorstep crying and threatening to hang himself if she didn't come out and talk to him. Recalling that night alone made her shrink away from him, even in the moments she longed to be closer.

"I guess what I cherish most is my diary," she said. "I couldn't live without it. Everything I wrote during the divorce is in there, all the nights my parents closed the bedroom door and I heard them calling each other totally bad stuff until my father finally left. Plus everything that happened with…you and me." She turned away from Kyle. "I don't know what I would do if I couldn't get everything out on those pages."

"How about you, Brandon?" Kyle asked. "What expensive item that Mommy and Daddy bought for you can't you live

11

without?"

"My car," he replied and shrugged.

"That's stupid, and not sentimental." He stopped pacing and dropped down, grasping his head in his hands. "I say I can't live without you two, and you both tell me you can't live without stupid, inanimate objects?"

"My feelings are not stupid!" Vanessa said.

"And how would I get either of you around town without a car?" Brandon added.

They bickered about this for a while, about what was really important in life, what friendship meant, and what they all meant to each other, until finally, porch lights clicked off all around them. Crickets chirped a late night song, and the moon hovered over the pond like a massive glowing balloon, sending a silver sheen over the banks. The night was a warm and humid precursor of the season ahead, foreshadowing many summer nights to come at the pond, many more long talks. But there was something in the budding summer air, some inexplicable and unspoken knowledge that this night, the last night of junior year, was somehow the most important.

"So you say that material stuff doesn't matter as much as our friendship," Kyle said, pacing again. He picked up the empty beer can, tilted it to get the few last drops, then tossed it to the ground. "Let's say we prove that."

"How?" Brandon asked. "I mean, whatever crazy idea is in your head is fine with me. Whatever it takes to get you to shut up and understand that Vanessa and I like the talks as much as you do. Whatever it takes to prove to you that we're your friends."

"Forever," Vanessa added.

"Okay," Kyle said. He sat down beside Vanessa. "Let's say then that we each take that one item that means so much to us, that one thing that we could never be without, and as a friendship

12

pact, as a tribute to these nights at the pond, we put them in a box and bury them. Right here."

Vanessa turned to Brandon. They were the reasonable ones, the ones who usually talked Kyle out of these crazy ideas. But tonight, whatever magic was at the pond, whatever sense of nostalgia remained there, seemed to make Kyle's request shine with an assuring brilliance. It was a way to keep them connected, to leave behind a piece of them, right at the pond, right in the exact place the memories had been born.

"It won't be like a time capsule or anything like that," Kyle went on. "Those you dig up again or let someone else dig them up years after you're gone. This box…it won't ever be found. It's like a forever secret. A hidden grave."

"I'm in," Vanessa said. "I'll totally put my diary in the friendship box. I'll just start a new one." It wasn't like she wouldn't know where the diary was. And besides, wasn't there a certain relief in letting go of the past and getting rid of the diary? Wasn't she cutting the last string that attached her to both the awful slices of time that made up her parents' divorce, and her pain when she'd broken up with Kyle a hundred times?

"I can't put my car into a box," Brandon said. "It's not small like a diary."

"As usual, your superior intelligence has beat me out," Kyle said, and rolled his eyes. "Put something just as valuable in there. How much is your car worth?"

"Ten grand, at least," Brandon replied, then went deep into thought, scratching his head. "We got this computer thing that might be worth a lot."

"Something small," Kyle said, and stood. "Meet me back here in ten minutes, and everyone bring their item. I'll get a box and a shovel."

***

When Vanessa returned to Blueberry Pond ten minutes later, Kyle and Brandon were both standing in moonlit ferns at a distance from the banks of the pond. She was out of breath from running to her house, then through her room and back to the pond. In her hand, she held her cherished diary, a small magenta book with a gold lock that had been busted over a year ago after she'd lost the key somewhere in Florida on spring vacation. She always worried that someone would read the diary, but burying the book would forever ease her mind. It was, as Kyle had said, like she was putting it into a hidden grave.

"Beneath the tallest pine tree?" Kyle asked, holding a shovel in one hand and a flashlight in the other.

"Wait a minute," she said. "What are you putting in the box?"

"Actually, it's not a box," Kyle replied. He bent down to grab something. "I was thinking a box would deteriorate and wouldn't be safe. So I found this." He held up an old yellow Tupperware bowl with a grooved, star-like cover. "My mother only uses it to bring baked stuff to church. Besides, there's nothing stronger than Tupperware, right?"

Vanessa laughed, but Brandon did not join her as he usually did. He stood separate from Vanessa and Kyle, his frame caught between the silver moonlight and the yellow back porch lights streaming from the cape that neighbored the pond. With his thin and wispy light hair illuminated from all sides, he looked almost angelic. Vanessa watched for a few moments, a nagging fear ballooning in her belly. Maybe it wasn't the best idea to part with their personal items. Maybe Brandon was thinking the same thing.

"I'm still waiting to find out what you both decided to put in the friendship box," she said finally. "Or I guess I mean the friendship *bowl*." She turned to Brandon first, hoping he would speak up.

14

Before Brandon could reply, if he was even going to, Kyle grabbed Vanessa's elbow and steered her toward the tallest pine tree, where they'd shared their first kiss. He hollered to Brandon that they'd be right back, though Brandon didn't seem to be listening. He just stared over the pond, his eyes blank and unfocussed.

"Is he okay?" Vanessa whispered when they were safely concealed under the lowest boughs of the pine tree.

"His parents gave him a gold watch for eighth grade graduation," Kyle whispered back. "It's really expensive, has diamonds and stuff on it. He only wore it once to a funeral or something, but he decided it was worth enough to put in the Tupperware bowl."

Vanessa clutched her diary to her chest and spun to look back at Brandon.

"He'll be okay," Kyle said, and reached out to touch her arm.

"I hope so." She turned away from Brandon and let her gaze fall on Kyle. His dark hair was feathery and combed back behind his ears. The longer strands fell to his shoulders, just brushing the fabric of his jean jacket. "Why are you touching my arm?"

"Because in the moments when we're not together as a couple, I'm completely lost and need to know you're still there." He squeezed her arm. "That you're still touchable."

"Cut it out," she said. "We're not getting back together."

He moved closer and rested his forehead to hers. "I always told you that I would drop the world for you if you only said the word."

"I know." He told her this all the time, so much that she was sure it was even written in her diary. They were together even when they weren't together, even when she knew to stay away. "You just make everything so difficult."

"True loves are the difficult loves," he said. "The ones that

15

come too easy never last."

"One of these days you'll make sense to me." She allowed him to brush his lips against her cheek and then stepped back, still clutching her diary to her chest. The thing seemed so vulnerable there, with Kyle's hand resting on her arm, just inches away from the contents. "I have your word that you won't go dig up the bowl and read my diary, right? That you won't read all the private stuff I wrote about you?"

"Why would I need to read it when I lived it?"

Vanessa almost corrected him but stopped herself. The truth was, there was more in her diary than he knew about, things that were only in the deepest depths of her heart and the steamiest recesses of her mind. Inside were the full details of every kiss beneath the pine tree, every touch in her bedroom, and every thought she'd had about someday going all the way with him. Her first time had to be with Kyle, in the woods, just behind Blueberry Pond. It had to be with him, nobody else. Only then would her first time have any true meaning.

"So what are you putting in the bowl?" she asked.

He pulled his hand away from her arm, dug into the pocket of his jeans, and opened his palm. Something small and silvery glowed in the moonlight.

"It's a magic cross," he said. "A family heirloom, sorta."

She slid her finger over the little silver cross in his hand. "Why is it magic?"

"Because it's pulled all the men in my family out of the muck," he said. "You know better than anyone that I come from a long line of drunks and total losers. This cross was supposedly passed down from each father to son and saved everyone just before they hit the rock at the bottom of the pit. Just before they drank themselves into nothingness and called it quits on life."

"It sounds important." She hesitated again, closing her eyes

16

as if the comforting darkness could pull her away from the seriousness of the friendship pact, or help her think of something just as important and memorable to secure in place of their items. "How about we just put our favorite tapes in the bowl? Like I could put Madonna, and you could put Journey, and Brandon could put U2?"

Kyle shook his head, just as she knew he would. Gently, he pressed his hand against her diary. "It has to be these things," he said. "And it means even more to me that our past together will be in the bowl."

"Forever buried," she whispered.

"But always there," he replied.

Ten minutes later, Vanessa watched Kyle dig a deep hole beneath the boughs of the tallest pine tree at Blueberry Pond. He knelt in front of the pile of dark dirt and bowed his head, praying over their sacrificial burial. He was silent for a few moments, then stood and took a breath.

"And so we stay here forever, at the pond," he said with a dramatic air, pulling the cover off the Tupperware bowl. "At Blueberry Pond, where we had first kisses and long talks and even shed some tears. Where we drank beer and laughed and smoked."

"Where we had dreams and looked ahead," Vanessa added.

"Where we decided that despite our differences, we would always be neighbors and friends," Brandon said.

"Always friends," Kyle echoed.

Vanessa laughed at the over-the-top words, and Kyle and Brandon joined in. There was a sort of lunacy in their friendship pact, in the permanent loss of their most valued possessions. There was nothing else to do but laugh, because it was too serious not to.

Vanessa kissed her diary and dropped it into the bowl.

17

Brandon held up the gold watch and carefully laid it into the bowl beside her diary. The watch was stunning, the face circled with round diamonds that glowed blue in the moonlight. Kyle rested his silver cross on top, bowed his head in another silent prayer, and sealed the bowl. He tucked the bowl into the dirt at the bottom of the deep hole and picked up the shovel.

"We never speak of this again," he said, and tossed on the first shovelful of dirt. "Not this summer, not senior year, not at graduation or after."

Vanessa wiped a tear. Brandon rubbed his forehead.

"And no matter what," Kyle said, "we will never dig this stuff up again."

CHAPTER ONE

23 Years Later

Kyle Macord stumbled into his apartment, knocked into the open closet door, and vomited inside the closet, directly into a pair of old sneakers. He ran his fingers through his hair and sank onto the rug, curling his body up like a defeated slug. He wasn't exactly sobbing, but tears caught in his eyes, and his throat swelled and burned with residual alcohol, vomit, and a fair amount of snot. Before him, Ava's red high-heels rushed over the beige rug, streaks and blurs through his vision. With colossal effort, he lifted his head to witness her laboring beneath the weight of two bulging red duffel bags. The red shoes stopped at the door.

"No," he mumbled. "No, no, no."

"I can't do it anymore."

"I'll go to those meetings." He shifted his weight back and forth like a knocked-down sailor on deck until he was in a full sitting position, staring up at Ava's scoop of blonde hair and one of her quirky hats, the gray one with the shiny gold buckle. He entertained the thought that perhaps he was slightly tilted to the left. Or maybe the gray hat was. Or maybe Ava was. "I'll tell them my name and admit I have a problem and say their prayer, and it'll all be good again. I swear it will."

"It's too late," Ava said back. "You didn't come back to the apartment again last night, and now today after work. I just can't do it anymore."

"I'm sorry," he said. "I had a horrible day at work yesterday, and —"

"It's always a bad day, Kyle," she said. "Always some reason why you go to the bar and come home throwing up and crying."

"What do you need from me?" he asked. "What will make this better for you?" His best strategy, as far back as he could remember, was to turn the conversation onto other people, get the focus off himself and his problems and ramblings. It was always best to know what other people were feeling, anyhow. He needed to know what was going on inside of someone else's head in order to release what was going on inside his own, match deep thought for deep thought.

"Kyle, I love you," she said in a voice that suggested otherwise. "But it's over." Red shoes gone. Door slammed hard enough to bust his skull from reverb.

He slumped back onto the floor after that, his cheek pressed right against the rough, matted rug. The apartment was suffocatingly hot, and as the humid air enclosed him, sticking to his already damp skin, he retched and pressed an arm to his stomach. Nobody was there to pick him up this time. Nobody was there to pull him to his knees, shake him and clean him up. Had he really expected that Ava's sole purpose in life was to shake him and clean him up every time he did this?

With a faint moan he stood up, tested the strength of his legs, and carried himself to the kitchen. He picked up a mug of coffee in the sink, tilted it into his mouth, and swallowed what was left from that morning. Despite the heat in the apartment, the coffee was cold. It tasted stale and sour and he retched again. He dragged himself to the cabinet, pulled down a bottle of aspirin, and ate three pills.

For a while he sat on the couch, staring ahead at the blankness of the wall. He was thirty-nine, no children, and now no girlfriend. Life was half over and he'd failed. It didn't come as much of a surprise to him that he'd failed; what came as a surprise was that he'd failed so quickly. Just ten years ago, he wasn't exactly successful, but had high hopes. He had hopes that he'd settle down with a wonderful woman, hopes that he'd succeed in life, hopes that he'd stop craving the warmth and comfort of a steady stream of alcohol when difficulties piled onto one another like horrific car crashes.

Last week he'd nearly lost his job at the Volkswagen dealership when he came in drunk and almost sold some poor old woman the wrong car, a car that hadn't even been for sale and was on the lot for repairs. It was mistakes like these that put his job as a car salesman in jeopardy, and his boss, for whatever reason, took pity on him each time and overlooked it. But one more mistake and that would be it. One more mistake and he'd be jobless.

There was always AA, but considering that would seal his label of failure. Stepping into an AA meeting, surrounded by stares of pity from strangers and engulfed in the stench of stale coffee, would be like admitting he couldn't do this himself, that he was weak. He needed to be his own second chance, his own positive whirling wind, his own fresh start. *Pick yourself up*, he thought. But he didn't believe his own pep talks anymore.

Ava walking into his life, the sister of one of his customers at the Volkswagen dealership, had been a blessing. He'd lost so many women over the years for one ridiculous reason or the other, because they wanted different things or were in different places. Or he was drinking too much and would pull away from a commitment, only to cling to a bottle of whiskey because it was easier. But with Ava, he'd felt something he hadn't felt in a while. She was the type of woman who would lift him up when he fell. The type of woman with a gold heart and a steel resolve.

Over the years, he'd perfected what he wanted in a woman. It was easy for him to pick her out, and if a million women were lined up in front of him, he would know exactly which one was his match. He'd always gone for the same type…a bubbly blonde with a true heart but a fiery spirit. His first love, when he was eleven years old and all through his high school years, was this kind of girl. He even wondered if every woman after Vanessa Lawrence had to live up to his memory of her.

He'd lost touch with Vanessa after high school when she'd gone to college in New York. He remembered that she wanted to be a fashion designer, but more than that, he remembered how much he'd loved her. He remembered how she looked, every fine detail of her face, how her curly lemon-blonde hair bounced when she ran. He remembered the taste of strawberry on her lips when they kissed beneath a pine tree in his old neighborhood. He also remembered that she was the first girl who saw him for what he truly was, and had constantly moved away from him because she knew better.

He stood from the couch and made his way to the bedroom, hoping some merciful angel would take pity on him and help him die in his sleep because he was too much of a coward to do the deed himself. He'd considered it, too many times to count, and enough times that he probably should have consulted a professional for help. He thought about what he'd do to end it all…one spectacular gunshot or an attractive display of bridge diving, something quick and dramatic, just as his life had been. But whenever he thought about the blood or the pain, he changed his mind before the next morbid detail fully formed.

He dropped down on the unmade bed, hung his head, and

said a silent prayer for Ava's safety. A prayer that she would have a good future without him. A prayer that God would lift him into the brighter horizon of the earth again. But he didn't feel like anyone heard him. He felt like God had left him a long time ago, but he never once believed God wasn't real. The belief he had stemmed from one simple thing his mother had said when he was a little boy: "Life is proof of God." That was all it took for him, as small as he was at the time, to believe in something so big and so invisible. Or maybe it was the strength in his mother's voice when she'd uttered the words by his bedside that night. She believed in God, with every ounce of her being, and Kyle knew if she believed with that much intensity and passion, God had to be real.

The full-body sting returned as he thought over his lost loves, Ava now among them. How many great women had he lost? Not enough for record books, but enough that he probably should have learned a lesson a long time ago. With another deep pain in his stomach, he clutched his hair in one hand and rested back in the bed. There was no one left to call, no one to turn to. He couldn't burden his mother with this, and his father had passed away three years ago. He had no brothers or sisters. His coworkers were just that, only people he worked with. He had nobody close at the car dealership. They were all tuned in to his status as the loser alcoholic on the job.

As sick as he was from stopping at the bar after work, he still craved another drink. Something to wash the sickness down his throat. A cure-all and mind-number. A dose of heaven in a glass. But what he really craved, more than anything else, was to go back to when life was on the cusp of greatness. When hope reigned. He wanted to step into a luminescent time machine, carry himself back through his thirties, and start the whole decade over again.

But that, he knew, was impossible.

CHAPTER TWO

Brandon Ballas slipped into bed beside his wife Jean. She smelled good tonight, as she always did, like flower petals steeped in a fruity concoction. That scent, coupled with her soft auburn hair and bright turquoise eyes, was what had first drawn him to her in college. Since then, they'd been inseparable. Jean had understood where he was going and seemed to know how to help him get there. She was a guiding light in a life he'd already planned out, and she escorted him in a direction they had in common: fall in love with your soul mate, get married, become successful and wealthy in steady careers, and make a family. Until that afternoon, that dream was their reality. They lived it like it was a daily routine: wake up, live the life of your dreams, go to sleep at night.

Usually Jean was reading a book in bed, something fictional and intelligent. But tonight, her focus was on Brandon, and she rolled into him, pushing back his thinning blond hair.

"Another project will come up soon," she said. "This is just a temporary setback."

"Nobody buys houses in a bad economy," he replied. "And if nobody is buying or building, nobody needs me to design houses."

"You're a good architect," she said. "Just because it's slow now doesn't mean you have to throw in the towel with Ballas and Monroe."

Ballas & Monroe was the architecture business Brandon had set up with his buddy Ferris Monroe from college, just after graduation. Throughout their college years they'd saved money doing odd jobs, then taken out loans with wealthy family members and scraped together enough to procure an office. They'd hired draftsmen, secured some projects, and built houses over the last fifteen years. The company had done so well that when Jean announced she was pregnant with their first child, Brandon told her she could quit her teaching job. She loved the job, but she loved being a mother more. They'd been well-off enough to live that lifestyle.

"I could go back to work," she said. "Logan and Andrew are old enough now."

Brandon shook his head. "Not yet," he said. "We still have some savings left, and that will get us through until it picks up or I find a job with another company. I owned my own business… I'm sure I can get my foot in the door with that, even if it's not exactly what I want to do for now."

"We have plenty of things we could sell, too."

Now she was treading in dangerous water, and Brandon pulled away from her. He loved her more than he loved himself, but talk of selling any of their expensive things sent a pulse of blood to his forehead.

"Just a minute ago, you were telling me not to throw in the towel," he said. "Now you practically have one foot in the poor house."

"I'm just being realistic." She pulled the covers up to their necks. "I don't want you to give up, but if you have to, I'm saying we have so much here we don't need: crystal chandeliers and extra couches, guitars that Logan never even plays, jewelry I never wear."

"You sell your jewelry and I'll never speak to you again."

Jean tapped her finger on his nose. "I find that hard to believe."

"It's a firm threat," he said, and laughed with her.

She snuggled close to him, and he was just about to press his lips to hers when a knock came at their bedroom door. He dropped his face into her hair and sighed.

"Mommy?" came Andrew's little voice. "Daddy?"

"Don't they ever sleep?" he said.

Andrew was eight years old, their youngest. He was a quiet boy, always had a book in his hand, and did well academically. But in parent-teacher meetings, his teachers always mentioned a problem with making friends, and on one occasion, Brandon and Jean had been called in when Andrew fled a group project about dinosaurs and hid in the bathroom. Brandon never knew quite what to do to help him with his bouts of separation anxiety and shyness. Andrew's eleven-year-old brother, Logan, was just the opposite. He hadn't really needed a thing. Brandon found it difficult to show Logan the love he needed when his younger brother seemed to require so much more. It was a difficult balance, and he hoped he was doing a good job as their father.

"Come on in," he said as the door creaked open.

"What's the matter, honey?" Jean asked him.

"Logan says we're going to lose our house and live with the bums. Is he right?"

Brandon never hit either of his boys, but he was angry with Logan for this. He choked on an accurate response until Jean took over.

"Oh, honey," Jean said, and scurried out of bed. "Logan is not being truthful with you." Brandon watched as she scooped Andrew up and carried him out of their room, back into his own room to settle him back in. His chest tightened in a way it never

26

had before, a massive crunch of fear tensing through him. He'd been well-off his entire life, from childhood to now at nearly middle age. His parents had always given him whatever he asked for, to the point where he knew he'd been the spoiled child people often went off about, strangers and family alike. When he was young, he had the nicest bicycle of all the kids on the street, the grandest house in the neighborhood, and was the first one in high school to drive in with a brand new car.

With this showering of expensive items throughout his childhood and adolescence, and graduating college so successfully before going on with an even greater business achievement, he hadn't had time to take a microscope to the one fear he'd always had, the fear that popped up every few years or so that he beat back down because it could never possibly happen. His greatest fear that one day, he'd be poor.

Jean was reassuring, but she didn't know the full truth. The business had been suffering for a few years now, since spring of 2009 to be exact, and Ballas & Monroe was barely keeping afloat. Projects came in less and less, even when they'd tried a disastrous dive into the world of mechanical architecture and hired an engineer. Brandon was most passionate about designing houses, and unless he was doing that, something felt wrong. Since the debacle with the engineer, he felt they were stretching to achieve a goal he wasn't even familiar with.

He sank his head back into the pillow, imagining some awful scene that hadn't even played out yet; Jean wearing a ragged blue sweater from a second-hand store, Logan crying over a broken bike that Brandon couldn't afford to fix, Andrew needing medical care but the family lacking any medical coverage. To spare Jean the internal stress and worry, he'd lied to her about the savings account, or at least made it seem like the savings was still intact, as they'd left it over the years: no less than twelve-thousand dollars, the equivalent of six months mortgage just in case the unthinkable happened. And though Brandon had left the unthinkable as just that over the years, now it was on top of him like a suffocating monster, and all he could do was stare it in the eyes.

He'd sank the bulk of the savings account into Ballas & Monroe for the sole purpose of keeping the last draftsman from being laid off. The guy, a man in his early thirties, had a two-year-old at home and needed the money. He needed the job. Brandon had pulled chunk by chunk out of the savings and used it to keep a regular paycheck going for his only employee. But he was scraping the bottom of the account now, and soon he'd be forced to go ahead with the layoff. He'd discussed this with Ferris, who didn't quite have the heart he had, and wanted to do a clean sweep from the beginning of the problems, leaving just the two of them on the sinking ship of Ballas & Monroe.

Jean walked back into the room, her designer nightgown silky and white against her porcelain skin. She'd aged well, not nearly as poorly as he'd aged. His hair had always been thin, and little by little it was falling away, exposing the shiny top of his scalp. In a few years he was sure he'd be bald, or worse, suffering from the hair-halo monstrosity some middle-aged men had going on. Poor and bald. Was there anything worse than that combination?

"Where were we?" Jean said, and slipped back into bed.

Never once, in all the years since college, had Brandon turned down love making with Jean. She was beautiful in such a way that he could be in any shape, weak or dying, and he'd still find a way to pull through and satisfy her. But tonight he closed his eyes and let out a faint, sleepy breath of air.

"Falling asleep," he said.

The light went off. Jean entwined her legs with his in the position they always slept in, and in a few moments, her warm sleeping exhales fell over his neck.

He tossed and turned after that, trying not to wake her but finding it unusually uncomfortable in the bed. His mind raced with what-ifs, and he kept playing that same scene of poverty and illness. He kept hearing Andrew's question over and over: "Logan says we're going to lose our house and live with the bums. Is he right?"

Brandon didn't know if Logan was right. Maybe that was why he was so angry with him. Logan had obviously overheard something he shouldn't have, so common with kids, no matter how hard he tried to keep it all behind a wall they would never be able to penetrate. Or maybe kids just picked up these things because they were so attuned to their parents' emotions. Maybe it hadn't taken more than a few poorly disguised words. Or maybe — and his shoulders sunk at the thought — Jean knew more than he thought she did and cried in despair when she thought nobody was listening.

Jean's advice to sell their expensive but unnecessary things wasn't so far off from a firm assurance he'd already given himself. They'd had money for many years. They had nice things. But even so, those things, now considered used or second-hand, would only get them through a few more weeks. There was no choice but to step off the fully submerged bow of Ballas & Monroe, let it sink with dignity, and swim off to find something else, something better, more solid and secure. And he hoped, as one last horror attached itself to his fear of becoming poor, that when all was said and done, they wouldn't lose the house. He'd designed the house himself, gone over every inside and outside detail with Jean. Their dream house. Crystal chandeliers in the front hall. Hardwood floors throughout. A balcony with a telescope. A cozy library. Two extra rooms for the two perfect children they planned to have then, and the dream (as it always had back then) had come true in the form of Logan and Andrew. Two blond little boys who made the house hum with spirit and life and the simple joys of being young and carefree. Now, the house wasn't worth what it had been years ago. Now, he would be lucky to break even with what he owed on it.

With the finality of his decision to close the business for good, his mind unequivocally made up, Brandon entwined his legs with Jean's again. He wrapped his arms around her waist, recalling eleven years ago when her waist had expanded when she was pregnant with Logan. Their first baby inside her belly, growing so fast that she seemed to swell a little more each day, and in this very bed he'd talked to his unborn child. Then, three years later, he'd done the same with Andrew. The three of them were his greatest treasures and the three people he would always live and die for, no matter what. He had to be strong for them. He had to provide for them and make sure they had warmth and food and safety. He had to make sure they had what they needed in life, from the serious business of medical care to the easy pleasures of bubble baths and hamburgers.

He closed his eyes as a tear spilled down his cheek and dripped into Jean's hair, not waking her.

Chapter Three

Vanessa Greene awoke in the middle of the night to a slamming sound somewhere inside the house. Her body shot up in bed and her heart thundered inside her chest. She reached beneath the bed, surprised at how quickly the thought had occurred to her, and felt around in the dark until her palm struck the cold steel of a baseball bat.

She'd heard about jelly legs but had never truly experienced the sensation until now. It was so pronounced and strange she wondered if she would even make it to the hallway. She carried on, lifting the bat with two hands above her head, ready to strike the second she saw movement. Through the faint light streaming from her daughter Emma's Disney princess nightlight, she could just make out a dark silhouette moving up the staircase, coming toward her. The footsteps were light on the stairs, sneaking. She edged closer, pressed her eyes closed, and readied herself to swing the bat against someone's skull.

"Mom, don't!"

The hallway light clicked on. The intruder wasn't a burglar or murderer—the intruder was her sixteen-year-old daughter, May. And Vanessa had almost bashed her head in.

"What the hell are you doing?" Vanessa said. May was fully clothed in a black skirt and lacy blue top. Dark makeup lined her eyes, and her lips were coated in candy apple red lipstick. "It's

31

three in the morning!"

"I—"

"Oh, come on," Vanessa said, and threw the bat to the floor. "Really?"

May didn't bother to make up a story. She didn't even have the decency to act like getting caught sneaking out of the house at night bothered her in the slightest. She just shrugged and started to whistle while walking past Vanessa to her room.

"Wait!" Vanessa said. "I don't even know where to begin."

"Can you begin in the morning, then? Because I'm tired."

"Where were you?"

May let out a huff, like she was already bored with Vanessa's discipline or lack of it, and lazily twirled a strand of dyed-black hair around her finger. "Out with God."

"God?"

"Out with God and Jesus. Praying."

"Go to your room," was all Vanessa could get out. She would have to deal with this in the morning.

"That's where I was going," May said. She disappeared down the end of the hall and slammed her bedroom door closed.

"You'll wake your sis—"

Too late. Vanessa spun as soft footsteps struck the floor behind her. "Mommy?" Emma said.

Vanessa bent down and smoothed Emma's long blonde waves. She picked her up and rested her on her hip, then wiped the yellow sleepies out of her eyes. Emma was ten but slight, and had the innocent heart of a six-year-old. If not for Emma's innocence to offset the atmosphere in the house, Vanessa felt sure she would have ripped out all the hair from her own head long ago, dealing with May's outbursts. Tonight's escapade was just one more rebellion in a long line of things May had done to stick splinters into Vanessa over the past year, since the trouble started with Vanessa's husband — May and Emma's father. Vanessa tried to understand what May was going through. Her separation from her husband was difficult and things were so obviously left up in the air. She wasn't sure where things were going and where and when things would end. The family, as it stood now, was in a never-ending state of turmoil.

"My little girl," she whispered to Emma. "Why are you up?"

"May is making noise again," she said. "She slams stuff all the time."

"I know," Vanessa said, and carried Emma back to her room. "But what did I tell you about teenagers?"

"I forget."

Vanessa laid Emma down on the bed, then pulled her purple bedspread up and tucked it in all around her. "Teenagers are special because they have a lot of different emotions. And sometimes all those emotions come out at the same time and go BOOM!"

Emma laughed. "May goes BOOM! all the time." Her eyes widened when she said "BOOM!"

"So we have to try to be patient with that, even if it happens late at night." She leaned over and kissed Emma's forehead. "Love you, cuckoo bird."

"Cluck cluck," Emma said, and closed her eyes.

Vanessa hadn't had the heart over the years to correct Emma that chickens clucked and cuckoo birds cuckooed. She stepped out of the room and was about to head back to her own bedroom when she decided to confront May rather than wait until the morning. By then, the seriousness of what May had done might have faded from Vanessa's mind, and she wanted that fuel in her veins when she handed out a punishment. May could have been killed or gotten into an accident. And if Vanessa guessed correctly, May was probably out with her long-haired, loser

33

boyfriend.

She didn't bother knocking, acquiescent to the outrage she knew she would receive by barging into May's bedroom. May was already in bed, but wasn't sleeping. She had her cell phone in her hand and was laughing at whatever she was looking at.

"We need to talk," Vanessa said.

"Don't you knock?" May replied, not looking at her. "You just come into somebody's room?"

"I own this house."

"No you don't. Dad owns the house, only he lets you stay here while he sits alone in that stupid little hotel room."

Before Vanessa knew what she was doing, she sped forward and ripped the cell phone out of May's hand. May cursed, but she ignored it.

"No phone," she said, and was going to stash it away but was wearing only a long T-shirt. "You're grounded from your phone."

"I'll use my old phone," May said, and shrugged. "Or I'll have Dad buy me a new one. I want the new iPhone anyhow."

"You're not getting any new phones."

They bickered back and forth, getting nowhere, just going round and round in an endless circle of cursing and yelling. Vanessa's punishments bounced right off May, until the only punishments left that felt fitting involved things that were probably illegal to do to your own kid. But Vanessa had reached the end of what she could tolerate. Every attempt to scold May was met with a laughed response, none of Vanessa's threats rattled her at all, and Vanessa even accepted that May probably hated her. True and real hatred.

"Listen...," she said, and made the mistake of trying to sit on May's bed.

"Get out!" May shouted. "Oh my God! Just get out of here!"

"I'm trying to figure out what to do here," Vanessa told her. "I can't do this with you anymore. I just can't."

"You just live your life and let me live mine."

"That's not the way it works." She stood and planted her hands on her hips. "You're my daughter, and until you're eighteen, I'm responsible for you. I can't have you sneaking out of here at night to...do whatever it is that you're doing with Warren."

May laughed, her usual shrilly, sarcastic laugh. "You think we're having sex?"

Vanessa lifted her hand but caught herself before she smacked May's face. How had that round, beautiful little face become a target?

"You're grounded for a month," Vanessa said. Tears grew in her eyes, burning and speedy like a match touched to kerosene. She had to leave the room before May saw this. "No phone, no going out. And Warren can't come over here."

"We'll just meet up at Dad's hotel room!" May hollered as Vanessa turned the doorknob and left the room.

Vanessa crossed to her bedroom and closed her door. She slammed the back of her head against the door wood and sniffled hard. Life was not just a mess right now, it was a veritable hell. She was in the last phase of a failed marriage, her teenage daughter hated her, and her career was almost nonexistent. And it all seemed to go back to that one decision she'd made two years after college—to sleep with Vincent Greene.

Life had been on the right track, trotting along as she'd planned. No, better than she'd planned. After college, life had gone off into a dizzying spiral of clubbing and literally dancing in the streets. New York City was a twenty-two-year-old's kaleidoscope; dancing and shifting multi-colors, changing patterns and sequences. During that crazy time, she'd met all the right women in the fashion industry and partied with all the right men. Until Vincent came along.

She'd been warned. Vincent Greene would help her get to the top, but he would destroy her life along the way. He was cool and charismatic back in the nineties, with sleek black hair and a dazzling white smile. His clothes were chic and immaculate, not because he was in the fashion industry, but because his family was in the industry. Vincent could not care less about fashion. All he wanted was power and money. But even with his influential family and unimaginable wealth, he couldn't stop fate, and when Vanessa told him she was pregnant with his child, he ran away for a full month before stepping back into her life and offering to marry her.

And that was that. With her focus on raising May (and then the surprise conception of Emma six years later), her career tanked and she ended up with nothing more than a job at Four Seasons Boutique, a clothes and accessories store in the center of town. She wasn't designing clothes — her dream career and what she'd gone to school for — and she wasn't earning enough money to keep herself going and self-sufficient, not while she was married to Vincent, and certainly not after a divorce.

Vincent's family was rich, and the house Vanessa lived in now was, from all outside perspectives, a mansion. But it wasn't Vanessa's. It had never felt like hers, and she'd certainly never contributed to the financial burden of owning such a luxurious home. Vincent had never really loved her enough to let her get comfortable in the house. She was the mother of his children, nothing more, and she wondered if, at thirty-nine, she'd ever even experienced true love. At least she hadn't in her adult years, when she was supposed to know what she was doing and how she was truly feeling.

She strode to her bed, no longer tired despite the late hour, and tossed down May's cell phone while plucking a tissue from a box on the nightstand. She dabbed at her eyes and sat on the bed, thinking over her life and how it had been one mistake after another. But she wouldn't change it or live it over, because at the root was May and Emma. And she loved them more than her own life, despite the problems with May.

At first, May's anger had seemed like normal teenage angst and aggression. May talked back to Vanessa, spent hours alone in her bedroom, and became increasingly moody. But lately, May had crossed a line to downright troubled teen. Vanessa wondered how to help her, considered counseling and the standard tough love scenario. Whatever it took, she would see it through until May came back to her, open-armed and giggling, as she'd always run to Vanessa when she was a little girl.

With all of this settling into the back of her mind, Vanessa reclined in bed and closed her eyes. Her thoughts whirled in visions of the life she craved in the fashion world, of all her old sketch pads, each one filled with designs of flowing dresses and colorful handbags, wispy sashes and wooly scarfs. Was there something still in this fashion designer dream? Some spark to kick it back from a long-dead yearning? It had been difficult enough in her twenties to break into the fashion industry, and that was with knowing people in the business. It was only a dream now, and though she knew the dream wouldn't come true, it was still a dream she liked to have. She'd held onto it for as long as she could remember, tucked it right under her arm along for the ride of life, and letting it go would be like tossing away all the components that made up her very soul.

The lateness of the hour finally overtook her, and she drifted in and out of sleep, every few minutes her eyes popping open with some new strategy to change her life. This went on until six o'clock, when the purple glow of dawn swallowed the stars outside her bedroom window. It was time to face the day, heat up some frozen pancakes for breakfast that Emma would wolf down but May would gag over. Then off to work, ringing up customers, folding blouses and hanging dresses. And after that she would come home, exhausted, and wonder how much longer this house would actually be her home, because she knew Vincent would pay her a hefty alimony but would never let her stay in the house. Then, late tonight she would fight with May, if May even stayed at home, and over and over this day would play.

Vanessa slipped out of bed and headed for the towel closet. At some point, fifteen years ago, life had seemed destined for success. And before that, dreams were sure as the stars. She remembered that feeling, even now. Or maybe, she thought as her hand grasped a thick red towel, she didn't remember that feeling at all. Maybe the feeling was so far in the past that it wouldn't catch up with her again. Maybe her dreams had gone straight but she'd gone sideways, never to meet up with each other. Never destined to align.

CHAPTER FOUR

Kyle fell to his knees in the church confessional. He signed himself with the cross, steepled his hands, and pressed them to his forehead.

"Forgive me, Father, for I have sinned," he whispered through the screen. "It's been…a lot of years since my last confession." He sighed and pressed his shoes together, bowing his head. "I've done some bad things over the years, but I don't know if I'd call them sins in the way God would. I think I've been a good person, but I keep doing stupid things." Father Brody didn't reply. "I drink too much," Kyle went on. "And people keep walking out of my life because I can't pull myself out of these holes."

He went on, giving more of a strained, verbal autobiography than a confession. Truly, he didn't think he'd sinned. He wasn't a liar, hadn't coveted, hadn't stolen or raped or hit. He didn't even think he'd treated Ava or any other woman poorly. All he'd done was refused to get the help he needed, entertained too many dark thoughts, and self-medicated the only way he knew how, with the only method that worked for him. And now, despite being a good man with a good heart, his life was falling apart. It felt right to come back to church, back to Father Brody.

Father Brody knew him well. He'd sat in on Father Brody's masses in his twenties, even went to confession during those years. As a child, he spent every Sunday at mass in St. Luke's

Catholic Church, paying attention to the words Father Brody spoke, even when other children went to the "kids" mass, or their eyes drifted away from Father Brody and onto the colorful stained-glass windows or the gold sun rays that sprayed through the upper panes like explosive starlight. Kyle couldn't pretend that he'd never once gazed at those beautiful windows, but mostly, he'd tried to be a good Catholic and listen to mass. He did it for his mother, standing beside him, her head forever lowered in prayer. It was the one thing that connected them, the one thing they did together as mother and son.

"...and I came to work drunk that day," he went on. "Coughing drunk. That's it." He choked back a sob. "I'm sorry for these sins and every sin."

"Would you like to offer an Act of Contrition, Kyle?"

"Of course."

After reciting an Act of Contrition and listening to Father Brody's absolve his sins and hand out a fitting penance, Kyle stood. He couldn't say he felt better than he had over the past few days, but he certainly didn't feel any worse. Just the scent of church comforted him, the old wood and faint incense. When he stepped out of the confessional, he let his eyes travel upward, focusing on the stained-glass windows, their intricate pattern of squares and crosses, their panes colorful like hard candy.

"Kyle, can I bother you to stay a moment?" Father Brody asked, indicating he should sit down in a back pew.

"I'm on my lunch break," Kyle told him. "I really have to get back before I get fired." Father Brody's kind smile was all it took to change Kyle's mind. Though Father Brody had to be in his seventies or even eighties by now, he still looked the same as Kyle remembered him; hair thick and white like puffs of clouds, cleanly shaven face, and eyes that were a muted, eerie blue and stared right through him as though reading every thought and emotion.

"I hope you don't find this forward of me," Father Brody said, clasping his hands together. "I've known you since you were a child, so I feel a certain need to make sure you're all right."

When Kyle didn't answer, Father Brody sat down in the pew in front of him.

"We have a group here," Father Brody went on. "They meet downstairs, every Tuesday and Friday night."

"I've thought about doing those groups." He tried to keep Father Brody's gaze but found it increasingly difficult. "I know how they work and I know myself. I wouldn't do well with that kind of thing. I can do it on my own."

"If you could do it on your own, you would have done it by now," Father Brody said in a gentle tone. "And this group isn't the traditional organization. It's not even about anything specific. It's just a group of people who get together and try to sort out their problems, using God and each other to guide them through."

Kyle considered it and nodded.

"Have you spoken to your mother about your issues?"

"I'm thirty-nine," Kyle replied. "The time for parental guidance has come and gone."

"That's not necessarily true." He paused for a moment. "Forgive me for saying this, but I do recall that your father had a similar problem."

"All the men in my family did." He didn't like where this conversation was heading. "And believe it or not, I'm probably doing the best out of all of them as far as keeping myself from losing it completely."

"I believe you," the priest returned. "But I also know your father, at one point, pulled himself out."

Kyle turned away. "My mother called it a miracle," he said,

and had to physically force the words out. "My father drank until I was sixteen, then the miracle happened, and he stayed clean for years before...."

"He passed."

Kyle blamed alcohol for the stroke that had killed his father, but more than that, he blamed himself. And he'd never told anyone...he'd just carried around the guilt all these years, his own personal cross to bear.

"Do you want to know what killed him?" he asked Father Brody. "What really killed him?"

"Of course, Kyle."

"I killed him."

Father Brody didn't flinch. He didn't even blink. Kyle supposed this was not the sort of confession Father Brody would believe, having known Kyle as long as he had. It was probably inconceivable that Kyle had killed his own father. But it was the truth...it was Kyle's firm belief.

"How did you kill him, Kyle?"

Kyle lowered his head and ran a hand through his hair. "When he relapsed, about a year before he died, he asked me for something...something he'd given me that he swore was the reason he beat alcoholism the first time. And I didn't give that thing to him. I couldn't."

"I see."

Kyle supposed it was the right time for a full confession. In fact, now that he was here, at church, the stained-glass windows above him, the wood scent in the air around him, and old Father Brody sitting in front of him, stoic and assuring, it felt like this was the place it was meant to happen all along.

"When I was sixteen, my father gave me a silver cross," he began. "He told me it had helped him beat the demons. He told me it had pulled every other man in my family out of the muck, just in the nick of time. He told me it was magic." He sniffled and shook the sob away. "But I made this pact with my friends and ended up burying the cross by a pond. Everyone put something personal and important into an old Tupperware bowl, and we swore to each other that we'd never dig our stuff up again, that we would forget we'd even done it, that it was a testament to our friendship." He sighed and let the rest tumble out with a sort of grace. "When my father relapsed, he asked for the cross back. I didn't give it to him and he died."

"I see."

Couldn't Father Brody say something else? Show some kind of reaction? Any reaction at all? Kyle had just told him something he'd never told another human being. Priests were probably used to that, but to Kyle, his actions had catastrophic consequences. He'd killed someone. How had he left that out of his earlier confession in the first place? Wasn't it the worst thing he'd ever done?

"And your heavy drinking started after your father died?" Father Brody asked finally.

"I've struggled with it since I was fourteen. But it got worse after he died, yes."

Father Brody stood and cupped his hand over Kyle's shoulder. "I want you to come Tuesday night at seven o'clock, downstairs. You'll meet with a woman named Annabelle. I'll tell her to expect you."

"That's it? Just a few Hail Marys and a church group?"

"Not entirely." He smiled. "I want you to seriously consider your role in your father's death. I want you to ask yourself if through the eyes of God, you really did anything wrong."

Kyle sat back in the pew. He knew it was fine to do this, that Father Brody wanted him to think this out. Of course he hadn't pulled a trigger or anything physical like that to kill his father.

43

But still, his father had fallen back into a drinking binge and had needed that cross. At the time, Kyle had been torn between honoring a friendship that had dissolved shortly after the pact was made, or helping his father by digging up the magic silver cross and handing it over.

Most memories of Kyle's life were blurry, just vague images here and there, but that night at the pond was perfectly clear, like a mental movie he could replay over and over. He remembered almost every word he'd spoken that night, remembered how warm the night was and how the moon was full and had made the pond look like a bowl of silver light. He also recalled that he'd been the orchestrator of the friendship pact, the one who'd said they could never dig up their valued possessions. He remembered telling Vanessa Lawrence that he wouldn't read her diary. He remembered how Brandon Ballas, his rich neighbor, had gone white after placing a gold and diamond watch, probably worth thousands of dollars, into the bowl.

"The bowl was never supposed to be dug up," he said, sitting forward. "I was trying to do the right thing by honoring that pact. I mean, the cross wasn't really magic, right?" He didn't believe in magic, not in a hocus pocus sense, anyhow. But maybe his father had, and that was what was killing him—this slow-bleeding stream of guilt.

"Magic, as I understand it, has to do with what people believe and the power of that belief," Father Brody replied. "So yes, the cross was magic, and no it wasn't magic at the same time. But that's a personal evaluation. Either way, you did what you felt was right at the time, and following your heart is never wrong."

Kyle nodded. Something released itself from within him; a spiritual removal of the pressure he'd had inside his chest for years. But he knew it wasn't quite the massive release he needed.

"Do you still keep in touch with these friends?" Father Brody asked.

Kyle shook his head. "I think they're both married now and have kids. One of them has a business in Fairfield, and the other one, the girl...." He pressed his palms to his forehead, unable to talk about Vanessa. Their friendship and romance had dissolved so fast, and as it faded, Kyle sensed that most of what she'd felt for him in those early teen years was gone. And that had been his fault, too.

"Ah," Father Brody said. "I see I've struck a nerve."

"An old but still open wound," Kyle said. "She put her diary in that bowl, and there wasn't a night that went by when I was sixteen that I didn't take a step out of bed and start to head out the door to dig it up and read what she wrote about me. Of course I never did."

"Of course you didn't." A woman with tangled gray hair stepped into the church, and Father Brody spun to greet her with an acknowledging nod. "I hope you'll come to the meeting," he said to Kyle in a low voice, squeezing his shoulder again. "And if for some reason you don't, I hope you find your own magic like your father did. I know you can do it. God will watch over you as you do."

He walked away, back toward the confessional, and Kyle stood and headed outside. Beside the church was an iron bench that faced the main road, and he sat down, kicking aside a stray potato chip bag.

He'd made the right decision by coming to church. More than the confession or reciting the Act of Contrition, the talk with Father Brody had put everything into perspective for him. He still wasn't sure if he'd go to the church group meeting, but at least it was something to fall back on should he slip up again...and he knew he would slip up. Digging up the past was the ignition switch that would launch him into long hours of drinking. There

45

was too much guilt there, and though some of it felt less pressing, there was always more guilt to release. Heavier guilt.

The silver cross. He told his father he'd lost it. There was wrath in that moment, his father shouting words at him that even in his thirties he hadn't heard before. He'd conveniently erased that lie from his original confession list to Father Brody—that big lie to his father—unless there really was some truth in the lie. The cross was lost, wasn't it…in a way? Someone could have dug up the Tupperware bowl and taken the contents. Brandon, sick with worry, may have come back for his watch. And Vanessa, a nervous teenage girl, could have dug her diary up only days after they'd buried everything. So truly, the cross was lost. It was gone forever.

Or was it? Maybe it was still there, buried beneath the tallest pine tree at Blueberry Pond. And if he had it back, maybe he could prove to himself that the cross wasn't magic, because right now, if it was magic, it would surely help him. If he had the cross back, he could close these open doors of rushing guilt. And if the cross wasn't magic, he could forgive himself for not giving it back to his father. It wouldn't have helped; it wouldn't have saved his father's life.

A strange fear grabbed him and he felt almost claustrophobic, thinking about the lost cross and how it was buried under the dirt, far away from him. The cross had to be powerful for him to remember its value after all these years. It had to be special somehow, even if in a way he didn't yet understand. He couldn't remember now why he'd even chosen that item to place in the Tupperware bowl. Maybe it was because he knew Brandon would put something ridiculously valuable in the bowl, something he could never match. Or maybe he did it to impress Vanessa Lawrence, because everything he did back then was to impress Vanessa.

But then he remembered why he hadn't dug the cross up long ago, and it was because of some peculiar but strong honor to uphold their pact. Even now, when he didn't know Brandon or Vanessa anymore, when they'd gone their separate ways as he always knew they would, when they were settled into their own lives and had families and probably didn't even remember the friendship pact. He almost laughed, remembering how he'd known, even back then, that the friendship wouldn't last. They were all so different; the only thing they really had in common was adolescence and a neighborhood pond. Brandon was ambitious, Vanessa was creative and smart, and Kyle was the odd guy out, just a sensitive, messed-up kid. Still, those two friends were the closest he'd ever had.

As cars raced by and a heavy gust of late spring wind blew through his hair, Kyle made up his mind. There was only one way he could go back to Blueberry Pond and dig up the cross without feeling like he was betraying a years-old trust, without having to stomach another helping of guilt. He could contact Brandon and Vanessa — easy to do over the Internet — and ask their permission. He could ask them if the bowl was even still there, if they even remembered the pact. Or maybe, now that he thought about it, the best way to bring all this up wasn't over some e-mail or Facebook page; maybe it was best to meet up in person. It was a crazy plan, but still felt right to him. It was the only way he'd either rest with some closure, or find the magic that his father had found. The only way to face his future, he now knew, was to unearth his past.

CHAPTER FIVE

Brandon's spoon clanged inside the coffee mug as he stirred his coffee around and around absently. He was thinking but not really thinking, his thoughts on so many separate issues he could not focus on just one, so the flurry stayed behind a carefully constructed wall of blank thought. He stayed like this as Jean packed up lunch boxes, as Logan and Andrew zoomed out the door to catch the bus, and as Jean came back from watching them and began her day by cleaning off the table. What may have been hidden days ago was now, Brandon suspected, open and in view, his inner fear exposed to the one person who knew him best.

"I hate Mondays," Jean mumbled as she picked up Logan's cereal bowl. All the raisins from the cereal were gone, but the bowl was still full of milk and the soggy remnants of bran flakes. "It's always so hectic in the morning."

"I used to be gone by the time they ate breakfast," Brandon replied. "So this routine is pretty new to me."

Jean piled bowls into the sink and ran the water to rinse them. Brandon watched her as she did what she always did, the daily routine he never got to see, all the little things she did before his return home from work. The dishes were done while he was away, dinner was cooked, laundry washed, wood floors swept. This brilliant woman who in college had a clear future and career plans was now a housewife in a time when she could be anything

48

she wanted. And he hated to think that deep down, he wanted her in that role. Not to impugn her abilities as a career woman, but because she kept things going better than he ever could. Because he felt like she was safe at home and happy taking care of Logan and Andrew and making sure her family had everything they needed. Wasn't that what Brandon did every day at Ballas & Monroe? Wasn't raising a secure family their shared dream since college?

"I'm going in at ten," he said, and pushed his coffee away, no longer wanting it. "Ferris and I will go over the legalities, close up everything, and start packing...whatever needs to be done at this point."

Jean picked up his coffee mug. "After that, I think it's best you take a week or two off. All the stress of closing down the business is taking a toll. I can see it in your eyes."

Brandon shook his head. "This afternoon I'll start looking into my other options. I have a few contacts, and if that doesn't work out, I'll dive into the newspapers and the computer listings. I can't say I've ever had to job hunt before, but how hard could it be?"

Jean laughed. "You'd be surprised."

She finished rinsing dishes and slid into the chair across from his. Their kitchen table was smaller than the dining room table, just a white round table circled by four high-backed chairs. They usually ate breakfast here, except for Sunday mornings when they all went out for breakfast at Milton's Restaurant down the street. Milton's served a magnificent brunch with trays and trays of food, ranging from breakfast eggs and bacon to lunch soups and salads. Brandon thought about eating at the restaurant every Sunday, Logan and Andrew pushing through the line to get to the pancake station, then sipping down chocolate milks at their table by the window. He hoped this wasn't one of the weekly expenses he'd have to cut from the budget now that things were so tight.

"I had something to talk to you about," Jean said.

Brandon saw indecision in her eyes, a tentative apprehension. Whatever she had to tell him, she was not sure of its benefit, and more unsure of how Brandon would reply.

"Go on," he said, sitting back.

"On the subject of looking for jobs, I phoned Lorraine Kutcher yesterday to inquire about openings at Vale Elementary. It turns out they have an opening for an aide, and she also said she would be happy to put me on as substitute for the higher grades."

"Absolutely not," he said and slapped his hand down on the table.

"Brandon," she said, and pressed her eyes closed. "This wouldn't be until the fall. The school year is over in a few weeks. And besides, Logan is almost twelve. They can stay home for a few minutes without me if I'm ever late, and—"

"This is what you want?" he said, cutting off the rest of her speech. "If I hadn't lost the business you would still be calling Lorraine Kutcher to look for a job?"

"Maybe," she replied, stronger. "God, Brandon, the boys are old enough now, and what do I really do all day? It's a waste for me to be in the house instead of out making us money."

"We'll get by," he said and was surprised when it came out as a shout.

"On what?" she stood from her chair. "The business is closing, and you said yourself that you'll never get the pay you had there with another company. Our mortgage is over two-thousand dollars a month, and with the savings account almost gone—"

Brandon held up his hand, stunned. "How did you know about that?"

"What? Do you think I just mop the floors all day and don't

50

have a clue about our money situation? That I don't know how to go online and check our accounts? The savings is gone, and soon the medical coverage will be gone. Just in case it takes a while before you find something, or you don't make what we need, I should at least put my name in for an assured job in the fall."

"I'll replenish the savings," he said. "I took the money out of there to keep Allen on, but I'll be sure to replace it. That'll buy us six months, and by then, something great will have come up for me. I don't want you to worry about this—it's my thing."

"Your thing?" Her face marbled maroon. "So we're in it together with raising the boys, but when it comes to our finances, that has nothing to do with me because I don't contribute to the bank account. Is that it?"

"Jean—"

Before he could explain or offer solace, she stormed out of the kitchen. Her footsteps banged up the staircase, and the bedroom door slammed upstairs. Brandon sat back in his chair and threw back his head. It was all falling apart, just as he suspected it would, and he hadn't even closed the doors of Ballas & Monroe yet. He hadn't even seen what other jobs were out there, talked to people he knew in the architecture business, checked out all the listings. Still, based on what Allen his draftsman had told him, things were rough in the job market right now. His field especially had been hit hard with the economic downturn, and he considered that he might have to sell a few valuable things to keep his promise and replenish the savings. That would buy him the six months he needed, a half a year to look for a high-paying job while still keeping his mortgage payments up.

He made a mental list of all the things he had worth value, the things that were used but still worth money, but the list was small. Logan's guitars were never used, but they were still Logan's possessions. What would Brandon have thought as a child if his father had come and taken away something he'd given him as a gift, even if he never used it? And Logan already suspected something was up. He didn't want the kids to worry as Jean was worrying. He could sell his SUV, but then he couldn't get around. The same with Jean's car. And trading down would only put him in some heap of junk that he'd end up putting money into anyhow. That was what his father had always told him: Buy new things, because buying old things will cost more in the long run. Buy the best.

He thought about a few more items, finding a reason not to part with each one, until he could no longer stand the thought of Jean upstairs alone, upset or crying. He footed the staircase and tapped on the door, then he stepped back in case she flew out in a rage. That wasn't Jean's style, but right now, anything was possible.

"Jean?" he said when a few seconds passed. "Can I come in?"

She hollered for him to enter, and when he did and saw what Jean was doing in their bedroom, it took a physical clenching of his fists to hold back his fury. On the bed, Jean had piled her jewelry into three separate stacks. He could tell by just a quick look that these piles were in order according to value. Her gold necklaces were in one pile, and the pile beside that were her rings and bracelets with gemstones. The last, smallest pile was diamond earrings and a platinum watch.

"What the hell are you doing?"

"Nobody here has a job right now," she replied. "And we have no money, as of July first, to pay the mortgage. The price of gold is high right now; I've seen all the commercials on TV about it. And I haven't worn yellow gold since the nineties."

Some of the gold necklaces she'd obviously acquired before he came into the picture. He didn't recognize most of that particular pile, but if she'd held onto them for that long, they must be valuable in a personal way. He scooped up the necklaces in his hand and reached out for her to take them back.

"We're not doing this," he said. "This is insane. We're not even late on a mortgage payment yet."

"You want to wait until they foreclose on us and stick an embarrassing sign on our front lawn?"

She didn't take the necklaces from him, so he tossed them down on the bed. "Nobody is foreclosing on us," he said, scrubbing the back of his neck. "I told you I'll put the money back in the savings account. And I'll start looking for a job this afternoon, okay? Please stop this."

Jean sank onto the bed. She covered her eyes with her hands, and Brandon dropped down beside her and scooped her up in his arms. She cried for a while, her body convulsing with each tiny sob.

"I'm sorry," she whispered at length. "It's just…I don't want to lose the house. I love it here."

"We won't lose the house," he assured, brushing his hand over her back. "Jean—you have my word."

After that she pulled herself together, wiping her eyes before disappearing into the bathroom down the hall. Brandon was anchored to the bed, listening to the water run from the bathroom. He was stuck right in the middle of his nightmare, frightened and immobile. Quietly, he stood and gathered up Jean's piles of jewelry, then placed all of it on the dresser, right in front of her tall wooden jewelry box. Whatever it took, she was not selling her jewelry. Not the ones from before she'd met him, and certainly not the ones he'd given her over the years. Her diamond earrings were a Christmas gift the first year of their engagement. Her sapphire bracelet was a birthday present the year she'd given birth to Logan. He was furious that she'd even considered selling any of it.

He checked the time and noted that he had an hour before meeting Ferris at Ballas & Monroe. To ease his mind, and to give Jean a sense that something was being done to rectify the situation, he went downstairs and sat down at the computer. A quick Google search took him to places he'd hoped he wouldn't find, a job on the other side of Connecticut that would be one hell of a long and painful commute, factory-based jobs for draftsmen that would be scooped up by people willing to take less pay, jobs for interior design which he found tedious, jobs for engineers, jobs in sales…the search would take some time. But he had a degree and years of experience, so it would happen eventually. He just needed time to find that one great fit.

Jean didn't come downstairs. The hour grew close to ten o'clock, and Brandon was about to close down the computer when he decided to end his time in cyberspace by checking his email and cleaning it out. When he clicked his mailbox, spam and junk filled the computer screen as always, which was why he rarely checked his personal emails. But as his eyes scanned the screen, he caught a name among the emails that was so distant he wondered if he'd read it right. The subject line read only: From Kyle Macord.

Before Brandon even opened the email, he knew what would be inside. There was only one thing that would bring Kyle Macord back into his life after more than twenty years of not speaking. There was only one thing they had in common, only one thing that Kyle could possibly need. And strangely, coincidentally perhaps, it was the same thing Brandon needed right now.

It fell upon him as both a saving grace and an awful memory. An early summer night back in the late eighties and a large pond in their neighborhood that had been aptly named Blueberry Pond for its brilliant blue water. He remembered that water so clearly, a deep blue that seemed to change colors along with the sky, matching shade to shade. Maybe it was the way the pond was positioned, or maybe just his own childhood imagination, but the place had always seemed magical. He'd spent many nights living inside that magic, talking to Kyle Macord and their neighbor Vanessa Lawrence for hours, bonding in the way only teenagers could. He remembered that he'd always felt like the odd man out—Kyle and Vanessa were so in love. They'd hidden themselves from his view more than a few times, hugging and kissing, sometimes arguing in passionate tones.

But that night, back in the eighties, Brandon had buried something valuable, something he never should have parted with. Kyle had an insane idea to make some sort of friendship pact and bury their most valued possessions. Brandon's first thought was to bow out, but there was something in the air that night, a full moon and the last day of the school year—some kind of crazy intensity that he usually only saw in Kyle but had felt beneath his own skin that night. So he'd done something equally as crazy, and buried, as part of their pact, an expensive gold watch.

The gold watch. For his own sanity, he'd told himself to forget about it—and he had. The watch was much too flashy for his taste back then, a thick yellow-gold Rolex with a ring of huge diamonds around the face. He'd worn it once to his uncle's funeral, and he had a bad association with it. The watch was the most logical item to put in the Tupperware bowl Kyle had brought that night, even if it didn't quite have the deep meaning Kyle and Vanessa's contributions had.

But the watch was valuable in a different way, and he was already perspiring with the thought of its worth. He sat back in the computer chair, still not hitting the mouse to open Kyle's email. He thought back on that watch and something Jean had just said upstairs: Gold was valuable right now. And back then, in the eighties, the watch was worth ten thousand; he'd heard his father say it, pompous and flaunting as he always was during family gatherings. Now, the watch would be worth at least that much, maybe more. Enough to replenish the savings account, even if he sold the watch for scrap, though he would try to sell it outright. The money, he suspected, would be enough to get him through the next six months, or even longer.

Taking a breath, he double-clicked the mouse and opened Kyle's email.

Brandon,

I'm taking a chance here that you remember me, and if you do, that you'll even want to hear what I have to say. Lately, I've been thinking a lot about you and Vanessa and our times back in the neighborhood. I was hoping that you two would like to get together with me to discuss something, and to just catch up. As far as I can tell, you're living in Fairfield now, and I'm not too far away in Stratford, so I thought we could meet for dinner sometime soon. Let me know as soon as you can.

Kyle Macord

It wasn't quite what Brandon expected, but all indicators pointed toward what he thought was truly going on. Kyle wanted to dig up the Tupperware bowl. What else could they possibly have to discuss? Kyle had put in a small silver cross, a meaningful contribution, but nothing of lasting significance, so he wasn't sure why Kyle wanted to dig up the bowl. Though maybe, now that he thought about it, Kyle had already dug the bowl up, and out of some kind of lasting guilt, wanted to return Brandon's watch. Or maybe he'd sold the thing long ago and felt the need to tell him about it. Whatever it was, it all came back to the expensive watch, and he had to meet with Kyle and find out what was going on.

Kyle,

Honestly can't believe I heard from you. And of course I remember you and the neighborhood. I would love to meet for dinner, just send me a place and time and I will rearrange whatever I have to so I can be there.
Looking forward to hearing back,

Brandon

He clicked send and shook his head as Jean walked into the room. "What are you doing?" she asked.

"Job hunting," he replied and stood. "But something else just came up that I think will help us out enormously." He planted a kiss on her cheek. "I have to go," he said, and didn't feel the awful chill he'd felt earlier when thinking about going into Ballas & Monroe to pack up. "But I'll be home for dinner."

"Is everything okay?" she asked, tilting her head.

"Fine," he said and pulled her into a hug. "Just trust me." He kissed her again, smiled, and headed out the door.

CHAPTER SIX

When Vanessa pulled into the driveway, Vincent's black Mercedes was parked just up ahead. She gripped the steering wheel hard. The last thing she wanted after working all day was to deal with Vincent or listen to whatever negative thing he had to say. Their arrangement of living in separate places had been working so well; May and Emma were slowly getting adjusted to visiting them in different locations, and the fighting was less all around. But with an impending divorce, she figured there were probably more than a few things that had to be tied up, so she stepped out of the car and headed for the front door.

Vincent was in the living room, sitting on their brown leather couch, looking strangely out of place in a house that he still owned. His appearance was immaculate as always; pressed dark suit, tidy hair styled with product to a slick and shiny finish, face cleanly shaven, eyebrows plucked, skin glowing. Vanessa almost cringed at the sight of him, even though he was probably the most handsome man she'd ever known. It was the soul that dwelled beneath that turned his good looks into something else, something dark and arrogant that couldn't quite be put into a category.

"Where are the girls?" she asked, tossing her purse onto the end table.

"I drove them to get something to eat so we could talk in

58

private."

"Something you need to tell me?" She crossed her arms on her chest.

"Yes." He nodded, not standing to face her or even moving. "I want joint custody."

"I figured you would." She let out a breath. She thought it was going to be something worse. "There's no reason for us to not do joint custody. You're their father and you deserve to be in their lives as much as possible."

"May already said she wants to stay with me," he said, not addressing what she'd just told him. "And she's old enough to make that decision, but I think it's best that she stays with you sometimes."

"No doubt," she replied. "If she's with you all the time, how will you ever find time to go out and party?"

"I didn't come here to fight." He tapped his finger on his knee. "I just wanted you to know that May is having a hard time with this, probably more than she's telling you."

"You think you know May so much better than I do? That I don't know she's hurting right now?"

"Look." He stood and crossed his arms. "This is difficult, I realize that, but considering how much I've given you over the years, I'd think you'd be a little more—"

"How much you've given me over the years?" She laughed, almost right into his face. "You mean how you had to sacrifice your cozy life of partying and snorting cocaine because I was pregnant with your child and you felt obligated to marry me? Or did you mean how you put me up in this house like it was a hotel and I was the lone lodger?"

"If you don't like it, move out," he said without feeling. "And I married you because I thought we could possibly have a life together, but you never let me forget, not for one day, that

59

I married you because you were pregnant. You could never get past it."

"Maybe because you brought it up constantly!"

She went into a rush of examples, from him telling her, even on their wedding day, how lucky she was that the condom broke or whatever the hell happened, because now she'd landed the most eligible bachelor in New York. Then she reminded him of the countless nights he'd left her alone with May so he could go out and party in the city, assuming she was happy just to be living in a grand house in Westchester County, New York. Or after that, when the marriage seemed over and Vanessa had miraculously become pregnant with Emma—like she'd planned it that way, even though she'd wanted out of the marriage as much as he did—and he accused her of skipping birth control pills on purpose.

The marriage was doomed from the moment Vanessa set foot down the aisle, and perhaps that was not the fault of either of them. There were too many incompatibilities, too many sacrifices, too many assumptions. And she'd never even loved him...that was the part that scorched her every day, the reality that stuck out more than any other. It had been a loveless marriage, a business relationship, a mere tolerance of each other for a greater purpose. It was incredible that neither had cheated over the years, or she assumed he'd never cheated. He was never one to let a chance to hurt her slip by, so she supposed he would have told her of any indiscretions.

By the time she was finished going off, he'd landed himself back on the couch, rubbing his head, no longer fighting back. It was pointless to keep doing this, she knew, and the only breath of relief she could muster evolved from the thought that it would all be over soon. The girls would be better off, and May had probably even seen it coming years ago, when she was old enough to understand. Emma was so innocent, though, so soft and vulnerable, but perhaps for that reason the divorce would be best. The fighting would cease and there would be more love to give. Still, it didn't feel entirely right to Vanessa that her youngest child's first lesson of love and marriage was to call it quits when the going got tough. There would always be some guilt there, and maybe she blamed that on Vincent as well.

"So I'll bring Emma back, and then May will stay with me tonight," Vincent said into the silence.

"If that's what she wants right now," Vanessa replied. "But I want her back tomorrow night. She can't get used to staying with you and your loose rules."

"And your rules are better?" He shook his head, but then shrugged, like he didn't want to get into another argument.

"I've been through this before," she said. "When I was just a little younger than May, my parents got divorced. I know how to do this the right way."

Vincent let out a sarcastic chuckle. "You obviously don't remember a thing of it, because you have absolutely no idea what May is feeling and what she's going through." He stood from the couch and picked up his keys from the coffee table. "From what she tells me, all you two do is fight, you won't allow her boyfriend to come over, and he's the only one who seems to understand her right now."

Vanessa wanted to tell him that May's boyfriend Warren was a loser and a liar, but she decided against it. Fighting with him was emotionally draining, and she just wanted him out of the house.

"I'll deal with May tomorrow," she said. "And then I guess you and I should probably have one last talk about the house."

Vincent's gaze softened. "We'll sell it," he said. "But with alimony and your job, you should be able to afford something adequate."

He walked to the door, and for a moment, Vanessa stood rooted to the spot. She wanted him out, out, out, but she also had a nasty bit of something still ringing in her ears from their argument. She followed him until he spun around in question when he saw her standing behind him at the door.

"Did you marry me because you thought we could really be a family?" she asked. "Or was it only because I was pregnant? I need the truth."

Vincent's hand was on the doorknob but he released it. "Both," he said, and she saw in his eyes that he truly meant it. "I assumed in the beginning that you wanted this lifestyle, all my money, the big house and the kids. I thought I gave all of that to you."

She shook her head. "I just wanted you to love me. Maybe not in the way you loved May and Emma, but in the way a husband should love his wife."

"And you loved me that way?" he returned. "Because it never really felt like it."

"Then maybe we both made the wrong decision."

He nodded—for once they were in agreement about something—and left the house. Vanessa stared at the closed door, and though it was a warm June evening, a chill crept up her body and settled inside her chest. She hated Vincent. She hated his gelled-up hair and his crisp suits and his love of money and parties. She hated the scent of his aftershave and the deep timbre of his voice. But still, he was the father of her girls, and they'd shared a house and a life for many years—and for that reason she wrestled with the loss in a way she didn't think she would. Divorcing was a stress she couldn't seem to bear, and she could feel all of it weakening her limbs, turning her sleepy as she grieved the finality.

She went into the kitchen and poured herself a glass of red wine, then sank into the couch in the living room, absorbing the silence. Would this be life now? The girls out with Vincent, no giggles around the house from Emma, no angry shouts from May. Vanessa wasn't sure how to do alone. She'd gone to college right after high school, always with people around her, then after college she cruised into the night life, then had May and got married. Now it seemed she was heading toward a quiet life she didn't desire, a loneliness that didn't fit with her personality.

The living room darkened. Vanessa sipped her wine. She was about to turn on the television when the door creaked open and Emma sped inside, kicking off her sneakers.

"Mommy!" she said when she saw her. "May is staying with Daddy! We have one of those Mommy and Emma nights!"

Vanessa nodded and patted the couch for her to come sit. She pulled her close, hugging her shoulder, and then clicked on the television to *iCarly*, one of Emma's favorite shows. Vanessa didn't mind the show. In fact, she needed the laugh right now.

They sat for a while, just the two of them, laughing and snuggling. With May so distant, and Vincent out of her life for good, Vanessa felt like Emma was all she really had now, for however long this lasted. She wanted to stay like this, sitting on the couch laughing, the moment forever frozen in time.

After the night of kiddie television and microwave popcorn, Vanessa tucked Emma into bed, readied herself for a lonely night in her own bed, and slid under the covers. She left the bedroom door wide open, so the little bit of light from Emma's nightlight would shine through, connecting them somehow. She thought about what Vincent and May were doing now, sitting in some fancy hotel room, maybe getting room service, laughing and bonding. She refused to think Vincent would bad-mouth her to her own daughter, but even if he didn't do that, he still took May's side on everything. Maybe May's boyfriend was with them in the hotel room. Maybe they were all against her, like she was the wicked witch and they were the innocent victims of her wrath.

She picked up her cell phone and checked it for any texts from May, though the time when May had sent texts to her was long gone. Then she checked her mail, letting the feed of emails run down the screen until one flashed by that made her bolt up in bed, wondering if she was imagining things. Quickly, she scrolled down to the email. It said: From Kyle Macord.

Kyle Macord. Just seeing his name on the glowing screen of her cell made some long-ago pain swell inside of her. Why was he contacting her? Her first thought was that someone must have died. That was all she needed right now, to hear that someone from her old neighborhood had passed away. She couldn't take anymore grief right now.

She touched the screen and read his message so fast that she had to re-read it a few times to ingest the contents.

Vanessa,

I know this probably sounds crazy, but lately I've been thinking a lot about you and Brandon Ballas and our times back in the neighborhood. I wanted to know if the three of us could get together for dinner to discuss something and catch up. I'll understand if you don't want to, but it's important to me so I hope you'll consider it. I don't know where you're living now, but I'm in Stratford and I think Brandon is in Fairfield. Last I heard you weren't in Connecticut, I think New York? Anyhow, let me know as soon as you can and I'll make the plans.

Kyle Macord

After the final reading, she gripped the phone and closed her

64

eyes. How long had it been since she'd spoken to Kyle Macord? Twenty years? Longer? And God, why was he attempting to reconnect right now? At this moment when her life was crashing down all around her? Kyle was the first guy to destroy her emotionally, and part of her even wondered if all failed relationships after him were because of what he'd done to her.

She reminded herself that they were just kids back then, high schoolers who excelled at drama and emotion. And Kyle was probably the most dramatic and emotional guy she'd ever known. He was the type of guy who wore his heart on his sleeve, said whatever was inside of his mind, no matter how it made him seem to anyone else. Even his email reminded her of the way he'd often spoken: "I know this probably sounds crazy...." Kyle Macord hadn't changed. She could tell that in the few sentences he'd written.

She wondered what had become of Kyle. He'd had more than a few problems with substance abuse and was probably the first person Vanessa had seen insanely drunk, crying on her doorstep, screaming about all the ways he would kill himself if she didn't come out and talk to him. And that, she recalled, was what had kept them apart in those middle teenage years. But their late teen years...that had been a different story.

In their senior year of high school, she remembered, they'd broken up yet again, only to find themselves with other people. It was only a minor tug of jealousy for her until Kyle got serious with the other girl. Vanessa wouldn't forget her name—Larissa Cadence—or the way the girl looked: puffy black hair and bright pink lipstick, dark mascara, and a leather jacket. She was the opposite of Vanessa, but seemed to connect with Kyle—in more ways than one. With a pang in her heart that was so, so different from the one Vincent always produced, Vanessa remembered that Kyle and Larissa had slept together in senior year, ruining

65

any chance of Vanessa and Kyle losing their virginity together, as had been Vanessa's plan since she even understood what sex was.

And that had killed her.

After that betrayal, she became looser with guys, losing her virginity to a long-haired guitar player a few days before the senior prom, even though she liked the guy but never actually loved him. Not in the way she loved Kyle Macord. But it had felt like a way to get back at Kyle, and after all of that, her relationship with Kyle had dissolved into nothingness—and not even their tight friendship or the long history they'd shared as childhood sweethearts could bring it back. She hadn't heard from Kyle since the summer after high school graduation, when she'd seen him taking his dog outside and stopped to tell him she was going to college in a month and that she hoped he dropped dead while she was gone. Truly, she was surprised he'd had the nerve to contact her through an email, even twenty years later.

She read over the email again a few times, but something kept nagging at her. Kyle had said he wanted to discuss something. If Brandon was involved, that could only mean one thing—Kyle wanted to discuss the friendship pact. Of all the pivotal moments in Vanessa's life, including crazy college nights, partying like a rock star in the city, and marrying Vincent Greene, the friendship pact stood out as the defining moment of her youth. When she'd placed her diary into a yellow Tupperware bowl and watched Kyle throw dirt over the hole and bury the thing by their neighborhood pond, she'd felt brave and liberated. Her past was essentially buried, and she'd felt free to finally move on from something that had dragged her down for years.

And that one thing, she just realized, was her parents' divorce.

Setting her phone down on her belly, she placed her left hand to her mouth to stifle a sob. She remembered her parents fighting,

66

calling each other horrible names, accusing each other of cheating and lying, arguing about money and who spent what and where they'd spent it. She remembered her only escape was to sit in her bedroom, back against her bed, hair dangling over her teary eyes, and write in her diary.

Now, looking back, she couldn't remember a word of what she'd written. All she knew was that getting rid of the diary seemed to release her demons. Though right now, in this moment, as she thought about Vincent accusing her of not understanding May despite having gone through the exact same thing, she wondered if she needed to invite those demons back, if only for a moment or two. If she could remember how she felt, maybe she could connect with May. Perhaps she would understand how it truly felt to go through that pain, and how she'd dealt with it at that age. All she could remember now were her parents shouted words and her reaction to write her fears and sorrow into her diary — leaking her sadness onto the pages.

Kyle had the diary. She'd always known he had it. Part of her, back then, even wondered if he'd made up the whole idea of the friendship pact just to get a peek into her private world, what she wrote about him, how she felt. He was always trying to find out how people really felt. She supposed that he had some kind of leftover guilt and wanted to tell her that he'd dug the diary up, and maybe, just maybe, he still had it and would return it at dinner when the three of them met up again. Her heart sped up at the thought of reading it, all these years later. She couldn't wait to look at the world again through younger eyes, look at turbulent times through a means that could no longer hurt her, only help her connect with the present.

She sat up in bed, hit reply on her phone, and typed:

Kyle,

I'll meet with you and Brandon for dinner. I'm in New York, but will drive to Connecticut if you decide to meet there. Let me know what you two decide. Looking forward.

~ Vanessa Greene

It was a short response, but that was really all he deserved. She would meet up with him, just to catch up, hear what he had to say, hopefully get her old diary back, but that was it. She still hated him for what he'd done to her all those years ago. Even if they were kids back then, she still could never forgive him. She thought about how close they all once were, and that alone warranted a get-together, even if it had all fallen apart not too long after they'd buried the Tupperware bowl. Brandon had gone to a different college — she was pretty sure he'd gone to Cornell — and they'd lost touch. But she didn't hate him. She hated Kyle.

She placed her phone on the nightstand, watched until the light dimmed and went out, then sat in the faint glow of Emma's nightlight until the emotions of the day overtook her and she laid back. Strange day, hearing from Kyle. Awful day, fighting with Vincent. Wonderful day, watching TV with Emma. Life was up and down, and she'd been down so long that she knew the only place left to go was back up, even if she only had a loose idea of how to get there.

CHAPTER SEVEN

Carmella's Restaurant in Connecticut was a good meeting place, fancy but not too elegant, and middle ground from Kyle, Brandon, and Vanessa's houses. The menu was of Italian food and great wine, the decor was warm and upscale, and the food, according to the feedback and testimonials, was extraordinary. Vanessa had learned all this after going onto the restaurant's website, right after Kyle had sent her an email about their intended meeting time and place: Carmella's Restaurant, Friday at seven.

It was Friday night, just after seven o'clock, and the ride to Connecticut had been excruciating with the traffic. As Vanessa pulled into a parking space and sat in the parking lot of Carmella's, she reminded herself of the importance of this meeting, how she longed for her diary, and how she wanted to know how Brandon and Kyle were doing after all these years. She was going insane wondering how they both looked, what life had done to them.

She was also nervous. Kyle Macord had shaped her childhood and teen years, and her talks with Brandon and Kyle were some of her most cherished adolescent memories. She couldn't pretend not to care about what they thought of her and how she'd aged and how she'd ended up, though she decided that she would not reveal the current state of her marriage. That was a personal thing, and though she'd grown up with Brandon and Kyle, she no longer really knew them. She had never known them as adults.

She sucked in a deep breath, stepped out of the car, and swung her pocketbook over her shoulder. She'd gone back and forth with bringing just a black carry purse or a bigger pocketbook, and decided that just in case Kyle had her diary, it would be best to have something bigger to conceal it in after leaving the restaurant. She wondered how he would present the diary, if it would be some drawn-out apology or just a quick handing over of her long-lost property.

There was also some question about how Brandon would handle the exchange. She recalled that Kyle and Brandon had been close when they all hung out at the pond, but she occasionally had to intervene when they clashed over their different outlooks on life. At those times she wondered if it was best to have her as part of their group. She'd been there to offset arguments, a soft and feminine presence, but she still felt like the odd person out, being the only girl. Maybe the two would have preferred male bonding time alone, without a girl around. Maybe their relationship would have been different.

The restaurant was dimly lit inside, the air conditioner already kicking, cooling the place at least ten degrees lower than Vanessa felt was necessary. She walked to the hostess, a tall brunette with her hair in a tight bun, and asked for the Macord party. As she was led through the restaurant, she wondered how quickly she would recognize Brandon and Kyle, and knew they would probably see her before she saw them. She'd been meticulous with her hair and makeup, and had even applied a face mask before bed the prior night, just to ensure her skin would be smooth, no wrinkles, though she was lucky not to have many of those yet. If she was tired, she might see a bit of sagging beneath her eyes, but usually some eye cream would fix that right up.

She'd been wrong—she saw Brandon and Kyle before they

saw her. They were sitting at a round table tucked away in the back of the restaurant, cozy and illuminated in dim gold light. She recognized Brandon right away, and the first thing she noticed was that his blond hair, fine textured even in high school, was thinning drastically. His face was pudgier, as though he'd led an affluent life, but he was not overweight. Though she could only see his side profile, she also sensed something of worry in his expression, though perhaps he was just nervous for the meeting as she was.

Kyle looked very different from his high school days. His dark hair was short now, not feathery and brushing the top of his shoulders as she remembered, though the shorter style made him look manlier. His face had always been young somehow, and the longer hair he'd had back in high school had given him a softer, juvenile look, like he was always a few years younger than he truly was. He was thinner than he'd been at sixteen, or maybe he'd just grown into the lengthiness of his body, Vanessa couldn't tell. Even so, Kyle and Brandon had both aged well, even if both had the appearance of two people who were in a current life struggle. She wasn't sure how she'd come to that conclusion, but it was something she was nearly certain of.

"Here you are," the hostess said as Vanessa approached the table.

Instinctively, she met Brandon's eyes first, and was pleased to see a familiar warmth there. It was as though no time had passed between them at all, like she was sitting beside him at Blueberry Pond, telling him her troubles and listening to his.

"Vanessa," he said, and stood.

Without words, Vanessa leaned forward and embraced him, surprised when tears sped into her eyes. Her body trembled as she tried to hold them in, and because Brandon was the kind and gentle person he'd always been, he held onto her as sort

71

of a shield, keeping her from the embarrassment of crying in a restaurant.

"Oh my God," she said when they broke apart. "I can't believe how great you look."

"You too!" he replied. "You look even better than you did in high school."

"Lying," she said, and laughed as she wiped tears.

She turned to Kyle, lifted her hand in a wave, then quickly sat down before he got any ideas to hug her. His deep brown eyes — still such an indicator of his inner thoughts — softened in understanding. So he did remember what he'd done to her.

"Vanessa Lawrence," he said and smiled.

"Vanessa Greene," she corrected. "I've been Vanessa Greene for seventeen years."

"Seventeen years," Brandon said and let out a whistle. "Makes me feel old just hearing that."

"You're married, too, right?" she asked Brandon, hanging her pocketbook behind the chair. "Two kids?"

"Two boys," he confirmed. "Logan and Andrew. And my wife's name is Jean. We've been married since just after college, going on…. God, I can't remember how long I've been married."

"Typical," Vanessa said, and laughed again.

She was careful not to look at Kyle, though she knew how immature that probably was. More than twenty years had passed since they'd parted on a negative note, but sitting across from him, suddenly thrown back into that period of her life, she couldn't help but regress.

"Kyle was just telling me that he never married," Brandon said, and opened his menu.

The news shocked Vanessa, and to keep herself from looking at Kyle and possibly displaying her reaction, she opened her own menu. "You never got married?" she asked Kyle, pretending to peruse the menu items.

"I'm in the 'almost' club," he replied. "It almost happened a few times, but was never meant to be, I guess."

She kept pretending to scan the menu while taking this in. Kyle Macord had never married. How could that be? He was attractive and uniquely sensitive. Something must have gone wrong somewhere.

"And no kids?" she asked him.

"No," he replied. "Which is difficult because I'm an only child—you probably remember—and I always wanted a big family."

Brandon lowered his menu. "It'll happen for you."

"Ran out of time," Kyle replied, and hung his head.

Vanessa looked at Brandon, an old reflex when Kyle turned emotional and they weren't really sure what to do. Again, it felt like no time had passed, and just for a moment, Vanessa felt the mess of years behind her fall away like they were never there.

"Your parents moved out of the neighborhood?" she asked Brandon.

"They moved to Florida a long time ago," he replied. "But they're up here so much to see Logan and Andrew it's like they never left. Does your mom—?"

"She got remarried to a guy who owns a fish market," Vanessa said. "They still live in Connecticut, up in Stonington."

"Eating fish all the time?" Brandon said.

"Pretty much."

A bouncy blonde waitress strode up to the table, interrupting Brandon and Vanessa as they shared a laugh. "Welcome to Carmella's," the waitress announced. "My name is Lola, and I'll be your server." She smiled, all teeth showing. "Would you like to start off with some drinks?"

"Just a water," Kyle said before anyone else could order.

"With no ice."

Vanessa stopped laughing. "Just a water," she said, following Kyle's lead.

"A water for me, too," Brandon said. "And I'd like to order Carmella's Famous Bruschetta Plate and some fried calamari for an appetizer."

"Brandon—" Kyle started.

"No, it's on me," he told him. "For my old friends."

"Very good," the waitress said before anyone could change their minds. "I'll be back with your drinks."

A few things were clear to Vanessa, just with the short exchange among Brandon and Kyle and the waitress. First, Kyle no longer drank alcohol, or had such a problem with it that he didn't even drink socially anymore. The second, the old feud between Brandon and Kyle and how much money they had was still there, simmering beneath the surface. And now Brandon was in a position to toss his money around when Kyle had set up this whole dinner and probably anticipated paying the bill.

"Thanks for the appetizers," Vanessa said to Brandon, then turned to Kyle. "And thanks for getting us all together tonight, Kyle."

Kyle's shoulders lifted in a silent laugh. Vanessa's gaze was fully on him now, taking in his gray dress shirt and the gold cross dangling from his collar.

"What's so funny?" she said.

"You were always the one who tried to keep the peace," he replied. "And it doesn't seem like that's changed."

"I think it's safe to say that people don't change all that much," Brandon put in. "They grow smarter, and maybe become more habitual, but all in all, the personality stays the same."

They talked about this as the drinks and appetizers came, then the subject switched around a few times to college memories

74

and current jobs before landing on kids and spouses. As Vanessa sampled the bruschetta and calamari, she stayed in conversation with Brandon as much as she could, and only spoke to Kyle when he asked her a direct question about May or Emma. She found it difficult to talk about them with Kyle, though with Brandon, she was matching parenting triumphs and tribulations back and forth, and with gusto.

"So do your parents still live in the old neighborhood?" Brandon asked Kyle.

Kyle was lifting a piece of bruschetta to his mouth but paused. "No," he said, shaking his head. "After my dad passed away, my mother moved in with my aunt."

Vanessa placed her hand to her heart. "I'm so sorry," she said and truly was. "I didn't know your father died."

"I'm sorry too," Brandon said. "I remember him as a great guy."

"Thanks," Kyle said. He placed his bruschetta down on the plate. "That kind of brings me to the reason I asked both of you here tonight."

A silence fell among them, but was broken when the waitress returned. "Ready to order?" she asked.

They each put an order in, and though Vanessa ordered the chicken parmigiana, she wasn't really hungry anymore. Her stomach felt off, and there was a leaping sensation in her chest that was upsetting her entire body. Kyle was about to present her diary, or at least he was ready to address the friendship pact.

"Thanks," the waitress said and walked away, leaving them in silence again.

Kyle cleared his throat. "Anyhow, of course I wanted to catch up with you guys, but I also had something I wanted to discuss with you." He tapped his finger on the table. "There's no point trying to ask this without giving you the truth, so I'm just going

75

to come right out and tell you both that I've had some problems in my life lately." He paused again, and when nobody spoke, he continued. "Do either of you remember...the friendship pact?"

Vanessa nodded. "I had a feeling that's what this was about."

"I did too," Brandon said.

"Good," Kyle said. "Then you remember that I put a cross in the bowl we buried our stuff in." He took a breath. "I need the cross."

"You mean...you never dug that bowl up?" Vanessa asked.

"You had to have," Brandon said.

"No," Kyle replied. "I told you two I wouldn't dig it up, and I didn't. But now...I need the cross for reasons I hope you two will understand. I wanted your permission to go back to Blueberry Pond and dig our stuff up. I'll return your things."

This wasn't what Vanessa expected at all. Kyle didn't have her diary, but now she truly needed to have it—she thought it would be in her hands by the end of this dinner meeting. And unless she read Brandon incorrectly, he thought Kyle had their things too.

"God," she whispered. "I can't believe that bowl is still there."

"I thought for sure you'd dug that up," Brandon said to Kyle, but the two didn't meet eyes. "And even if you didn't...there's a chance it won't still be there. For all we know, the pond isn't even there anymore."

"Why wouldn't the pond be there?" Vanessa questioned.

"The pond is still there," Kyle said. "At least, it was when my mother moved out of the neighborhood a few years ago. And nobody but us knew about the bowl, so it has to still be there." He glanced around. "Unless one of you told somebody."

"I never did," Vanessa said. "To me, it was best that I forgot about my diary. It was therapeutic to forget about it."

"My parents never knew I buried the watch," Brandon said.

He took a sip of water and his eyes traveled away. "To this day, they probably still think I have it with my jewelry."

Kyle's eyes traveled away too, moving around to each nearby table as though checking to make sure nobody overheard their conversation. Vanessa felt sure there was something beautiful in this story, a secret kept so long and by people who hadn't even spoken to each other. People who didn't even *like* each other because of failed friendships and romances.

"So I have your permission then?" Kyle asked.

"You can mail me the diary," Vanessa said, nodding. "I'll give you my address." Brandon seemed to struggle with his decision. He stared down at the uneaten food on the appetizer plates, twirling his thumbs in front of him.

"I want to go with you," he said to Kyle at length. "You'll need some help, and I don't trust that the watch will make it through the mail."

"I can drive it to your house," Kyle said.

"No," Brandon said in a stronger voice. "I'm going with you."

"You don't trust me with it?" Kyle said. "Is that it? Because my problems right now aren't money related."

"Guys," Vanessa said before Brandon's return. "I think it's best that you go together to dig the bowl up. Think about this. A grown man, digging a hole by a pond? The people that lived over there were old and are probably dead by now. If somebody new lives there, they might not be happy with somebody digging around their property. You'll need a lookout, Kyle."

Brandon and Kyle exchanged a glance.

"Fine," Kyle said. "He can go with me. But I planned on going Sunday, late."

"I'll meet you at your house," Brandon said. "We can take my SUV and bring shovels and stuff."

"Sounds grand," Kyle said, and grabbed another piece of

bruschetta. "Let's just hope we don't get your expensive SUV dirty. That would be tragic."

Brandon shook his head. "You haven't changed, Kyle. You haven't changed at all."

Vanessa couldn't help but laugh.

Chapter Eight

As soon as the waitress placed the black bill holder down on the table, Kyle pounced on it. After all these years, the time had finally come when he could one-up Brandon when it came to money. He could prove that he had the means to back up his dinner invitation to Carmella's Restaurant and pay the bill for all of them. When they were teenagers, it always seemed like Brandon would amount to so much more than Kyle, and of course he had, but Kyle did not need Brandon to know exactly how much more.

"I've got it, Kyle," Brandon said from across the table.

Kyle waved his hand. "I invited you guys, so I'm paying." He'd expected Brandon's offer, and was even grateful for it, because he would get the chance to decline.

"At least let me put in for the appetizers," Brandon contested. "I told you that I was treating for those."

Kyle shook his head again, opened the bill, and stuck his credit card inside. Done.

"Thanks," Brandon said, giving in.

Vanessa thanked him as well, and he tried to smile at her, but she turned away from him, as she'd been doing since she walked into the restaurant over an hour ago. He must have really shattered her for her to hold onto the grudge for all these years, and though he couldn't blame her for that, he wasn't sure exactly what he'd done wrong. He knew she hated him, and that it had been his fault, but he was foggy when trying to recall all the facts. In senior year, they'd dated other people, and their relationship dissolved after that. He found it odd, because Vanessa knew, as he had always told her, that he would drop anything or anyone if she wanted to get back together. Back then, she had been his entire world. Nobody else even came close.

And she was still stunning. When she arrived at Carmella's Restaurant, it took him a moment to realize it was her because he expected a middle-aged woman. She'd always been a beautiful girl, but now she was an elegant, fashionable woman, confident and poised, bright and still youthful. He supposed her rich lifestyle in the fashion world was responsible for her ageless appearance. Although she was vague, she had mentioned something while they ate appetizers about marrying a man called Vincent Greene, whose family was well-off and in the fashion industry. Kyle found it odd, however, that Vanessa had slipped into that family but now worked the register at a small boutique. He always imagined her designing clothes...that had been her dream.

Brandon, on the other hand, had turned out exactly as Kyle thought he would. He owned his own business, doing architecture, just as he'd always wanted to. He had money, a good marriage, and two perfect children. He had a big house, an SUV, and fancy clothes. The only thing Kyle had that Brandon didn't was all his hair, though Kyle knew at any time his hair could start receding or thinning.

"So send me your address, and I'll meet you at your house Sunday night," Brandon said to him. "We'll drive to the pond, get the stuff, and hope that we're not seen."

The remnants of dinner lay all around the table; the basket of rolls that had arrived just prior to the entrees, Vanessa's refilled glass of ice water, and Brandon's empty plate. Looking around,

Kyle was struck with a sudden sense of finality.

"And that's it?" he said. "We get our stuff and go our separate ways again?"

Brandon and Vanessa exchanged a glance.

"We'll keep in touch," Brandon said.

"Sure," Vanessa added.

When the bill was paid, the three of them gathered their things and made for the door. Kyle held the door open for Vanessa, and when they were outside he halted, purposely holding up their goodbyes and departures. He was able to squeeze out two more quick conversations about how long it would take each of them to get home and how much they'd enjoyed the food at Carmella's Restaurant, until the inevitable end of the evening loomed and the conversations died. As Vanessa swung her pocketbook over her shoulder, ready to leave, he felt a familiar tug inside his chest. He wasn't quite ready to say goodbye to her forever, especially with so much still unfinished between them.

"I'm going to walk Vanessa to her car," he said to Brandon.

"Of course you are," Brandon said, and shook his head. He reached out and embraced Vanessa. "We'll send you the diary," he said in her ear. "And of course we'll be in touch after that."

"It was so good to see you again," she said, her eyes soft on his as they broke apart. "We'll get together again so I can meet your wife. She sounds great."

"She is," Brandon told her. "We'll all get together soon." He spun to Kyle. "Don't forget to send me your address." He shook Kyle's hand. "And thank you for dinner. It was the best night I've had in a while." He smiled at both of them and spun to leave.

Vanessa watched him walk away, then shot Kyle a look that clearly said she didn't really want to get into the conversation Kyle anticipated having with her. She started for her car and he followed in her wake, not talking until she stopped in front of a shiny black sedan.

"What do you want?" she said, and spun to face him.

"It's just...all through dinner you seemed like you hated me, and I wanted to address that."

"You wanted to address it."

"Yes."

For a second, he thought she was going to just hop into her car and drive away, never to speak to him again. He felt sure he deserved that, but when she didn't leave, he stepped closer, a peace offering gesture, a sign that no time had passed between them. "We were kids back then," he said, reminding himself, as he caught the flowery scent of her perfume, that she was a married woman now. "I apologize for whatever idiotic thing I did back then to make you hate me so much now, all these years later, even when you're married and we're mature adults."

The harsh lights in the small parking lot, which he was certain were making his own age lines evident, did not change her appearance in the slightest. Her skin was clear and soft white, ethereal. She wore a fun yellow dress, the color of butterfly wings. He remembered that she'd always loved bold, bright colors, and before he could stop himself, he had a major flashback of her hair in the early years of high school, tied back with a thick neon yellow ribbon.

"Your hair isn't curly anymore," he said.

"I had a perm back then," she replied. "And I'm sure you've seen recent pictures of me on Facebook. Isn't that where you got my email address?"

"I had to pay fifteen different people to hunt down your email address," he said, and then laughed at her shocked reaction. "I'm kidding. I found it on Facebook, but I didn't really look at your pictures. I hate Facebook."

"That doesn't surprise me," she replied. "Anyhow, thanks

for dinner." She spun back to her car.

"Wait," he said. "You didn't tell me if you forgive me for… whatever I did."

She turned back to him, the anger in her eyes unmistakable. It was probably making it worse that he didn't know what he'd done, though he had an idea, so he decided on a strategy to ask questions and gather evidence by her responses.

"Let me ask you this," he started.

"Don't start with turning it around on me. You seriously don't remember what happened? Does the name Larissa Cadence mean anything to you?"

"Larissa…her last name was Cadence?"

"You don't even remember her last name?"

She started for her car again, then disengaged the alarm and put her hand on the door handle. Kyle's mind turned back, and just as he suspected, the reason for Vanessa's anger stemmed from when they'd both dated other people in senior year.

"You were dating that Ronald guy with the messy red hair," he said. "What was I supposed to do, Vanessa? Just wait around until you wanted to get back together again?"

"His hair wasn't red, it was strawberry blond."

"It was red," he said back. "Red as a clown's."

"It wasn't!" she returned. "And besides, I didn't even go out with him for that long, because he wasn't like…."

"Me?"

The air between them electrified and then stilled. It felt to Kyle like he'd just been swept through a time portal, dropped right into a sweet and sizzling spot of heat they always shared. Vanessa's eyes stayed on his for the longest they had all night, soft and blue and filled with passion, the way he remembered, but then that burning anger rushed back into them. She whipped her pocketbook around to her front as though ready to toss it inside her car, but the force knocked the bag from her grasp and the contents spilled out onto the pavement.

"Damn," she said. "Damn it!"

Kyle thought her curse was an overreaction, but he bent down to help her stuff everything back into her purse—compacts of makeup, scraps of paper, mints and gum, and what looked like a tiny magnet colored in with a pink flower.

"Thanks," she said as they stood.

"No problem," he replied. "Is the magnet from one of your kids?"

"Emma," she replied. "We made them for each other. She has one too. It's supposed to be…it's for when we're not together and one of us misses the other. It's a magnet so we're always connected."

"Oh, Vanessa," he said. "That's just great."

She nodded, and he saw something he hadn't seen earlier, a sadness that was so pronounced he couldn't believe he'd missed it all night. When they were kids, he would have picked up on this immediately.

"She's a great kid," Vanessa said. "I love her more than anything in the world. It's just…I don't know, the teachers keep telling me she has developmental problems, and I shouldn't keep doing things like the magnet, that I should try to push her to grow up a little, be more independent."

"I'm sorry," he said, not knowing what to say. He didn't know much about children. "But as her mother, I'm sure you should follow your instincts with how to raise her, right?"

"Yeah," she said faintly.

"Listen," he said, and took a breath. "I'm sorry about what happened back in high school. Truly sorry. The best I can remember, you dated someone else, and then I got involved with Larissa. It was the wrong move, for a lot of reasons. She was bad news, got me into some things I shouldn't have been involved in."

"It's done," Vanessa replied. "It's in the past."

"And I'd say we should leave it there, but I don't want to forget that you and I were close at one point."

"Whatever, Kyle."

He sensed that no matter what he said, she would always carry that hurt with her, even if it happened so long ago. At least now he knew what was going on with her. At least now he could leave Carmella's Restaurant with some sense of closure.

"Now that we got that out, would you consider going to the pond with us to get our things? The three of us, just like it used to be?"

"I don't think so," she replied. "That's a part of my life I should probably leave behind."

"I understand," he said, and felt the sting of his final goodbye with Vanessa Lawrence.

"If you change your mind, though, you can email me."

"Okay." She opened her car door and tossed in her pocketbook, but then hesitated, resting her hand on top of the door. "Why didn't you marry Larissa Cadence?"

Kyle let out a faint laugh. "I don't think she was the marrying type." He thought back to what little memory he had of Larissa and her wild personality. "From what I can remember, we broke up the summer after graduation. She went to live with her brother and his girlfriend or something like that. It was almost a blessing."

"And why nobody after that?"

He shrugged, fighting away the urge for a drink. It was in moments like these that alcohol didn't even seem like a substance anymore, but something that was necessary for survival, a tool or weapon to get him through something rough. Alcoholism seemed less of a disease, and more like a response and remedy. Without letting on, he said a silent prayer for strength and tried to carry on.

"I actually just got out of a long relationship," he said, and carefully wiped the image of Ava from his mind. "We almost got married, but I've had some problems to deal with so she ended up leaving. It's sort of a trend with me."

"I'm sorry," she said. Something in that moment linked them, he could see it in her eyes, but then she smiled in a way that said it was time to leave for good. "I wish you the best."

"You too," he said. "I'm happy that your life is going well, that you're married and have two great kids. I'm happy that your life went just the way you wanted it to."

She turned away, not responding, and slipped into her car before he could try to give her a parting embrace. She whispered a soft goodbye, and the word sat there for a fleeting moment inside his chest.

As she closed the car door and started her car, the lights from the parking lot highlighted a watery sheen in her eyes, then a silent drip of tears. Kyle watched her drive away, and as her car turned out of the parking lot of Carmella's, the warmth in the air seemed to change to something icy and empty. He was standing in the middle of a cold storm, some spiral of grief left behind in Vanessa's wake. And strangely, it felt just like it had in high school, all the times she'd left him because she knew better than to get involved, that he would destroy her life. He probably would have.

Had she felt all that too? The beautiful turbulence and the passion of what used to be between them? Was that why she'd cried? There was no way he'd ever know for sure. He stuck his hands into his pockets, lowered his head, and shuffled to his car. It was too late now to go to his church group's Friday night meeting, and though he'd only attended one meeting so far, he felt the group's presence was much needed right now. He had anticipated needing a drink after dinner with Brandon and Vanessa, and had a planned method of prevention with prayer. But he hadn't anticipated Vanessa crying, hadn't anticipated the pain of hearing about her children and the other man she'd settled into a life with. He hadn't anticipated the coldness.

And for those reasons, and because of the woeful tug inside of his chest, he sank into his car, prayed for forgiveness, and drove straight to the bar.

CHAPTER NINE

It had been difficult to navigate back to New York through traffic and tears. Vanessa had cried for so long that her head was heavy and achy and her nose was running. She'd ran out of the little pack of tissues she kept in her glovebox, and had resorted to using Dunkin' Donuts napkins. The dinner with Brandon and Kyle hadn't turned out the way she thought it would. She anticipated reminiscing with them, getting her diary back from Kyle, and then leaving with the fake promise everyone makes after these get-togethers — that they'd all stay in touch. But it hadn't gone like that.

Kyle didn't have her diary. Her diary was still buried beneath the dirt by Blueberry Pond. And knowing what she knew about time and how it changed the world, she was almost positive that new people lived in the house by the pond. She'd never really been sure who owned Blueberry Pond, but if the old people who lived there did own it and had passed away, the new owners of that house weren't going to let two grown men dig up their property. She supposed she could have brought up knocking on their door and asking permission, but Kyle already seemed like he was in stealth mode and wanted to dig up the bowl on his own secretive terms. He hadn't even wanted Brandon to come along.

But why did Kyle need the cross so badly? As she pulled onto her street, she thought back as hard as she could, and pieces of that night at the pond came to her, something about the cross being magical. Did Kyle believe this now? As an adult? Based on what she'd seen at the restaurant, and what he'd said about the problems in his life and his girlfriend leaving him, she surmised that he had a drinking problem. He was probably clinging to some last belief that the cross would help him through. She had to admit that digging up the cross for that reason was something Kyle would do. Kyle was definitely the type to believe in magic and miracles.

She pulled the car into the driveway, but didn't shut off the engine. The lights were on inside the house, and the TV flashed through the living room curtains. May was babysitting Emma — something May had protested vehemently — and she knew an argument awaited her when she stepped inside the house. Just for this moment, she wanted the peace of knowing her family was safe in the house while she sat just outside, warm in her car. Just for a moment, she wanted to forget that she was going through a divorce, that her oldest daughter loathed her, that her youngest daughter had development problems, and that she'd just spent the night with two old friends who thought she had the perfect life.

She hoped Kyle hadn't seen her cry. If he had, and if he'd pieced together everything as she had about him, then he would know that things were not perfect in her life. He would know that seeing him had sent her backward through time and space, and that she'd landed in a big heap of memories that involved him and only him. The memories were bold, colorful flashes here and there; holding hands with Kyle at a sunny picnic, kissing beneath a tree by the blue-watered pond, holding each other in her bedroom, surrounded by the screaming colors of the eighties. Falling in love as only teenagers could, with reckless abandon, living and dying for one another because there was nothing so

89

great to live for in that moment but each other.

That was how she'd loved Kyle Macord.

With all his passionate talks and strange questions about life and the future. With his impulsive friendship pacts that lasted nearly a lifetime. With all his unique views on life and love. With all his beliefs in God and magic and friendship. Even with his violent bouts with alcohol. She'd loved him in spite of, and probably because of, all that craziness. Thankfully, life hadn't changed him the way it had changed her. Thankfully, he was just as she'd left him.

Minus the haircut, she thought and laughed, remembering his long dark hair. It was insane that he was a man now. Kyle and Brandon. Men.

Her mood was lifted, thinking back on Brandon and how good things were for him. He'd married a wonderful woman and they had two perfect little boys. He was living his dream, working as an architect. If she could have, back then, made one wish for how Brandon's future would turn out, she would have wished for him everything that he had now.

She rolled down the car window and let the early summer air fall against her cheeks, drying her tears. There was something in the memory of Blueberry Pond and her times there with Kyle and Brandon that was comforting—a soft pillow of nostalgia to rest upon. Even though their reunion dinner at Carmella's Restaurant hadn't gone the way she thought it would, there was still something soothing in hugging Brandon and interpreting the emotion in Kyle's eyes. Merging the past with the present was healing in a way she had not anticipated.

Her moment of peace and quiet was broken by the shouts of a teenage girl. May, probably disgruntled about something irrelevant as always, sped out of the house.

"What are you doing out here?" May said, zooming up to

the car. "Like I want to just sit around the house while you do nothing out in the driveway?"

"I wasn't doing 'nothing,'" Vanessa replied, and grabbed her pocketbook.

"What, were you trying to kill yourself or something?"

Vanessa didn't bother with a response. She stepped out of the car, locked it, and walked beside May up the front path.

"I'm going out," May said. "It's Friday night, and I've been stuck in the house all night while you went out and I didn't. What were you even doing all that time?"

"I went to Connecticut to have dinner with some old friends. I tried to tell you that before I left, but you weren't paying attention, as usual."

"I was pissed that I got stuck watching Emma again. It's not fair."

Vanessa stopped on the front porch. May's words and tone, for the first time in a while, struck something inside of her that wasn't seeped in anger.

"You don't like watching your sister?"

"I have a life," May replied. "I have friends and a boyfriend. Every day after school, I watch Emma until you get home from work at seven o'clock. I cook her dinner. I help her with her homework. It's not fair."

May pushed open the front door and disappeared inside, leaving Vanessa alone on the front steps. Deep inside of her, and maybe because she'd revisited her past that night, she recalled a similar argument with her own mother. Her younger sister Morgan became her responsibility when she was sixteen, after her parents got divorced. It was another thing May had in common with teenage Vanessa.

Vanessa had lost touch. And it hadn't happened in the way of a generation gap, it had happened with the combination of

May's rebellious nature and Vanessa's abandonment of her past self. Though that explanation appeased Vanessa, it did little to rectify the current situation. She was a mom now, and she was very responsible in that role. She wanted to do it right.

May appeared in the doorway, cell phone in her hand. "Warren is picking me up in five minutes. I'll be home when I get home."

"Is Emma asleep?"

"She fell asleep on the couch about nine o'clock. I put a blanket on her because the central air keeps kicking on, and it was freezing in the living room. She had macaroni and cheese and baked beans about seven." She stepped onto the front porch, past Vanessa, and sat on the front step.

"Thanks," Vanessa said. "For watching your sister all night. I really needed the night out."

May looked over her shoulder. "Okay," she said, narrowing her eyes.

"Be careful tonight."

"You're freaking me out," May said. "Why are you being so nice?"

"I'm always nice, you're just too busy hating me to notice." She thought about sitting down beside May, but decided it was best not to push this. "I went out with some old friends tonight and started to remember what it was like to be in high school."

"Funny," May said. "I thought you were born thirty-nine."

"Not really."

She waited, but May didn't keep up the conversation. At least this was a start.

Inside the house, Vanessa found Emma sleeping on the living room couch in front of the television, a fluffy pink blanket wrapped around her. She rubbed Emma's shoulder in smooth circles until Emma's eyes fluttered open and her mouth turned up in a sleepy smile. Emma lifted her arms and Vanessa carried her, with some difficulty, up the stairs and to her bedroom. She tucked her in, brushed back her hair, and kissed her warm forehead.

When she went to her own room to get ready for bed, she reflected one last time on the evening. She hoped Kyle would get his silver cross back, knowing now how it felt to need something so personal and important returned. She wanted her diary now more than ever, and almost wondered if Kyle Macord had contacted her at this particular time in her life for a reason beyond simple coincidence. Maybe it was some kind of message, from the universe or higher power, reminding her that she'd once been a teenager and was not so much different from May.

As she pulled off her dress and slid into a long blue nightgown, she thought about Kyle's request to go with them to Blueberry Pond when they dug up the Tupperware bowl. If she went there with them, not only would she feel that connection to her past again, but she'd also have her diary in her hands the very moment it was unearthed. She would see its exhumation, whether it had survived or had withered away, and wouldn't have to worry about it getting lost in the mail or Kyle reading the contents. After all these years, she still didn't want him to see what was inside. She remembered that one entire page had been dedicated to Kyle's attributes, with dozens of hearts doodled onto the paper, and though she couldn't remember what she'd written inside each heart, she knew that each one held some little reason why he was the one she'd always be with.

As she slid into bed between the cool sheets, she decided she would send an email to Kyle in the morning, telling him that she would join him and Brandon when they dug up the Tupperware bowl. She just hoped that when they returned to Blueberry Pond, the passing of time would not hinder their quest. With probable

93

new neighbors, a few things could go wrong, and though she tried to shake those thoughts away, they kept at her until she fell into a restless sleep a few hours later.

CHAPTER TEN

Vanessa watched as Kyle and Brandon tossed shovels into the back of Brandon's white SUV. It was Sunday, just after nine o'clock, a warm June night. Vanessa waited for Brandon to nod to her, then stepped into the back of the SUV and closed the door. Brandon and Kyle hopped into the front, and Brandon started the engine.

They'd all met up at Kyle's house at nine o'clock, exchanged greetings in the driveway, and then listened to a plan devised by Kyle: pack up shovels, drive to Blueberry Pond, assess the situation, and, if the area was clear, go to work digging up the Tupperware bowl. Vanessa would be their lookout, a job she wasn't really looking forward to. Something about the plan seemed excessively criminal. What they were doing was not exactly legal.

"You know how to get there from here?" Kyle asked Brandon.

"Parkway?"

Kyle nodded.

"I can't believe we're doing this," Vanessa said.

"Same here," Brandon replied, turning off Kyle's street. "How do I explain it to my wife if I get arrested tonight?"

"She doesn't know what we're doing?" Vanessa asked.

"I haven't told her," he replied. "Did you tell your husband?"

"No."

Kyle turned to look at her. "It's something that's always been just among us three," he said. "I appreciate that you guys kept it that way."

Vanessa gave him a slight nod, just to acknowledge what he said, then diverted her gaze. She found it difficult to talk about Vincent around Kyle, and she wasn't sure if that was because she'd essentially lied to both Kyle and Brandon about her husband and their problems, or because Kyle was an old boyfriend. Either way, it was best to avoid the conversation at all.

"If we get caught, do we confess to what we're doing?" she asked to change the topic.

"No," Kyle replied. "But don't ask me for a back-up story, because I haven't figured one out yet. I'm not that good at lying, being a Catholic boy and all."

Brandon laughed. "Yeah, from what I remember of high school, you were the perfect Catholic boy."

"Maybe not back then," Kyle said, and laughed along with him.

The SUV turned onto the highway, picking up speed, and Vanessa rolled down her window. The breeze pulled through her hair and she closed her eyes, letting the warm air dance over her face and forehead. Kyle and Brandon were talking about random things, the weather and how they were lucky it hadn't rained, and she listened for a while before opening her eyes.

In the distance, off the highway, colorful lights glowed from stores and restaurants, an area she remembered now that they were so close to where she used to live. It was different, the scenery. What she remembered as *Caldors* was now *Kohl's*, and where she remembered a *Bradlees*, there was now a *Bed Bath & Beyond*. On land that was once vast green fields now stood *Chili's* and an *Olive Garden*.

"They really built this area up," Brandon said, pointing to the

96

Chili's. "It used to be so desolate."

"It's big business now," Kyle said. "Corporations, restaurants, stores. Although with the economy so rough, they haven't built anything new in a few years."

"Car sales slow where you work?" Brandon asked.

"Picking up," Kyle returned. "Volkswagens sell themselves anyhow."

"Spoken like a true car salesman," Brandon said and smiled.

Brandon pulled off the highway onto the exit ramp. Conversations ceased, and Vanessa suspected that being so close, Kyle and Brandon might be having second thoughts. But Brandon kept going, driving down a street that Vanessa remembered as her old bus route. This area had not changed much, but it was difficult to tell in the dark. When Brandon reached the side street that led to Vanessa's old house, he slowed down.

"Where do I park?" he asked Kyle.

"The Masons' house. One house away from the pond."

"Do the Masons still live there?"

Kyle shook his head. "I think Mrs. Mason died, and Mr. Mason is in one of those old people apartment buildings."

"That's too bad," Vanessa said. She remembered the couple as not being very old, but now, all these years later, they would have to be in their seventies.

The first thing she noticed when Brandon swung the SUV to the side of the road in front of the Masons' house was that the wood fence that used to be around the Masons' yard was gone. She remembered that as sort of a shield for their property, and without it, the yard now seemed so open and exposed. Slightly up ahead, she could just make out the tiny white cape that edged Blueberry Pond, though from the angle they were parked at she could not see the pond.

"The cape next to the pond is still the same color," Brandon said. "That's a good sign. Most people, when they buy a new house, change the color."

"Is that an architecture thing?" Kyle asked.

"Just an observation."

Brandon turned off the engine, and they sat in silence for a moment. "Well," he said finally, "I guess we should get this over with."

Quietly they opened the back, retrieved the shovels, and snuck along the curb toward the pond. Vanessa, serious in her role as lookout, kept her eyes on every surrounding house, noticing little details that may help them later: what houses had lights out for the night and what houses had dogs that might start barking. The neighborhood was foreign to her now; bushes stood where there used to be only grass, siding had been installed on houses that used to be painted, and there was even a new round above-ground swimming pool behind the house a girl named Fawn had lived in. But when they approached the tiny white cape by the pond, all of that seemed like nothing compared to the differences now in front of her.

"Wow," Brandon whispered, stopping.

The row of flowers and whimsical decorations that used to line the brick walkway beside the cape were gone. The driveway used to be loose stones, now it was paved. A huge, newly constructed garage stood in back of the driveway, blocking out the pond. It was clear that the house had new owners; people who did a lot to their property and took care of it like nothing Vanessa had ever seen. Even the front steps looked different, closed in by some sort of screen, and the porch lights above the enclosure were fancy modern-style lanterns.

"I don't like this," she said.

"See that?" Brandon whispered, pointing to something massive and shadowy beside the garage. "That's a mini backhoe.

I'm going to guess that whoever lives here now is a contractor or something. He probably did all this work himself."

"He changed the entire place," Kyle said.

The three of them looked at each other, and through the faint white light streaming from the cape's front porch, Vanessa shook her head. "It's not a good idea," she said.

"I have to," Kyle replied.

"I agree with Vanessa," Brandon said, staring up at the house. The sunporch, where the old man used to sit with his lemonade and crossword puzzle, was lit up, though it seemed vacant. "New people live here now."

"We knew that was going to happen," Kyle said. He turned and started for the pond before they could stop him.

Vanessa followed, Brandon just ahead of her, and when she turned the corner behind the garage, Blueberry Pond came fully into view. Though it was dark, she could tell the pond hadn't changed at all. She couldn't help but smile for that.

"Kyle," Brandon said, nearly running to catch up with him. "Wait."

But in the silence and darkness around the pond, Vanessa felt a reassurance. The pond was a good distance from the house, and the tallest pine tree even farther. She hoped Kyle knew exactly which pine tree that was, though. They all seemed the same size now.

"Kyle!" Brandon said in a sharp whisper.

They'd come up behind him, only now there was no light at all, not even from the moon, and Vanessa could not tell where anyone was standing until a bright light sliced through the surroundings.

"Are you crazy?" Brandon said.

"You knew I was crazy years ago," Kyle replied, standing beside a tree, a lit flashlight in his hand. "You think in twenty-three years I've improved?"

"This is insane," Brandon said. "Turn that off."

"I will once we start digging." He glanced at the house, then turned his gaze upward. "This is the tree," he said, and stuck the tip of his shovel into the dirt.

"Wait," Vanessa said. "How can you be sure it's the right tree?"

"Because when we used to kiss here, if I looked straight ahead from the trunk, my eyes were dead on Fawn McKinley's front door." He pointed across, then spun to Brandon. "You ready to dig?"

"I don't know."

"You're the one who wanted to come with me."

"Guys," Vanessa said, and stomped her foot to the ground. "Just start digging before we make too much noise and somebody comes out. Turn the flashlight off. I'll keep watch."

She took three steps forward and focused on the white cape, the illuminated sunporch, and the back door. There was no movement inside the house, though somebody was obviously home. Behind her, Kyle and Brandon didn't seem to be digging yet as she'd instructed, and were just talking in hushed voices about the projected position and depth of the bowl. She wished they would hurry.

Finally, the flashlight clicked off and the unmistakable sound of metal plunging into earth echoed through her old neighborhood. Something shadowy moved across the back window of the house and she spun around.

"Wait a second," she whispered. "Somebody is moving inside the house."

"Dig quieter," Kyle whispered to Brandon.

"How the heck am I supposed to do that?"

"Shh," Vanessa said. "If someone comes out, what do we do?

100

Run?"

"Cut through the back of the pond, through the woods," Kyle replied. "That comes out near the Masons'."

Vanessa nodded and spun back to the house. If they had to run, she was thankful that she'd worn flats, though sneakers would have been a better choice. Kyle and Brandon began again, and the movement from inside the house seemed to stop. Vanessa rocked on her heels for a few minutes, unsettled but vigilant, until she noticed something had changed in the surroundings. The porch light across the street, at the house that used to be Fawn McKinley's, was on.

It was probably nothing. Maybe someone had to let their dog out or had to get something out of their car. And from the McKinley house, the woody area behind the pond would not be visible in the dark, though the light from Kyle's flashlight would have been noticeable when it blasted through the surrounding trees.

A few minutes passed, and Vanessa struggled with the unsettled feeling. Something was wrong, something felt off in a way she could not explain. Distantly, from inside the white cape, a phone rang.

"Guys," she whispered. "We should hurry."

"It doesn't even seem like we've broken ground," Kyle said. "I think maybe I used to be much strong—"

Vanessa jumped backward as the cape's backyard floodlights burst on, sending thick white light over the woods and the pond. The back door of the house shot open and slammed against the wood with such force that the top of the door fell off its hinges. A monstrous man with bushy dark hair stepped outside.

"What the hell are you doing!" he hollered.

Vanessa stood still, not able to make any movement.

"Get the hell off my property!" the man said, rushing at them.

A warm, sticky hand slid into Vanessa's and tugged her backward, toward the woods. She kept running hand-in-hand with Kyle, through the woods in a route she knew well, even if not consciously; weave through the trees, straight across the back of the pond, then hang back slightly near the rocks. As she ran, low branches and broad leaves slapped at her face, and though she was in shape and went to the gym at least a few times a week, her lungs and throat were on fire. Maybe it was the combination of flight and fright, but by the time they reached the edge of the woods, she already felt like she couldn't go any further or she'd pass out. Her face stung and her feet throbbed as she spotted the silhouette of the SUV just ahead.

"Hurry!" Brandon said as the lights flashed on the SUV.

With the first rational thought she'd had since the floodlights of the cape flashed on, Vanessa grabbed the shovels from Kyle and Brandon and hopped into the back of the SUV. She couldn't tell if the huge, lumberjack-looking man that lived in the cape had followed them through the woods, or if perhaps he'd detoured and would come crashing down the street, but her instincts told her to get everything into the SUV as fast as she could. She pushed the shovels onto the floor of the SUV as Brandon and Kyle jumped in. Brandon started the engine, and the SUV darted out onto the street, speeding down the road as Brandon and Kyle huffed and wheezed from the front seat.

They made a right turn off her old street, straight down her old bus route, then a left turn onto a short road she remembered as leading to Sal and Josie's Pizzeria. A few minutes later, as her breathing slowed and her lungs finally stopped burning, Brandon pulled into the parking lot of Sal and Josie's and parked the SUV in the back of the lot.

"Oh my God," Vanessa said.

Brandon sat silent in the front seat. Kyle slammed his head

back against the headrest.

"That was the stupidest thing I've ever done in my life," Brandon said at length. "No, wait a minute. Putting a ten-thousand dollar watch into a Tupperware bowl and burying it was the stupidest thing I've ever done in my life."

"I'm sorry," Vanessa said, mostly to Kyle because she knew how important this was to him. "But at least we tried."

Kyle lowered his head.

"Did you see that guy?" Vanessa asked.

"I saw him," Brandon replied. "If he had caught up with us, I think he probably would have killed us."

"With his bare hands," Vanessa said. "Thank God we remembered how to navigate through the woods and did it better than he did...if he tried to catch us, that is. I'm not sure what happened after he started shouting."

Brandon let out a little laugh. "Thankfully I didn't have a heart attack or something. I'm definitely not young anymore." He sucked in a raspy breath and blew it out to prove his point. "But for a second there...I guess it felt sort of fun to get chased away like that."

"Fun?" Kyle said. "You think that was fun?"

"I didn't mean it like that. I just meant it was fun to act young again."

Kyle shook his head, then planted his face in his palms. "We need to go back," he said. "With a better plan."

"Kyle," Vanessa said softly. "It's over. We tried, but the guy that lives there now is nuts. And I have a feeling the people that live in the McKinley's house now might have seen us and called him, so it's not just one person we have to look out for."

"Then next time we'll wait until everyone is asleep," Kyle said. "I have to get that cross back, whether you two come with me or not."

Vanessa locked eyes with Brandon. She wasn't sure what to do for Kyle, but was sure that he was on a mission, one he was going to see through, even if right now the outlook was bleak. Brandon must have been thinking the same thing, because he just shrugged as though he didn't know what to do for Kyle either.

"I have something to tell you guys," Kyle said. He lifted his head but didn't make eye contact, just gazed ahead at the bright red and green lights of Sal and Josie's Pizzeria. "Just before my dad died he asked me for the cross—the one in the Tupperware bowl—and I didn't give it to him. He was an alcoholic, and he needed that cross to pull him through, because it had helped with every other guy in my family. I'm sure that the stroke that killed him was because of his drinking, and the cross might have helped him pull through. I feel like I was the one who killed him because I didn't give him the cross."

"I'm sorry, Kyle," Brandon said.

Vanessa reached out and cupped Kyle's shoulder. "I'm sorry, too," she whispered.

"Thanks," Kyle said and lowered his head again. "But that's not all of it. I've got the same problem as my father, so I figured the cross would help me beat it. And if it didn't, at least I wouldn't feel so guilty about not giving it to my dad, because it wouldn't have helped him either."

"Understandable," Brandon said. He met eyes with Vanessa. "So that's why you wanted the cross so badly. You should have just told us that from the beginning."

Vanessa pulled away from Kyle and sat back. Now that they were giving confessions, she decided it was time to come clean. "I wasn't entirely honest with you guys either," she said. "When Kyle emailed me, I thought he had my diary, and that was the only reason I agreed to meet up with you two. I needed it back because I'm having some trouble with my oldest daughter and wanted to see what I had written in my diary when I was her age…when my parents were going through a divorce. I wanted to see how I handled it, how to connect with her right now."

Kyle turned to her. "You and your husband are—"

"He's been living in a hotel for two months," she said. "We're going through a messy divorce."

"Oh God," Brandon said. "I'm so sorry, Vanessa."

"Don't be," she replied. "It's for the best, believe me." She wanted, more than anything, to see Kyle's expression, to see how he was taking her confession, but found she couldn't look at him.

Brandon sighed. "My turn," he said. "The reason I wanted to go with you, Kyle, is not because I didn't trust you, but because I didn't want to take the chance of losing the watch. I need to sell it to get me through the next few months until I can find a job. My company just went under."

"Oh my God," Vanessa said, and palmed her heart. "Brandon, I'm so sorry!"

"Sorries all around," Kyle said. "I really can't believe any of this."

The three of them fell silent. Vanessa couldn't remember ever feeling this way, so helpless in not only her own problems, but her friends' problems as well. And she really did consider them her friends, then and now, but maybe even more now, because time and circumstance had somehow pushed them back together.

"Kind of strange," Kyle whispered. "We all needed our stuff at the same time."

"True," Brandon said. "So what's our next move?"

"You're in for plan B?"

"Do you have a plan B?"

"Not yet," Kyle said and laughed. "But is anybody up for pizza? All that running made me hungry, and it looks like Sal and Josie's is open until eleven." He pointed to the distant sign on the door.

"I can't believe this place is still here," Vanessa said. "And yes, I could eat."

When Vanessa stepped out of the SUV, she shivered as the late night air fell over her skin. Brandon lingered by her door and reached into the back. He pulled out a white wrap-around sweater and draped it over her shoulders.

"It's Jean's," he said. "But it's getting cold, so…."

"Thanks," she said. "I can't wait to meet her. She must be really great to have landed a guy like you."

"She's about one-hundred times greater than I am," Brandon said as they walked to the door of Sal and Josie's. "If that gives you any idea."

Kyle held open the door for her and she stepped inside, glad for the sweater because the air conditioning in Sal and Josie's made it feel even colder than it was outside.

"I'm paying this time," she said to them. "For my old friends."

Kyle nodded. His jeans were splattered with dirt from his dash through the woods behind Blueberry Pond, and when she glanced down, she was surprised to find her own clothes were dirty too, as though a spray of mud had come up at some point and painted her jeans in various shades of brown and black.

"What a night," Brandon said as they walked toward a booth in the back.

He started talking with Kyle as Vanessa gazed around the restaurant. Much was the same as she remembered, posters of Italy on the walls and fake plants in the corners, although she thought the restaurant had red seats and now the seats were mauve, like they'd remodeled in the nineties. Still, the place always smelled like garlic and spices, and she couldn't wait to eat. She slid into a booth and Kyle slid in beside her, Brandon across from them.

Kyle reached across her and picked up three menus from the menu stand. "I guess we have a lot to talk about," he said, distributing the menus. "Like how our last few years have *really* been."

"Well," Vanessa said, and opened her menu. "The girls are with Vincent tonight at his hotel, so luckily, I have a lot of time to talk. Unless we get kicked out of here," she said, noting the time.

"I told Jean I was going to clean out the office, and I think she went to sleep after I left, so I have time too," Brandon said.

"Good," Kyle said and leaned back. "So who wants to go first?"

CHAPTER ELEVEN

At midnight Vanessa stepped out of Brandon's SUV, back at Kyle's house. She'd spent nearly two hours at Sal and Josie's Pizzeria with Kyle and Brandon, eating pizza, drinking Cokes, and talking about life. Brandon had told them all about his failing business, how he'd used his entire savings to keep his draftsman on, and how he needed to replenish the savings to get him through mortgage payments until he found a well-paying job. He had a high mortgage and wanted to keep his house if he could, but it would take a while to find a job with the salary he required.

Kyle told them of his battle with alcoholism, how he'd be clean for a month or so and then lose it because he had some bad thought, bad day, or guilty feeling. He told them more about his father's death, his struggle with digging up the Tupperware bowl or honoring the friendship pact, and about how he'd kept his faith and religion through all of that. He also told stories of loves he'd lost because of his drinking problem, and how he wondered if maybe he was using his drinking as an excuse because he just hadn't found the right woman yet. He admitted that he missed the woman named Ava who had just walked out of his life, though he didn't feel the loss as greatly as he expected he would. His focus now was staying off the alcohol.

Vanessa returned Jean's white sweater to the back seat of the SUV, wrapped her arms around Brandon, and held him close.

She found herself in such a state of melancholy that she couldn't let go of Brandon for fear of it all pouring out of her in messy tears, and wasn't sure if this was because she was tired or because of the emotional night they'd all shared. From the beginning of their reunion it had felt like stepping backward in time, then being whipped back into the present, and then tonight, dipping back again into the past just a little. It was a life review, and she knew Kyle and Brandon felt the same way she did.

"Thanks for dinner," Brandon said as she held him. His hair held the faint scent of pizza from Sal and Josie's. "I can't wait to do this again."

"Soon," she said, and let go.

He reached out and shook Kyle's hand, then clapped him on the shoulder. "We'll figure something out," he said. "We'll go to the pond in the middle of the night, or when nobody is home… we'll get your cross back for you."

"And your watch," Kyle said. "And Vanessa's diary."

"I'll call you," Brandon said, and stepped back into his SUV. He rolled down the window and waved, then pulled the SUV out of Kyle's driveway and was gone.

Vanessa stood beside Kyle, shoulder to shoulder, until a shiver ran up the base of her spine and settled inside her chest. They'd been alone together the night at Carmella's Restaurant, and had even stood close like they were now, but that was before he knew she was going through a divorce. She wasn't sure if he would address that, or ask for more details than she gave at Sal and Josie's. Somehow, it seemed like there was so much more to say to him.

"I guess I should be going," she said, not looking up at him. "I have a long ride back to New York."

"Come inside," he said. "Just to see my place for a few minutes."

She wanted to say she didn't think it was a good idea, that there might be old feelings still between them, but she didn't. She just nodded and followed him to his front door like some invisible rope had wrapped around her waist and was tugging her there.

"It's not entirely my house," he said, pulling out his keys. "It's a two-family house, and the owner lives on the top floor. He's a security guard so he's gone all night."

"So you rent?"

"Yeah," he replied, and swung the door open. The apartment smelled like stale coffee. "But I've been here a long time and he hasn't raised the rent, so it's too good of a deal to move."

His apartment, on the inside, was drab, and gave the overall illusion of being stuck inside a cardboard box. The living room was virtually colorless, beige and tan and eggshell, nothing on the walls and no decor at all. Just a tan couch, a television, and to the right, a small kitchen.

"It's not real fancy, I know."

"It could use some color," she said. "Bright reds and oranges, like fire. That would really pick the place up." She sat down on his couch and he sat beside her. "You could do it easily with colorful throw pillows on the couch and some artwork on the walls."

"Mmm," he said and looked around, probably to humor her. "You had a way with color, I remember that." He tilted his head. "But you never became a fashion designer, even though you always wanted to, and you even married someone in the business. How come?"

Vanessa stared ahead at the blank wall above the television. "I got pregnant with May really young, and that took over everything. I wanted to be a good mom, and that meant putting May before myself, and I wouldn't change that for anything. Plus…Vincent's family never offered me anything. They never helped me out at all. I think they always hated me because they thought I tricked him into marriage, though nobody ever came right out and said that…except Vincent, of course."

"Nice."

"He's a real piece of garbage," she said, and yawned. "Do you have some coffee or something?"

"Of course," he said and stood. "I'll be right back."

Vanessa watched him walk to his kitchen and pull brown mugs out of the cabinet. His jeans were muddy and saggy, and he wore a dark blue T-shirt that was just a touch too loose for him. He looked a wreck, but underneath all that mess, he was still attractive. Not attractive like Vincent, not debonair and fashionable, but attractive in a youthful, boyish way with a touch of the edge that he'd always had. His outer look somehow meshed with his inner self, resulting in a dark appeal outwardly, a sensitive and deep persona within. He was oddly discordant but beautiful, like an orchestra tuning up. That had always been the draw with him, and Vanessa sensed that alluring mix was still intact all these years later. She was also fully aware that it still pulled her in.

They spoke back and forth about the evening while Kyle prepared the coffee, then he came back into the living room and placed her coffee down on the coffee table, along with a few packets of sugar.

"So the night you left Carmella's Restaurant, you were crying because of what's going on in your life right now?" he asked, sitting down beside her.

Vanessa shook the sugar packets, ripped off the tops, and dumped as much as she could into her coffee. "I was hoping you hadn't seen that," she said. "But I was crying for a few reasons. Mostly because you thought I had the perfect life, and right now, it's just the opposite of that."

Kyle sipped his coffee. "Let me ask you this," he said. "What's your definition of the perfect life?"

"I don't know," she replied, thinking. "I guess working your dream job, marrying your soulmate, and raising loving children."

"So you've already done one of those things, and there's still time for the rest."

Vanessa laughed. "When we went to Carmella's and you talked about not getting married and having children, you said you ran out of time. What makes it different for me with finding my soulmate and working in my dream job? We're the same age."

"I have a few battles to win before I even start thinking about raising a family. Plus, nobody wants to deal with a middle-aged alcoholic salesman, so if you look at it that way, I'm out of time." He sipped his coffee again, placed the mug down on the coffee table, and surveyed her. "You, on the other hand, can change careers whenever you want, and I can't imagine any man in the world would ever turn you down."

Vanessa considered his theory. There wasn't any rule that said she couldn't change careers, even if she wasn't in her twenties anymore. And even if it wasn't specifically a job as a fashion designer, there were other jobs in the field that would excite her. Maybe after the divorce, she could rearrange her lifestyle, finally land a true career, and concentrate on doing the things she'd missed out on because she'd married so young. She could still be a good mom, perhaps an even better mom, because she'd be so much happier without Vincent and without being stuck in a dead-end job.

"I could be a fashion consultant or something," she said. "Or do a fashion blog, or write for a magazine...I could do a lot of things."

"There you go, then," Kyle said, and smiled.

They spoke about jobs as it sank deeper into the night, then changed the subject to Brandon and how sorry they both were that things were not going so well financially for him. It had been a long time since Vanessa connected with someone the way she connected to Kyle, and she reprimanded herself for ever letting him slip out of her life. Maybe if he hadn't, things would have been different. Maybe she wouldn't have been the wild girl she'd been in college and after college. Maybe she would have ended up marrying Kyle. But then she wouldn't have May and Emma, and imagining those two beautiful girls in any different form was impossible. She was pleased for fate, pleased it had given her May and Emma, just as they were.

"...and she lived here but didn't give up her apartment," Kyle said, talking about Ava and his recent breakup. "That should have tipped me off that she wasn't into it a hundred percent."

Vanessa stifled a yawn. It was nearly two o'clock, and her coffee was already wearing off. "Did you love her?" she asked.

Kyle shrugged. "In a way," he said. "But the same way I loved the others, and I don't know if that would be an 'in love' sort of thing." He stood and picked up the empty coffee mugs. "Did you want to sleep on the couch and go home in the morning?" He glanced at the clock on the cable box. "Or I could sleep on the couch and you could take my bed."

Vanessa considered it. "I don't think that's the best idea," she said after a moment. "But thanks." She stood and waited for him to finish cleaning up their mugs. If she stayed, traffic would be horrible in the morning, and she didn't feel like dealing with Monday morning commuters as she drove back to New York.

"I could make you breakfast in the morning," he said, coming back into the living room.

"You cook?"

"I've had long stretches of time on my own," he said like it was no big deal. "So I sort of took up cooking out of both necessity and boredom."

She laughed, then rested a hand to her mouth as she yawned again. "I'm sorry," she said. "I really should get going."

Kyle walked her outside. The night air did little to rouse her, and by the time she reached her car, she regretted turning down Kyle's offer for a place to sleep for the night and a home-cooked breakfast in the morning. But she admitted to herself, standing in front of Kyle in his driveway, that her decision had less to do with morning traffic and more to do with the fact that she wasn't sure what would happen if she spent the night in Kyle's apartment. Memories, she was coming to realize, were very powerful things.

"So thanks for the pizza at Sal and Josie's," Kyle said. "It made me think about old times. Although lately, it seems that's all I really think about."

"Me too," she whispered. "Things were so much easier back then, even if at the time we thought things were so tough."

"If only we could go back," he said, and sighed. "Do things differently. Not screw up our lives so badly."

"I don't know if anyone has done it right," she replied. "Or if we're even meant to get it right."

He nodded in agreement and took a step closer. Through the white light streaming from his front porch, the cross that hung around his neck glimmered like a golden star. Vanessa reached out and touched it, letting her fingers run down the length.

"This one isn't magic?" she asked.

Kyle met her eyes, and for a moment he seemed stuck on an answer. "It's a...it's a symbol of my faith, so in a way it's magic. I don't have much, but I do have my faith."

"When was the last time you drank?" she asked, still touching the cross.

"Friday night after we all met for dinner at Carmella's."

"Oh, Kyle," she said and pulled away.

"I know," he said. "But you have no idea how difficult it was for me to see you again. And when you drove away crying, I thought it was because...."

"What?"

He turned away. "I thought maybe you cried because of... us. Because of seeing each other again after we were each other's first loves and first kiss. All of that."

"It was," she said. "Part of it was that. How could it not be?"

He turned back to her, his eyes filled with the intensity Vanessa remembered. "I'm sorry for the way it ended between us. If you had told me you wanted to be with me back then, I would have dropped the world for you. You know that, right?"

"No," she said, and shook her head. "I thought you were in love with Larissa Cadence. And that hurt too much to forgive you for it and take you back. It hurt so much that it stayed with me all these years."

"If I could go back and change it, I would."

"It's too late," she said. "And life went on the way it was supposed to." She reached behind her and opened her car door. "I really should go, but call me during the week and let me know what our next move is with the friendship pact."

"Okay." He reached out and touched her sleeve, just as she was about to step into her car. "You always hug Brandon," he whispered. "But you never hug me."

"Things are different between us."

"Even now?"

She couldn't risk telling him the truth...that the attraction was there, had always been there. Maybe more now because she was older and wiser and knew what she wanted. But she was going through a divorce, and getting involved with Kyle again was probably not the best idea. Having two men of different but equal intensities in her life would be unbearable.

"If you want a hug, I'll give you a hug," she said.

"I don't want a hug."

He slipped his arm around her waist.

"Kyle," she whispered as he pulled her close. "Please...."

But when his lips went to hers, she didn't resist like she knew she should. She kissed him back, her heart thumping with such pressure she was sure he could feel it against his chest. She wished she could remember exactly how he'd kissed when he was sixteen, but it seemed so long ago. They were different now in the roles they'd always played, but as she kissed him, moving her mouth against his, she decided that in this case, different was good. If she could let the past go, it could be a new start.

But right now, she wasn't quite ready for a new start.

She pressed her hand to his chest and stepped away. "I'm going through a divorce," she said, and bit her lip. "It's not the right time."

"I had to give it a shot," he said. "I had to see if it was still there."

"It's still there."

"I know." He smiled. "I'll call you this week."

She slipped into her car and gave him a quick wave, then backed out of his driveway and gunned the engine. Tears grew in her eyes, but she couldn't help but smile through the watery haze. For as dark as Kyle Macord had always been, right now, he was a much needed light.

CHAPTER TWELVE

Tuesday morning, Brandon slept late. When he finally woke up, he knew by the silence in the house that the boys were already at school and that Jean was probably done cleaning up and was reading down on the couch. He'd spent the entire day yesterday finishing up the final cleaning out of Ballas & Monroe, and hadn't had much chance to think back over his weekend with Kyle and Vanessa. But now, as he lay in the quiet of his own sunny bedroom, he could revisit the adventure in his mind, remember it on his own terms.

From the moment he saw the white cape beside Blueberry Pond, he knew he wasn't getting his watch back. The kind of people who put that much work into their property weren't going to just let somebody come and dig it up, and he even suspected that the guy who'd chased them away had probably had a similar battle with others who visited the pond under the illusion that it was still open ground, free space. Sunday night he'd considered that the guy was crazy, but thinking back on it now, what would he have done if three people were standing in his backyard that late at night? Maybe not scream and run after them, but he'd certainly call the police if they appeared to be digging up his property.

And then there was the dinner at Sal and Josie's, when the three of them had truly opened up about their lives and their struggles.

117

It struck him, hearing about Kyle's battle with alcoholism and Vanessa's divorce and problems with her children, that what he wanted more than anything was to help his old friends. The watch was important, but if the watch was in the Tupperware bowl alone, by itself, he probably wouldn't want it quite as much. The draw was digging up the bowl that contained all the items of the friendship pact, because what was inside was a remedy to what afflicted the three of them now. It was almost as though Kyle had known, back then, that they would need these specific items back at some point, and had decided to store them all away safely, beneath a tree, beside a pond.

He laughed at the thought of Kyle Macord as some sort of clairvoyant, but it did ring true in a way. Kyle had been a sensitive, introspective kid, and still seemed that way as an adult. Maybe his instincts had pulled him in a certain direction that night so many years ago...or maybe they'd all felt it. He remembered that night as different. Magical.

He rubbed his eyes and sat up in bed, checking the time. It was nearly ten o'clock, and he figured this was what unemployment felt like, in the early stages, before the interviews started up. He dreaded that, because even though he'd sent out a few resumes, nobody had phoned him yet. He supposed his resume was too sparse—only one job, owner of his own business—and he wondered if that would be beneficial or work against him. Either way, he'd been truthful. He could have stretched things out or lied if he'd wanted to. Everyone did that, or so he'd been told, but he wanted to land the right job and didn't want to risk getting caught in a lie once he was settled into a place he liked.

Beside him, on his nightstand, lay his cell phone. He reached for it and checked for possible calls or emails from prospective jobs. Only one call and voicemail...from Kyle.

Already, he thought, and laughed as he started to listen. From the quick voicemail Kyle had left, it seemed he had a plan to go back to Blueberry Pond and wanted Brandon to call him when he got up. Brandon memorized Kyle's cell number from his voicemail, and called.

"Hello?" Kyle said after a few rings.

"Hey," he said. "It's Brandon."

"Well, look who decided to wake up today."

"Ha ha," Brandon said. "Why are you in such a good mood?"

"Hang on a second. I'm at work and in earshot of coworkers."

Brandon kicked his covers down to the bottom of the bed, something Jean despised but was his habit in the morning. He wasn't sure when this routine started, but assumed it was something he'd done in childhood, when his mother would come in each morning to clean the bedding.

"Okay," Kyle said, coming back onto the phone. "Guess who I kissed Sunday night?"

Brandon laughed. "I could never guess."

"Vanessa Lawrence." Kyle went on like he hadn't caught Brandon's joking sarcasm. "Can you believe it?"

"You realize you sound like you're sixteen, right?"

"Yeah," Kyle said and laughed. "Great, isn't it?"

Brandon shook his head. When he'd left Kyle and Vanessa alone in Kyle's driveway Sunday night, he would have bet anything that Vanessa would end up staying over there, possibly starting something up again with Kyle. The two, back in high school, had been so in love that Brandon thought for sure they would end up married. They were the traditional joined-at-the-hip couple, the on-again, off-again relationship that everyone knew about, the keepers of a love that made them seem much bigger together than they were apart.

And now that Vanessa was divorcing her husband, he couldn't blame Kyle for trying to start all that up again. Vanessa was a beautiful, intelligent, sensitive woman, the type that only came around once or twice in a lifetime. Brandon had only once thought of her in a romantic way—a year or so before the friendship pact—a night when Kyle was sick with a stomach thing and Brandon had been alone at Blueberry Pond with Vanessa. She was upset over something Kyle had done, and Brandon put his arm around her to comfort her. There was almost a kiss, he remembered that clearly, the type of kiss that would have happened out of teenage hormones and emotion and not real romance. Plus Vanessa belonged to Kyle, even when they weren't together, and Brandon always respected that. Now, even though Vanessa had turned into an attractive, assured woman, Brandon was happily married and would never think of straying.

"So just the kiss?" Brandon said.

"She says it's not the right time, because of her divorce going on," Kyle replied. "I respect that. I mean, that's what I should be doing, right?"

"Yes," Brandon said. "Definitely."

"Okay," Kyle said, like he needed the reassurance. "So, here's what I came up with. This Saturday night—"

"I can't just keep disappearing late at night," Brandon said in a low voice. He tilted his head to listen, making sure Jean wasn't upstairs. "The business is all cleaned out, so I have no more excuses to just leave the house that late."

"Then sneak out," Kyle said. "My plan is that we go in the middle of the night, when everyone is sleeping. Vanessa can stay further out this time, by the garage, and let us know if she sees or hears anything. But I think if we go at three a.m., we'll be fine."

"That guy is going to come out shooting next time. I just don't know if it's a good—" He paused as the floor creaked outside the bedroom. "I have to go," he said. "But I'll call you back later."

"That's fine," Kyle replied. "I'm just walking around outside

120

on the lot anyhow."

"That's all you do is walk around in the fresh air all day?"

"It's how I keep thin," Kyle said and laughed.

Brandon placed his hand on his stomach. "Maybe that would be a good job for me, then," he said, and laughed with Kyle. "Talk to you later." He ended the call and placed his phone down on the nightstand. "Jean?" he said, knowing she was just outside the bedroom door. "You out there?"

The bedroom door didn't open, though he heard another creak just outside in the hallway and knew she was standing out there. He wondered how much she'd overheard, and how much explaining he'd have to do. Maybe, now that he was spending so much time with his old friends, he should just come clean to her, although he knew she would tell him to stay out of it, that it was dangerous to go trespassing at the pond.

"Jeanie?"

Now he was alarmed. She'd heard him, so why wasn't she responding? Quickly, he pulled on a pair of sweatpants and opened the bedroom door.

Jean was sitting against the wall at the end of the hallway, crying. "Jean," he said and sped to her. "What's the matter?"

"Nothing." Her shoulders shook as she sobbed.

Brandon ran into the bathroom and ripped a few tissues out of the tissue box. He sped back to the hallway, dropped down beside her, and handed her the tissues. As he did, he noticed that in her right hand, she was clutching what looked like a small piece of paper. When he went to grab it, she pulled it away, out of his reach.

"What's that?" he asked. "Why are you crying?"

Jean sniffled. She dabbed at her eyes with the tissue. "Do you remember when that attractive woman with the house remodel in Westport asked you if you were married?"

121

"Yes," he said.

"And you told me about it right away, and told me you would divorce me before cheating on me?"

"God, Jean," he said, and felt all the air knocked out of him. "Why would you think…?" She handed him the piece of paper in her hand, and when he opened it, he saw it was a receipt for Sal and Josie's Pizzeria from Sunday night. Vanessa had paid the bill and must have stuck the receipt in her pocket, thinking it was her own sweater, forgetting it was Jean's.

"I took the SUV yesterday afternoon to bring Logan to soccer," she said. "This receipt was inside the pocket of my sweater. I've never been there."

Relief swept over him. He could explain this.

"Okay," he said. "First of all, stop crying. Nobody around here is cheating. I don't even have the money right now to go out and cheat."

"It's not funny."

"I wasn't trying to be funny. Honestly, I lied to you about where I was Sunday night."

"Oh really," she said.

"Jean—"

She stood, tissues falling from her grasp, and walked away, into the bedroom. "Jean," he said, following. "Listen to me."

"You let some other woman wear my sweater?" Her full body shook as she stood beside the bed. For a horrific moment, he wondered if she was going to start packing her things. "I could smell perfume on it, and there was dirt all over the backseat of the SUV. What the hell is going on, Brandon? I thought we were stronger than this."

Brandon sat at the bottom of the bed, on top of the roll of blankets he'd just kicked down. He patted the mattress for her to sit beside him, and she did.

"The woman's name is Vanessa Lawrence. Actually, Vanessa Greene. She's an old friend from when I was young. You don't remember me talking about her?" Jean's eyes shifted as she thought. There was something of recollection in her expression, and he was pleased. "We used to hang around with a kid named Kyle Macord, and he contacted me recently." He wasn't sure what to say and what to leave out. The friendship pact was secret, and now that he was faced with revealing something he'd never spoken about outside of his time with Kyle and Vanessa, he decided he wanted to keep it that way. "I can't get into the nature of his emails," he said, "but I can honestly tell you that I'm not cheating on you with Vanessa. In fact, I think Vanessa and Kyle have started something up again, based on what he just told me."

"Kyle was the person you were just talking to? You said something about guns?"

Brandon thought back. "Sort of," he said. "No, not really. I was only joking about something."

"Please tell me what's going on." Her voice was strained and pleading. "Because it looks pretty bad from all the evidence."

"It's not bad," he replied. "Not really. It's just something that Kyle, Vanessa, and I did that's sort of a secret."

"Did you kill someone for money or something? Bury them?"

"God, no," he said, and laughed. "It's me we're talking about here."

She laughed too, but it was punctuated with a tiny sob. It took him a minute to catch his disbelief that his own wife thought he could be a killer, just because they were low on money right now. Did she really believe he could murder someone?

"We all got together Sunday night," he said. "And we ended up by Sal and Josie's, which is right around where I grew up. You can check that out if you want. I swear to you that I'm not involved in anything like murder or adultery. After all these years, I would think you'd know me better than that."

She seemed to contemplate his words, which he wished she hadn't needed to. Was that a failing in their marriage that he'd missed all these years? A severe lack of trust?

"So she wore my sweater?"

"It was getting cold, so I let her wear it, and she was very grateful. When we left the restaurant, she must have put the receipt in the pocket. You can ask her if you want. She wants to meet you."

"I don't think so."

He wasn't sure what that tone was. Anger? Jealousy? But he'd reached the end of what he could stand for now, and needed to get his day going. Jean had stopped crying, and he'd explained himself the best way he could, without giving up a secret that he now realized was more powerful than he ever expected it would be. A secret that held three people close, and at a time when each of them needed that closeness and friendship.

"I love you," he said, and kissed the ball of her cheek. "I love you and Logan and Andrew more than anything in the world. I hope you know that."

"I love you too," she whispered.

He headed for the shower, because if he didn't, the conversation would go backward and he'd have to explain more, or it would escalate into a fight. He couldn't believe she was letting it go so easily, though he had to believe that somewhere, she trusted him. In all the years they'd been in love and married, he'd never once given her reason to believe he would cheat.

As the shower water spilled over him, fast and steamy, the thought occurred to him that Jean had the receipt from Sal and Josie's in her possession since last night. It was painful to process that. Lying in bed last night, as she read her book, she suspected he was cheating on her, but hadn't said anything until she overheard his phone conversation with Kyle and broke down in tears. Would she have always kept it to herself? Never shown him the receipt? Just walked around with it in her grasp, a constant reminder that he'd betrayed her, but she loved him enough to stick around? In that moment, he felt a love for her so strong that if she ever did leave him, he was sure he would melt away into nothingness. And just as he thought that, the bathroom door opened and closed, sending a burst of chilly air through the bathroom and down into the shower.

"Jean?"

Without a response, Jean pulled the shower curtain aside. Naked, she stepped under the hot stream of water, met his gaze, and pressed her body against his.

CHAPTER THIRTEEN

Thursday after work Kyle drove to his mother's house, as he always did on Thursday nights. His mother lived with his Aunt Bev in a small house, about a fifteen minute drive from Kyle's apartment. Aunt Bev kept his mother busy since Kyle's father had passed away, and Kyle was grateful for that. Besides their shared religion, he didn't have much in common with his aging mother anymore, and had always considered himself more like his father...passionate about life, but much too weak to handle the difficult times.

Aunt Bev's house was a feather-gray traditional New England cape. Inside, all the rooms were downstairs except the two upstairs bedrooms. It was the perfect little house for his mother to live in, much smaller than the one in the old neighborhood by Blueberry Pond, and less work for her to deal with. She was sixty-nine, and Aunt Bev, who had never married, was just a few years older at seventy-two, but had always successfully handled any problems on her own.

"I made you beef stew," his mother said, holding the front door open for him as he walked the cobblestone pathway. Her gray hair was pinned up at the sides, leaving just a few tight curls against her nape.

"Thanks," he said, and stepped inside. The house smelled like cooked meat and vegetables, and Kyle was starved. He kicked

126

his shoes off by the door and headed for the kitchen. "Where's Aunt Bev?" he asked. She wasn't in her usual place on the sofa, watching court shows.

"Helping out at a church function," his mother replied. "They needed one more person to run the bake sale."

Kyle sat down at the table, and a few minutes later his mother placed a steaming bowl of beef stew in front of him.

"So how has your week been?" she asked, sitting down with her own bowl of stew.

"Eventful," he replied, and grabbed a biscuit out of the basket on the table. "You'll never guess who I went out to dinner with last weekend."

"Ava?"

"No," he said, and shook his head. "That's over with. She hasn't even called. I went out to Carmella's Restaurant Friday night with Brandon Ballas and Vanessa Lawrence."

His mother tilted her head. "Really?" she said. "I didn't think you'd talked to them in years."

"I hadn't." He buttered his biscuit and took a bite. "Both of them look good, but both of them have some things going on right now that aren't real cool."

"Vanessa Lawrence is going through a divorce," his mother said casually. "And one of her kids is developmentally delayed."

Kyle stopped eating. "How did you know that?"

"I still talk to Vanessa's mother once in a while." She went back to her stew. "Although I haven't talked to Brandon's mother since she moved to Florida. She doesn't even send a Christmas card. God forgive me for saying it, but she was a pompous woman who always looked down on us."

Kyle shrugged. He knew that Brandon's parents didn't like to associate much with his family when Brandon and Kyle were younger. Even during neighborhood picnics they would keep their distance, knowing that Kyle's father had a drinking problem and that Kyle himself was going down the same troubled road. It was no secret that some of the other parents thought of him as bad news.

"Brandon is going through some financial stuff right now," he said. "He's closing down his architecture business, and doesn't think he'll find a job that pays enough to support his family."

"And did you offer to help out your old friend?"

"People don't do that, Mom." She never understood that there was a line with money that most people didn't cross. "I would offend him if I offered to give him money."

"We have a quarter of a million dollars just sitting in the bank from when we sold the house and your father's old cars," she said. "You should make the offer. It's the right thing to do."

Kyle contemplated it while he ate his stew. The thought had occurred to him, when they'd all sat at Sal and Josie's talking about their problems, that he had extra money in the bank that he never touched and didn't really need. He was comfortable in his job, comfortable in his apartment, and drove a decent car. Of course, none of those things were flashy or expensive, but he didn't care to live that way, never had. Brandon, on the other hand, didn't know how *not* to live that way.

"So Vanessa and I talked a lot." He wasn't sure how to get into this, but he needed some advice, so he decided to just dive straight in. "She stayed for a while the other night, and when she left…we kissed."

His mother stuck her fork into the air like it was a dagger. He was familiar with the technique. A lifted fork was a warning. "It's not a good idea to get involved with a woman who is going through an emotional time. And I'm almost positive that it's wrong to get involved with a woman before she's legally divorced. A million things could happen, and all of it would spell

128

trouble for you or her."

"That's what I figured."

When he'd kissed Vanessa, he knew she was still a married woman and that she was probably not emotionally intact from all the recent trauma in her life. But he couldn't help himself, and as they'd stood by her car in the dark, he had grabbed her waist before he knew what he was doing, almost as though it was habit. When she kissed him back he was surprised, but fully gave himself to her until she pushed him away. He wasn't sure where they would go from there, but if she wanted to rekindle what they once had, in any shape or form, he would wait until her divorce was final. He'd always loved her, always thought of her as the one who got away, and would still drop the world for her if she only said the word.

"I don't even know why you'd want to start something up with that girl again," his mother said. "God forgive me for saying it, but she never did treat you well."

"It was me who didn't treat *her* well." There were so many things his mother didn't know about that time of his life. "I deserved everything."

She made an indistinct noise and went back to her stew. In the past he would have disregarded his mother's behavior, but now that he was thinking about bringing Vanessa back into his life, he wondered what his mother's deal was. Did she hate Vanessa? And if she did, then why?

"Can I take a look at my old yearbooks after we eat?" he asked.

"They're in my closet," she replied. "I'll get them later."

After dinner, Kyle sat down in the living room with six yearbooks in front of him on the coffee table. He had all of them, from seventh grade to twelfth, even though he wasn't in the books much when he was an underclassman. He flipped open the first one, seventh grade, and found Vanessa's picture. She was so young that he could barely remember her looking the way she did, before her hair was curly, just straight and feathered back at the sides. He flipped backward to the "Bs" and found Brandon, looking kind of geeky with shaved blond hair.

He went through all of the books until senior year, when he stopped at a picture of Larissa Cadence. Had she really been such a harsh-looking girl? He couldn't remember why he'd found her attractive, though he did remember why he'd gone out with her. She was a party girl—he could recall that so clearly now that her face was in front of him, staring out forevermore from the yearbook page—and she'd always had beer or pot. Back then, he craved those things probably more than he craved Larissa Cadence.

He did have a fuzzy memory of his first time with Larissa. He'd been ridiculously drunk at some girl's house that he didn't know, in an upstairs bedroom, while a small party boomed below. Larissa hadn't been a virgin; she'd lost her virginity to an older guy who knew her brother, but Kyle had been drunk, and he couldn't remember if he'd been nervous. He recalled an unfamiliar bed, the sweet smell of marijuana, and a breathless moment of bliss. But the memory streamed into one long wisp of thought and descended back into his mind; a necessary memory, though not one that played often.

As he thought back on his time with Larissa Cadence, it struck him peculiar that he had so little memory of her—the first girl he'd slept with—but he had so many of Vanessa. Of course he'd grown up with Vanessa, but it seemed to him that he'd spent a fair amount of time with Larissa. There should have been memories there, but mostly he had just blurred pictures in his mind of wild parties, curls of cigarette smoke, and pot. Larissa was more of a loose vision depicting a crazy period of time than a cherished old girlfriend.

He flipped to the back cover of his senior yearbook, and was surprised that most of his classmates had signed the book, except for Vanessa. If only he hadn't been so stupid back then, his first time could have been with Vanessa, a girl he would always remember, and not with some girl he could barely recall, even with her picture right in front of him. Maybe Vanessa would have signed his yearbook with hearts, and it would have said something like: "I'll love you forever—Vanessa."

But didn't he have a second chance now? Hadn't destiny strangely rearranged itself to give him that? And not only did he have a second chance with Vanessa, he had another chance to make things right with Brandon, to keep up an old friendship, help each other out as buddies did. He had to admit that he liked Brandon much better now than he had in high school. Brandon was pompous back then, even if he hid it well. But time had changed Brandon, and though Kyle suspected that if he'd run into Brandon only a month ago he would have hated him, now, at this moment, Brandon was just a sensible and decent guy, struggling with life. Now, at this moment, Brandon and Kyle were on equal ground.

"Find what you were looking for?" his mother said, coming into the living room.

"Yeah," he replied, and shut the senior yearbook. "I just wanted to see some old pictures of Vanessa and Brandon."

"I have other ones, too," she said. "Hang on, I'll be right back."

Before he could question her about the pictures, she left the living room. He stacked the yearbooks on the table, starting from seventh grade to senior year, and sat back. When his mother returned, she was carrying a gold box the size of a shoebox, with the words "Kyle's Birthdays" written across the top in black marker. She placed the box down on the table.

"You told us you didn't want anymore birthday parties after your thirteenth, but we did have a few friends over on your sixteenth," she said. "You remember that, right?"

"I think we just got pizza," Kyle replied, thinking back. He pulled the top off the box and removed a stack of photos. "And I do remember that Vanessa and I were dating at the time."

"She couldn't keep her hands off you," his mother said, and frowned. "I had gone into the kitchen for some sodas, and when I came back, the girl was up on your lap."

Kyle laughed. "I don't remember that," he said. "So is that why you don't like her?"

"She was trouble," she said, and sat down on the couch. "She wanted to do things with you that no decent girl of fifteen should want to do with a boy."

"Believe me, she was a good girl compared to most."

The first few pictures were family pictures at his old house, his grandmother and his Aunt Bev lounging on the sofa beside a few blue balloons, then a few of Molly, his black Labrador retriever, sniffing through a pile of gifts. As he flipped through, he came to his tenth or eleventh birthday, a group of kids sitting at a table at his house, all with colorful party hats on and bowls of melting ice cream in front of them. He recognized Vanessa, her blonde hair in a ponytail, and Brandon, looking glum over something as he slouched in his chair.

The pictures went on and on, and he made a small pile of the ones with Brandon and Vanessa, hoping to show the photos to both of them when he saw them Saturday night. Some of the photos he remembered, most he didn't. Some brought back good memories, and some reminded him of things he would have liked to forget, like stupid haircuts and ridiculous clothing. Life was so different now. Time had sped forward, changing Atari to X-box and Walkmans to iPods. The flow of time hadn't yet caught up with him, and he wondered if he was one of those pathetic middle-aged people still stuck in their youth, refusing to acknowledge the gifts of modern technology.

Finally, at the end of the pile of pictures, he came to a photo of his father. It was Kyle's sixteenth birthday party, his last one before he stopped them entirely, and his father was sitting in the background, watching the party from afar. Not only was his father in the picture, but in the foreground were Brandon and Vanessa, just as Kyle remembered them, close to the last year of high school. His father seemed to be staring at them as they watched something on the television, and Kyle had a vague memory of watching music videos that day.

"Can I keep this?" he asked his mother, showing it to her.

"You can have it," she said, and pointed to his father. "I remember he was exhausted that day. We just had a snowstorm and he had to shovel while you all stayed inside and watched TV and ate pizza."

Kyle didn't remember that at all. But the frozen moment in time, right in front of him, tugged his insides until he felt a sting in his nose and had to squeeze the bridge, just to keep from crying. Here was his father, alive and well, only months before Kyle had made the friendship pact with Brandon and Vanessa and buried his magic family heirloom.

The guilt hit him with the force of a pounding storm, and the image of his father remained fastened to his thoughts, glued in his mind. There was only one way to remove it. Only one way to remove the guilt and wipe all of it clean.

"I have to go," he said and stood.

"Kyle, please don't...."

His mother's urgent tone led him to believe she knew exactly where he was going, but he pretended not to hear her. He kissed

133

her cheek, gathered up the pictures, and headed for the door.

"You'll go straight home now, right?" she asked, following him.

"Yeah," he said.

"I want you to call me when you get there."

He nodded, knowing how easy it would be to stand outside the bar and call her from his cell phone. "Thanks for dinner."

He sped out the door, holding the photos against his heart, already tasting whiskey on his tongue.

Chapter Fourteen

"This is the last time I'm driving to Connecticut this late at night," Vanessa said from the backseat of Brandon's SUV. "So we better get the stuff this time."

"Technically, it's morning," Kyle told her.

The clock on Vanessa's cell read 2:45. She'd been playing a game for the last few minutes to keep her awake on the ride to Blueberry Pond, but now stashed the phone away as they pulled up in front of the Masons' old house. Kyle's latest plan was to drive to Blueberry Pond at 3 a.m. and sit in the SUV with the lights off for a while, making sure everybody in the neighborhood was asleep. At any sign of lights or people, Brandon was to start driving immediately. If everything stayed quiet until 3:15, they were going to sneak through the woods, back to Blueberry Pond, and make another attempt to dig up the Tupperware bowl. This time, Vanessa would keep watch much closer to the white cape.

"Brandon, you okay?" Kyle asked. "You haven't said a word since we left my house."

"Just don't like leaving Jean and the boys home alone at night."

"I know," Kyle told him. "This is the last time."

Vanessa sat back in the seat, battling heavy eyelids. She'd arrived at Kyle's house early, around ten o'clock that evening, because she knew if she left any later she'd run the risk of falling asleep at the wheel or falling asleep at home and not making the trip at all. Vincent was taking May and Emma to New York City in the morning, and he had them overnight until Monday, when he promised to drive them both to school in the morning. It was actually perfect timing for her to be out of the house for the night.

But Brandon was not as fortunate. Earlier he'd told Vanessa and Kyle that he confessed to Jean that he was going out in the middle of the night, and she wasn't crazy about the idea. Since that announcement, Brandon had been droopy-eyed and grouchy, despite two cups of coffee and Kyle's constant talking. He hadn't told his wife where he was going, but Vanessa suspected, from the way Brandon was acting, that he was done lying to his wife. This was probably the last time he would attempt the trip to Blueberry Pond.

"I've got some pictures to show you," Kyle said. He didn't seem tired, just the opposite, like they were sitting in the SUV in the middle of the day. "From my birthday parties."

By the light of her cell phone, Vanessa went through the old pictures, laughing at her '80s hairstyles. Most of the pictures she couldn't remember Kyle's mother taking, although she did remember Kyle's sixteenth birthday. It had been just the three of them at Kyle's house, her and Brandon and Kyle, eating pizza and watching music videos on MTV. There had been a snowstorm that day, and she'd walked through the snow up the street to Kyle's house. She had never really known if she and Brandon were the only guests at Kyle's party because of the storm, or because he'd only invited the two of them.

The pictures perked Brandon up, and by 3:15, he seemed ready to get the dig over with. Quietly, they removed two shovels from the back of the SUV.

Vanessa followed behind as they began on a path through the woods that edged the pond. The beam of Kyle's flashlight led the way through the tall silhouetted trees, around the rocks, toward their destination at the other end of the pond. It was like moving around a great big U, and though it was the dark of night, Vanessa knew the route well, as though there was a map somewhere in the back of her mind. The most unnerving part was not the dark woods, but the lack of conversation with Kyle or Brandon, just trudging along through the woods, wordlessly, without their verbal support. She wondered if this was still a separate, solo mission for each of them, or if it had become something they were doing for one another. Right now, she felt like it was a group effort. She wanted to retrieve Kyle's silver cross and Brandon's watch just as badly as she wanted her old diary.

"Much darker than last time," Kyle whispered when they reached their destination.

Every window in the house was black, and when Kyle moved the flashlight away, the darkness swallowed the house entirely.

"Let's not waste time," Brandon whispered back.

Vanessa took her mark, at least ten feet closer to the house than she'd stood the last time they attempted the dig. The air was scented with the sweetness of June flowers, so thick and strong she wondered if she was standing right beside a flower patch or downwind of one. Without delay, she heard the sound of shovels hitting the ground, and she prayed the sound would not carry.

Five minutes in and all was going well. There were no lights on inside the cape, and though Vanessa could not see through the dark all the way across the street to the Masons' house, she was certain no lights had flickered on over there, either. She hadn't heard any dogs barking, hadn't seen any cars driving down the road. Her old neighborhood was silent tonight.

"Almost there," Kyle whispered after what felt like hours. The flashlight clicked on, sending a stream of light over the grass, as though he had it resting on the dirt.

"Turn it off!" Brandon said in a sharp whisper.

"I need to see how far down we are!"

As they bickered, Vanessa let her gaze skim over the still water of the pond, and wished she could walk closer, right to the edge. In her mind's eye, she saw the pond in daylight, golden sunbeams bouncing over tiny waves, blue water rippling from a soft summer breeze. The place always had a certain magic, even now, when life had proved conclusively for her that magic did not exist.

She wondered what had become of her old house in the neighborhood, so far down the road, and recalled that her mother had sold it to a young couple years ago. That couple probably had children now, still too young to sit shoulder to shoulder and discuss their teenage troubles at Blueberry Pond, but probably young enough to sprint after fireflies as she had done when she was small. There was always some mini adventure waiting at the pond...the deep croak of a frog playing hide-and-seek with the world, or the cracked ice to avoid while skating in the wintertime.

As she smiled in remembrance, a noise in the distance caught her attention and brought her back to her job as watch girl. She wasn't even sure what the noise was, could barely detect it over the sound of shovels scooping dirt, but whatever it was, it warranted closer inspection. She moved a few feet forward, toward the house.

Through the night she heard the sound again, a scraping noise from inside the house, as though someone inside was gathering items from off the floor or moving things around. She paused to listen, her muscles tight, and then ran back to Kyle and Brandon.

"He's awake," she said. "I hear him inside the house."

She could just make out Kyle's tall silhouette as he stopped shoveling.

138

"Maybe he just got up for a drink of water or to use the bathroom," he whispered.

"Shh," Brandon said. "I hear it too."

Through Vanessa's own fear she sensed Brandon's, and the instinct to flee took hold of her. Just as she set herself up for a dash back to the SUV, Kyle held out his arm to hold her back.

"We're almost there," he said. "It's got to be just another foot down."

"I don't think it's here anymore," Brandon replied. "We would have hit it by now. Let's just go. This is insane."

"In case you don't remember, I'm the one who buried it," Kyle told him. "And I'm sure it's just another foot down."

"Like you can remember twenty—"

"Guys!" Vanessa said. "Shut up and either finish up or let's go. We don't have much time."

Just as Kyle lifted the shovel to finish the job, the creak of a door echoed through the night. Vanessa grabbed his forearm.

"Wait," he whispered to her. "Don't run."

The last time they'd tried to dig up the Tupperware bowl, the man who lived in the cape by the pond had run out like a lunatic, screaming at them. This time, though less violent so far, somehow seemed worse to Vanessa. She supposed he'd heard something outside while he slept, but wasn't sure what it was. And if he saw that they were back again, strangers who had now completely torn up his backyard, he would probably fly out with his thoughts only on murder.

"Hello?" the man said from his back porch. "Is someone out there?"

His tone was unsure, not quite shouting. If he turned on the back light he would see them clearly, just as he had last time. Vanessa jerked her body to move away, but Kyle clutched her elbow. She couldn't see where Brandon was, but hadn't heard him run back through the woods, so she assumed he was right behind her.

She stood still, holding her breath as the seconds passed, until finally, the back door of the cape creaked and closed. She exhaled as Kyle's grip on her arm loosened.

"We're leaving," Brandon whispered.

Vanessa couldn't see Kyle's expression, but she knew what he was feeling. This was the last time they were going to attempt this dig, and they'd come so close, nearly to the finish line, only to have to leave again. Kyle had surmised that he was only a foot away from the Tupperware bowl, and to leave right on the edge of unearthing their items was probably torturous for him. Still, they'd been caught again, and were lucky enough this time to get away without having to run, without the risk of some psycho chasing them.

"Not going," Kyle said. "We've come too far."

"Kyle," Brandon said in a firm but gentle tone, "we have to leave now."

But Kyle, it seemed, was a man possessed. As Vanessa stared on in astonishment, Kyle lifted the shovel and plunged it into the ground, one last attempt to scoop up what he could before being chased away — one last chance to strike the plastic bowl.

And that last attempt was a horrible mistake.

As soon as Kyle threw the shovelful of dirt onto the existing mound, the back door of the house flew open. The floodlights kicked on, illuminating the woods and the pond. Vanessa had only a glimpse of the enormous man, dressed in nothing but dark sweatpants, before the light burned through her eyes and she had to lift a hand to shield her face. This time, it seemed the man was too shocked to shout. There was an obvious mound of dirt on the ground, and a deep hole in his property.

Brandon was the first to run. He tore off in an explosive

stream, so fast that Vanessa barely had time to turn her head and watch him go. But Kyle was rooted to where he stood, almost like the hole was his property. He was standing his ground.

As Brandon's frame disappeared through the woods, Vanessa tried to pull Kyle away by the neck of his T-shirt, tugging until he finally gave in and ran with her. Behind them, she heard the man holler, shouting obscenities, his footfalls close at their heels. They'd wasted too much time, and now he was right behind them.

But when they reached the middle of the woods, it became clear that the man had either let them go or was unable to navigate the woods as well as they could. As they raced, Vanessa noted the lack of heavy footsteps behind her, the end of the shouting and swearing. She didn't slow her pace, but her shoulders loosened in relief as the light from the house faded and the dark of the woods obscured her vision ahead. Kyle squeezed her hand, swung her in a different direction, and they kept running.

"I have to go back," Kyle said, slowing his pace near the end of the wooded area. "You leave with Brandon, and I'll—"

"No," Vanessa said. The dark mass of Brandon's SUV loomed ahead on the street. "You're coming with us."

"This is the last time!" he shouted. "You both said this was the last time!"

Vanessa felt his despair to the depths of her stomach. Just as they reached the SUV, ready to jump in and take off, Vanessa paused and made a decision. Panting, she turned to Kyle.

"Stay…here," she said. "I'm going to…end this."

"What?"

She spun in the opposite direction, making up her mind to do one of the craziest things she'd ever done in her life. She bumped her speed up to a fast jog and passed the Masons' old house, moving toward the tiny cape beside Blueberry Pond.

141

"Vanessa!" Kyle called after her. "Come back!"

This was the last time, she reminded herself. If not tonight, then never. She wasn't driving to Connecticut anymore, and they all needed their things. They'd nearly had them. And there was only one way to end this now, only one way to get Kyle his beloved, magical cross and Brandon his expensive watch.

A few lights in the neighborhood flickered on. Dogs were barking. As Vanessa slowed and stepped onto the front walkway of the cape, she had the sense that people were out watching, awoken just before dawn from the shouting and swearing. She ignored the tense sensation of eyes on her, ignored her instinct that Brandon probably wanted to drive away and leave her there, and continued to the front door enclosure. She stood just outside the screen and rang the bell, then took one step backward.

At first she heard nothing, so she rang the bell again. After a series of bangs through the house, the porch lights burst on, and the front door swung open.

Up close, the man who owned the house was even larger than he appeared from a distance. His upper body was massive, his bare chest wild with wiry dark hair. A thick black beard hung from his chin, and his narrow dark eyes stared blankly at Vanessa. He towered over her, nearly a foot taller, though she was tall at five-foot nine. She was not accustomed to looking up more than a few inches at anyone.

"Excuse me," she said.

"What?" he said back. "It's the middle of the night, and I don't know you."

"I realize that." Unconsciously, she took a step backward. "I apologize for the intrusion. It's just that my friends and I need something that's on your property, and we'd like to get it so we can stop coming by and waking you."

His eyes slitted in rage as he connected her to the damage of his property.

"I'm trying to be nice here," she said. "So I hope you'll do the same."

Footsteps fell over the walkway, just behind where she was standing, and she knew Brandon and Kyle were coming for her. She twisted her arm behind her and held up a hand to halt them. Their presence would screw this up — a female needed to take care of this situation; a soft form that this behemoth would not holler at or try to attack. At least she hoped he wouldn't.

"What's the matter with you people that you come out and dig in my yard?" he said in a rough, deep voice. "I oughta call the cops."

"Please don't do that," she said, trying to keep her tone gentle, feminine. "The truth is, we used to live around here when we were kids, and the people who owned the house before you let us hang out at the pond." She pointed around the house, to Blueberry Pond. "When we were younger, we buried something there, and right now…we need to dig it back up again." She didn't want to give too much away. Brandon's watch was worth a lot of money.

"All these kids been coming 'round here for years," the man said, rubbing his beard. "I run them out, but they think it's just all right cause they been doing it for years and their parents been doing it. But it's my pond. It's my woods."

"I get that," Vanessa said. "And I understand where you're coming from. So if you'll just let us get our stuff, my friends will fill the hole back in for you, and we'll be gone. We won't come by again. I don't even live in Connecticut."

He seemed to contemplate it for a moment, eyes shifting left and right as he thought.

"What'll you give me for messing up the yard?" he asked finally.

143

"Excuse me?" For one horrific second, she thought he was suggesting something sexual.

"You dig up my yard, you give me something to fix it up. You want your stuff back there, you pay for it."

"Money?" she asked.

"A hundred bucks."

"*What?*"

He yawned and threw back his thumb. "You wanna dig up my property over there, you give me a hundred. And you better fix the damage or I'll call the cops."

"Fine," Vanessa said. "I'll leave the money in your mailbox when we leave." She didn't think she had a hundred bucks in cash on her, but maybe Kyle or Brandon did, or Brandon could run out to the bank.

"You gotta name?" he asked. "In case you try running away without paying?"

"Vanessa Lawrence," she said, giving her maiden name. "But I'm not going to run away without paying." She turned to leave, heading for Brandon and Kyle, who were standing just on the edge of the yard in the distance. When she reached them, they were both wide-eyed.

"It's okay," she said, trying not to laugh at their stunned reaction. "We can finish digging, we just have to fill the hole back up and...leave a hundred bucks in his mailbox."

"A hundred bucks?" Brandon said. "Is this guy out of his mind?"

"Why did you do that?" Kyle said to her. "You had me worried sick over here."

Quickly, she explained that this was their last chance, that she had no other choice but to ask permission. It had worked, so they couldn't be angry with her, she reminded them. They could finish the job now, get their things, and go on with life.

They'd left their shovels by the hole, and when they got back to the pond, Kyle wasted no time and grabbed a shovel to start digging. This time they kept the flashlight on, Vanessa aiming the beam at the hole, and the process was much easier. Kyle dug and dug, more like a machine than a human being. Brandon tried to help, but Kyle, determined, did most of the labor.

It went on for too long. The hole was deep, much deeper than Vanessa remembered. Kyle, obviously exhausted, kept wiping his forehead with the back of his hand, then shifted his track and dug side to side, covering the entire area. With every shovelful of dirt tossed aside, Vanessa grew more and more discouraged. Something wasn't right, and as the faint lavender of morning brushed over the dark sky, she met eyes with Brandon.

"Kyle," Brandon said, resting his chin on the shovel handle. "It's not there."

Vanessa could not look at Kyle. She hadn't had the courage to say what Brandon had just said, though she was thinking the same thing.

"It's got to be here," Kyle said, shaking his head.

"Somebody must have dug it up or something," Brandon said. "Because it was right here, and it wasn't this far down."

"It has to be here," Kyle said again.

Vanessa rested her hand on his forearm. It was the kindest way to tell him to stop digging. It was over.

Below her, daybreak exposed a hole in the ground so deep and wide, it could have housed a coffin. The bowl, even if they'd been off a little in their calculations of its position, would have been unearthed if it were still there.

"Maybe the old people who used to live here saw us that night and just dug it back up and threw it away," Brandon said. "I think their back light was on that night. I kind of remember standing in a lot of light, so they could have seen us. Or maybe

145

something else happened to it over all these years."

Kyle didn't respond. He tossed the shovel beside the huge mound of dirt and sank to the ground. Vanessa squatted beside him.

"Let's cover it up and go," she whispered, and rubbed his shoulder.

"It has to be somewhere," Kyle said. "Somebody has to know what happened to it."

Brandon stood behind them, shining the flashlight into the hole back and forth, as though taking one last shot that maybe they'd missed something. He sighed, clicked off the flashlight, and sat down with them, right on the dirt.

For a while they all sat in silence, a halo of brightness ahead on the horizon, the pond eerily quiet as daylight and morning dew settled around the banks. Vanessa, sandwiched between Brandon and Kyle, watched the sky and water, wondering where her diary was now, who had it, or if it was long gone, thrown away years ago. The hope she'd had days ago was erased, and what was left was emptiness. And that wasn't even the worst emotion. Brandon and Kyle didn't have their things, either. Brandon had lost a watch worth thousands of dollars that he desperately needed to save his house, and Kyle had lost his family's precious heirloom. She suffered the pain of both of them.

"We shouldn't have done the pact," Kyle whispered at length. "It was my fault that you guys lost your things. I'm sorry for that." He lowered his head.

"We were kids," Brandon told him. "And if it makes this any better for you, at least it reconnected us. Maybe that was what it was supposed to do all along. It was a friendship pact, right? And we stayed friends, so really…it did what it was supposed to do."

"Yeah," Kyle said and sniffled. "You're right."

Vanessa pulled her legs to her chest. She rested her head on

Kyle's shoulder, and in that moment, as bleak as the day had dawned, she was struck with a peculiar sense of happiness and closure. The diary was gone, but everything else felt full circle to her in a way she could not explain.

"It really is a beautiful pond," she said. "Magical, always."

Kyle nodded and rested a dirty hand on her wrist. "And so we sit at Blueberry Pond," he said, gazing over the water. "After all these years."

"A lot of years," Brandon added. "But it feels like no time has passed at all."

Vanessa shifted and rested her head on Brandon's shoulder. She grasped Kyle's hand in hers, letting the morning sun warm her cheeks as her thumb glided against Kyle's. They sat like that for a long time, until Brandon finally let out a tired chuckle.

"I can't believe Vanessa just walked up to that guy's front door," he said.

"Somebody had to save the day," she replied.

"Speaking of him," Brandon said, "we should get going before he comes out screaming."

"I wish he didn't live there," Vanessa said. "Honestly, I could stay sitting here forever."

Brandon smiled. "It would be easier that way, wouldn't it?" Quietly, he stood and grabbed a shovel. He dragged the dirt from the mound back into the hole, and shook his head when Kyle attempted to help him.

The fullness of a warm day beat over them as Brandon sank the last bit of dirt into the hole and smoothed it over. They stood for a moment, arms at their sides, staring down over the dirt as though it were a grave, which, Vanessa supposed, it really was and always had been.

"I guess we say goodbye now," Kyle said to nobody in general, just gazing down at the ground. "Goodbye to our things, goodbye to Blueberry Pond."

"But not goodbye to each other," Vanessa added.

Brandon smiled at her, and she sensed that within that smile was the promise to keep in touch; the promise of a lifelong friendship. He gestured toward the street, for them to get going.

Vanessa walked away between Kyle and Brandon, and when she reached the garage beside the tiny white cape, she glanced back once at the pond. She didn't have a memory of leaving the pond behind when she was younger. When she'd left for college, she had other things on her mind, things more important than saying goodbye to a neighborhood pond. But now she said a silent and proper goodbye, knowing she wouldn't be back, that a part of her life that had been closed and reopened was now sealed up for good.

"I'm leaving him the shovels and twenty bucks," Kyle said, and pointed to the steel mailbox in front of the house. "That's good enough." He jogged off toward the mailbox.

Vanessa met eyes with Brandon. "You think he'll be okay?" she asked.

"If somebody can prove to him that the cross wouldn't have saved his dad from dying." He watched across the yard as Kyle dug into his pocket for cash. "And that it won't save him, either."

Vanessa nodded. "I'm going to stay with him for a while after you go back home. I'll call the girls, check up on them, and then stay the day with Kyle." She was surprised when Brandon laughed in response. "What?" she said.

"He told me that he kissed you the other night." He kept his eyes on Kyle, who was stuffing cash into the mailbox. "It's just funny how things have a way of working out."

"It was just a kiss goodbye," she said, and smiled. "I have no idea what will happen from here. But I do agree with you that things always work themselves out. Even if someone as crazy as

Kyle Macord is involved."

"True," Brandon replied. "And he's just crazy enough to keep this thing going, isn't he?"

"The bowl, you mean?"

Brandon nodded. "Something tells me he won't give up. That's just how he is."

Vanessa knew Kyle wouldn't give up. There had to be some explanation, some reason why the bowl was removed from its secret hiding place. She accepted that her diary was gone, and assumed Brandon accepted his watch was gone. But Kyle was never the accepting type.

"Do you think the bowl is gone forever?" she asked Brandon.

"No idea." He draped his arm around her shoulder. "But if it's still out there, Kyle will find it."

"There's not a doubt in my mind that he won't."

Kyle walked back and met up with them, and the three of them stepped onto the road, heading back to the SUV, away from Blueberry Pond.

CHAPTER FIFTEEN

Kyle hadn't spoken much since they'd left Blueberry Pond. He sat in the front seat of Brandon's SUV, staring out at the restaurants and stores moving by in colorful blurs, thinking about the last few hours. His muscles were sore and spasming, all the way from his arms down to his legs. He was so tired that the motion of the vehicle was sending him off to sleep for three seconds, only to rouse him when Brandon hit a bump in the road. He craved a bed, a pillow, and a full eight hours of glorious sleep.

Though his body was weak and his muscles tired and spent, his mind was still going. The Tupperware bowl was gone. He'd started to come to terms with that about a half hour before he'd stopped digging, and kept on, just in case. He knew how far down the bowl was, knew its exact position, and knew, when he did not hit it at a certain point, that it wasn't there anymore. But what he couldn't shake was why the bowl was gone. Who had removed it from the ground? Nobody knew about it, and nobody had been there that night except Brandon and Vanessa. There was a mystery brewing, one that he could possibly solve, but he was too tired right now to gather anymore thoughts.

For now, and for his own sanity, he would have to assume that his father's cross was gone forever. The logical conclusion was that the contents of the Tupperware bowl — or the entire bowl itself — had been chucked away. If the entire bowl was thrown

150

away, unopened and just considered garbage, then there was a chance his silver cross would always be beside Brandon's watch and Vanessa's diary. That was how he chose to think about their personal items. Still together.

When Brandon pulled the SUV into Kyle's driveway, Kyle battled both relief that he was home and could sleep, and a deep ache that he was parting ways with Brandon and Vanessa. Of course they said they would keep in touch, that they were friends forever now, but would they really? He knew how life worked, especially when people were older and had other things in their lives. Blueberry Pond was their last link. Now that was gone.

But he did have one more thing to take care of.

"I have to talk to Brandon alone for a second," he said, turning to Vanessa in the back seat. "But could you wait outside so I can say goodbye to you?"

"Actually," Vanessa started, and placed a finger to her lip. "I was kind of tired, so I thought maybe I could stay."

"Oh." He shook awake. Fully awake. He dug into his pocket for his house keys and handed them to her. "The gold key. Just turn it to the left and push the door in. I'll be right there."

Vanessa reached out to Brandon, grasped his hand, and held it for a few seconds before letting go.

"I'll call you this week about getting together for dinner with Jean and the boys," he said to her. "I know you're sick of the ride, so maybe we'll do it in a few weeks or next month."

"Sounds good," she replied. She stepped out of the SUV, waved one last time to Brandon, and proceeded to Kyle's front door.

"I'm going to assume you need some kind of advice here," Brandon said, watching Vanessa slip inside the house. "So you should probably know that she told me she wants to spend the day with you."

"That's good," Kyle said. "But that wasn't what I needed to talk to you about." He rubbed his forehead, not sure how to approach the subject. "Listen, I know you needed the watch, and I really feel like it's my fault that you don't have it now that you need it. So…if you need money, just to hold you over, you can borrow whatever you need. Actually, you could have it, but I'm sure, knowing you, that you'd rather it be a loan."

Brandon stared straight across at him, eyes narrowed, as though Kyle was playing some kind of joke.

"After my father died, my mother sold the house and all of his vintage cars," Kyle continued. "We have thousands in the bank that we don't need."

"You're kidding, right?"

"No." The temperature in the SUV, with the sunbeams beating through the windshield, felt like it was rising ten degrees per second. "I'll let you talk it over with your wife," he said, placing his hand on the door handle. "And you call me to let me know what you want to do."

"Wait," Brandon said, and tapped Kyle's arm to stop him from leaving. "I'll take the money. As a loan."

"You don't want your wife to know where you got it."

Brandon nodded. "I'd appreciate if you kept it between us."

"Of course."

Silence fell, until finally, Kyle opened the car door. "On the subject of advice," he said, hopping out and leaning against the open door, "when Vanessa said she wanted to spend the day with me, do you think that meant she wanted to…you know, spend the day with me?"

"You never really make sense," Brandon said. "But if you're asking what I think you're asking, then I'm not sure. Just keep in mind that she's going through a tough time with her divorce and that she's still married. I'm guessing a saintly Catholic boy such

152

as yourself wouldn't want to sleep with a married woman."

"You'd guess wrong on that." He lifted his hand and waved. "Swing by the dealership this week, and I'll give you the money. Just call me to let me know how much you need and when you'll be by to get it."

"Thanks," Brandon replied. "I'll call you."

Kyle closed the door and walked around the SUV, but just as he stepped onto the cement pathway to his front door, Brandon rolled his window down.

"We need a new place," he said out the window.

"A new place?"

"How about Carmella's? We could meet there, the three of us, once a month. Just to talk and hang out."

Kyle smiled. "Good idea," he said. "I'll see you."

Brandon rolled his window up, then reversed out of the driveway and drove away.

CHAPTER SIXTEEN

Vanessa sat on Kyle's couch, waiting for him to finish up whatever business he had going on with Brandon. She surveyed the room while he was outside, taking in the sparseness of the place, the dull beige walls, the lack of pizzazz or color. He had the basics—just as she had noted last time she was here—a television, a small bookcase, and an older stereo system. She sat wondering if it was the same stereo he had when he was younger, until finally, the door opened and Kyle stepped inside. She closed her eyes, just to let him know she could stay awake no longer, then sank her head onto the arm of his couch.

"Hey," he said. "I was going to make you breakfast."

"Just hand me a pillow and make me breakfast later," she mumbled.

"Come on," he said, and tapped her shoulder. "Go in my room. I'll sleep out here."

Vanessa grabbed her cell phone off the coffee table and lifted her body from the couch.

"Did you get in touch with May and Emma?" Kyle asked, pointing to her phone.

"You remember their names?"

"Of course."

"Yes," she said. "I texted May. Everything is okay for now, so I can get some rest."

He indicated a room off the living room and Vanessa followed behind him, talking about May and Emma, as he guided her to his room. The walls were drab in this room, just like the rest of his apartment. The place needed color, a woman's touch, and it became clear to her that Ava, his recent girlfriend, had not really intended to stick around too long. If she had, the place would still hold some hint of her essence, some flare of brightness and femininity.

"Have you ever dated anyone with kids?" she asked as Kyle pulled the covers down on his bed.

"One time," he said. "But it didn't last long. She had a son—I think the father actually died in a suicide and never really knew the kid—but it didn't work out between her and I, so I didn't get a chance to meet her son. She was one of those girls—I guess kind of like Larissa Cadence, now that I think about it—who was just a touch too wild for me."

"I can't imagine anyone being too wild for you." She sat down on the edge of the bed and kicked off her shoes. "So, you would be okay with dating someone with kids?"

"I'm not one to mess with God's plan for me. If I end up with a woman who already has kids, that's just the way my life was meant to work out. I wanted kids of my own, but kids are kids, so I would definitely be happy in that situation if I ended up in it."

She knew he meant what he said, but also detected his dark moon demeanor—he was nearing forty and did not have kids of his own. He would make a good father, and maybe being in that role would help cure him, chip away some of the plaster that had always held him where he was, stuck among past demons. Having children had done that for her. It had softened her, even after she'd spent her early twenties in a whirlwind of parties, in a lifestyle she never truly felt comfortable in, but once in it, never imagined there was a way out.

155

"Kids really change you," she said. "After I had May, I settled down a lot. In college, I was kind of a wild girl." She paused, reflecting on that behavior and what had been at the root of it. "There was this guy in high school who broke my heart so badly that I went out and did all these awful, crazy things, just to get away from that pain."

"A guy in high school." He leaned his back against the wall. "So you're saying it's my fault that you did crazy things in college. Not that everybody in the world isn't crazy in those years."

"I don't want to get into this."

"You're already into it," he said, and crossed his arms. "You brought it all up."

She stood from the bed. "You want the truth, then? You ruined my life." It hadn't come out angry, because she wasn't sure if that's what she felt. Since they'd reconnected, she was past being angry with him. "You went out with Larissa Cadence and that ruined my life."

"Whoa." He held up his hand. "We've already covered all of this. We were teenagers."

"So what? You were still Kyle and I still loved you and you knew that. Do you have any idea how hard it was for me to hear that you slept with Larissa?"

"That's what this is all about?" He reached out to her but she pulled away. "You weren't really mad that I went out with her, you were mad because I had sex with her?"

Hearing the words aloud changed Vanessa's mood and direction. She sped out of the bedroom and contemplated leaving. She wondered why she had even stayed. Earlier she'd told herself that she should stay to make sure he was okay, that she was tired and had been up all night and needed a place to sleep, but those were just excuses. If she really pushed herself, she could have driven back to New York. The draw was Kyle.

The draw had always been Kyle.

"Vanessa," he said, and walked into the living room. "We need to talk about this. I think you're just overtired right now and upset, because I'm overtired and upset too." He rubbed his forehead. "And I have worse ways of dealing with things than you do, so I really need some closure here."

"You mean that I made you feel guilty, so now you're going to go out and drink, right?"

"I've had a bad night," he replied. "I thought that's why you stayed here with me. So that I wouldn't go out and drink."

"That's what you thought?" She rushed at him. "I'm not going to do this with you, so get all of that right out of your head. I'm not going to babysit you or pick you up and put you back into bed after you've drank yourself sick. Not as your friend, and certainly not as anything more than a friend. I'm not like all those other women who did that, until they got so fed up with it that they just walked out on you. I'm not going to do it."

As she stared up at him, her hands trembling in rage, she was thrust back into another time and place...a different argument, but the same result each time. She could never be together with him, and this argument was proof of that. Since they were young, it had always been this passionate fighting, breaking up and getting back together, an endless circle of unpredictability. In high school it was intoxicating, but now it was physically draining.

"I know it's difficult to understand why I feel the need to drink when things bother me, but—"

"Because your father did it? That's how he dealt with things, so you feel like that's how you're supposed to deal with things?"

She saw in his eyes that she'd crossed a line. He stepped back, away from her, and for a moment, she thought he was going to his bedroom, leaving her behind.

"You don't know anything about my life and how it turned

out," he said finally. "I gave you the sugarcoated version, okay? I've lost jobs, I've lost women, I'm an emotional wreck, and a pathetic, vomiting drunk. So don't tell me that I ruined your life, when you ended up married with two children, living in a mansion. At least you didn't turn out like I did."

Vanessa had no return. She wasn't even sure who was right or wrong, or if there was a right or wrong. They'd both led difficult lives, even if the lives were different in many ways. Though now, she felt a touch of relief that they'd both let out what they were feeling deep inside. The angry bits, at least.

"Maybe it's best that I leave," she said.

"Fine." He moved closer to her. "You want to walk out on me for good, I guess I deserve that, right?"

"Of course you deserve it," she replied. "And you want to know why?"

"Tell me."

She exhaled. Confessions of the heart were difficult, but now, it seemed, was the right time. "Do you know what was in the diary I buried? Why I didn't want you to read it? For a year I wrote about how badly I wanted my first time to be with you. It was supposed to be me and you, in the woods, by Blueberry Pond. But you did it with Larissa and that killed me. I hated you for that. I still hate you for that."

He opened his mouth to respond, but then turned away.

"And that's everything," she continued. "That's why I never talked to you after high school. That's why I slept around in college and ended up getting pregnant with Vincent Greene's child. Maybe my life wasn't as bad as yours in some ways, but every way it went wrong, I blame you for. I thought we were going to get married...even though I was young and naive, I thought we had that kind of love. You can say you're sorry all you want, or tell me that you were just a stupid teenager, but I'll never forgive you for it. Never." She stormed past him to get her shoes and leave his apartment, but he reached out and grasped her elbow.

"Vanessa," he whispered. "I honestly don't remember that time with Larissa as well as I remember all my firsts with you. First time holding hands, first kiss, and first time falling in love... those things are more important than sex, aren't they?"

"I don't know," she replied, and really didn't. "All I know is that I want to leave now. Being with you, after all this time, isn't good for either of us." She continued to his bedroom, knowing he would follow but still focused on getting the hell out of his apartment.

"Please don't leave," he said when they reached his bedroom. "I didn't know any of what you just told me about the diary, and if I had, I'm sure everything would have been different for us. Just stay with me so we can talk about it."

As she slipped on her shoes, he slid up behind her and touched her arm.

"Don't," she said.

"You and me, after all these years...we're not done." He moved his hand to her shoulder, his breath falling into her hair as he spoke into her ear. "You can't tell me that we're done. Not with all of this still between us."

"Please don't," she said.

She spun to face him and was surprised when her body fell against his. In the next second, before she could tell herself not to, she was kissing him.

The kiss was angry and heated, not the kind of kissing she'd ever done before...not with him, not with anybody. Everything she put out he was returning—there was no indecision or hesitancy, just a stream of mingled rage and passion as heads turned and lips touched in a beautiful choreography she deemed uniquely their own.

His hand moved to lift her shirt.

"Wait," she whispered. "I don't want to do this just because we have a past together, or because I'm getting divorced and you just came out of a relationship. I don't want it to happen for all the wrong reasons."

"I would think those would be all the *right* reasons."

"No," she said. "Kyle, I'm still married."

"You're getting a divorce." His lips brushed her throat. "Let's just pick up where we left off. Let's pretend no time has passed."

"But time has passed...."

Her body was sending her mixed signals. She wanted Kyle and was letting him undress her, but she hadn't been with anyone except Vincent for over sixteen years, and was terrified. Having sex with Kyle would be taking a sharp turn in the road, heading in a totally different, uncharted direction.

But time and experience had given Kyle superb seduction skills, and just as easily as she'd slid into his kiss, she slid into his bed. The next moments went by in a blur of tossed off clothes and deep kisses, until finally, with a total abandonment of the present moment in time, Vanessa surrendered to him entirely.

CHAPTER SEVENTEEN

The alarm clock beside Kyle's bed read 2:13. Vanessa supposed, as she lay in his bed, that by the length of time they'd spent making love that morning, they'd only had a few hours of sleep afterward. She'd never gone so long without talking to May or Emma, and was feeling a sort of ache in her stomach from the distance between her and the girls. As her head rested against the pillow, she stared across at Kyle. He opened his eyes.

"Morning," he said in a groggy voice. "Or is it afternoon?"

"Afternoon," she said back. His chest was bare except for his gold cross dangling from his neck. "Just after two."

He gazed across at her, and she gazed back. In all her years with Vincent, she couldn't remember this kind of connection, something that ran so deep that it felt comfortable, even timeless. But she was skeptical of making comparisons right now. It didn't seem healthy, like she was replacing something before it had truly gone away for good. She'd just made love with a man other than her husband, technically cheating, and the thought that she was still a married woman sent a surge of guilty acid through her throat.

Worse than that, the imagined vision of Vincent sleeping with another woman before the divorce was final pained her in a way she couldn't understand. If she truly loathed Vincent the way she thought she did, she wouldn't care about his sexual encounters

161

with other women. She wished she hadn't flipped the scenario around in her mind, and tried to change gears, focus on Kyle.

"Do you remember when we were really small?" she asked him. "Like your first memory of when we played as kids?"

"Of course," he replied. "Blueberry Pond, catching frogs with nets and then putting them back into the water. We were probably four or five."

She kept the gaze, her head still resting on the pillow. "It felt weird going back again, didn't it?"

"Back to the pond?" he asked. "Or did you mean...back to us?"

"Both, I guess."

Kyle's eyes turned in thought. "Weird in a way I can't explain," he replied finally. "Lying here with you now, I feel like I'm suspended in midair between one place and the other."

"That's how I'm feeling too." She sat up. "I have to get my cell and check on the girls."

"While you do that, I'll run out to the store and grab some food for us. We both haven't eaten since last night."

Now that Kyle mentioned it, Vanessa addressed her slight queasiness from not eating in nearly twenty-four hours. It had been so long since she'd disregarded everything for the sake of letting loose and letting go, and perhaps now she was just too old to do that anymore. It took a toll on her, going without food, spending the morning making love, venturing out so far from home. All she wanted was to talk to the girls, eat, and head back to the house, even if she wouldn't see the girls until tomorrow after school. Connecticut, a place she used to call home, now seemed so far away from everything she knew.

"Believe it or not," Kyle said, stretching as he slid out of bed, "my specialty when I cook is stir-fry and Asian cuisine, that sort of thing. Is that okay for you?"

"That's fine." Anything sounded good right now. "Can you direct me toward a shower, too?"

After setting her up for a shower, Kyle grabbed his keys and headed out the door. Vanessa sat down on his bed, leaned her back against the pillows, and dialed Vincent's phone. She was passed around a bit as May came on and then Emma, but hearing both of their voices lifted her spirits, knowing they were safe and having a good time with Vincent in the city.

In the shower, as the hot water streamed over her head and down her skin, she battled a growing confusion. Earlier, the confusion had been there, and maybe she chose to ignore it because kissing Kyle had felt so good. His fingers unbuttoning her shirt, then the pressure of his body against hers…all of it had temporarily numbed the morals she'd spent a long time building and achieving. She wasn't a cheater, but did her morning of passion with Kyle truly qualify as cheating? She and Vincent had lived in separate locations for two months, and their divorce was…what was even going on with the divorce?

The divorce seemed stalled, and she wondered why that was. The solution to the fighting had been to sleep and exist in different places, and the obvious result of that arrangement had been talk of divorce and joint custody concerning May and Emma. But nothing had really happened legally. She hadn't been in touch with any lawyers and was sure that Vincent hadn't either, because he hadn't said anything and had served no papers. To put her mind at ease about this, she decided to ask Vincent what was going on the next time she met up with him to discuss the finalities. And when everything was final, she would then have to figure out what she would do about her relationship with Kyle.

She loved him and always had, but their love was complicated. It wasn't a permanent love and never had been—all evidence suggested that Kyle hadn't been able to keep anything permanent in his life since high school. Women had come and gone, and Vanessa's only distinction was that she'd been the first one. But she was older now and Kyle was too. They'd learned their lessons, or should have by now, though a part of her wondered if maybe he'd lived under the same curse she had — unable to truly give away a heart that once belonged to someone else in such a powerful way that nothing else ever seemed to compare.

The water went cold, and she realized she'd spent too long pondering things under the rush of hot water, as was her habit. Quickly she grabbed a bar of soap from his soap holder, lathered, then rinsed and stepped out of Kyle's shower. The apartment was quiet, her cell phone displayed no calls, and for a moment she enjoyed a sense of calm. It was a welcome relief after her struggle to keep her confusion over Kyle and Vincent in the back of her mind. She wondered how long she would stay in this strange mix of emotions, loose and easy from bouncing back to the more comfortable part of her life, but confused by the two men who'd dominated her thirty-nine years of existence.

After drying off, she spent a while on the couch, flipping through the channels on Kyle's television. She wasn't much of a TV person, and really only watched with Emma, all those kiddie shows that made her laugh and forget, if only for an hour or so, that life was much more serious than sitcoms would suggest. At a quarter after three, Kyle returned with two bulging brown bags, greeted her, and then headed to the kitchen to start food preparations. She went in to bother him a few times, peeking over his shoulder at the frying pan of colorful vegetables and strips of chicken, but was shooed away each time.

Finally, she sat down across from him at a small table and was presented with his culinary masterpiece: green snow peas, vibrant carrots, sautéed broccoli, and seasoned chicken over white rice. He'd mentioned a few times that he longed to cook

164

for her, so she eagerly started on her food, both out of extreme hunger and a desire to taste his cooking.

"So?" he said when she took her first bite.

"Unbelievable," she replied truthfully. "In high school, I wouldn't have guessed in a million years that someday you'd be able to cook like this."

He laughed, looking pleased with himself, and then started on his own plate of food.

They were silent as they ate, though there were so many things Vanessa wanted to say, so many questions she had for him. Where did they go from here? Would he be willing to wait until her divorce was finalized before diving into something? Was a relationship the best thing right now? She decided to ease into a conversation, and started off with small talk.

"So I guess I'll drive back to New York after dinner. I have to go into work tomorrow at nine-thirty, if I even still have a job from taking today off."

"I don't go into work until Tuesday," he said, and took a sip of water. "I work Saturdays, so I get Monday off most weeks, unless we have a big sale at the dealership."

"You like your job?"

"Love it," he replied. "I mean, I know it's nothing glamorous, but that works for me. I'd rather be comfortable in sales than trying to work myself up some corporate ladder constantly." He watched her take a bite of her food. "I know I've never been the ambitious type, and I don't know how that works for you. It seems like Vincent was pretty ambitious."

"You're not Vincent," she replied. "And nothing is…it's too soon to be discussing how I assess your level of ambition." He was already in a place she wasn't sure she wanted to be in yet. "I mean, Kyle—"

"We said we were going to pick up where we left off." He

placed his fork down on the table. "We spent the day together, and—"

"There are a lot of problems." She reached across the table and touched his arm. "I'm still married, and I need you to wait for my divorce. Then we can discuss where this is going. I have two children, and I don't know what to do about them meeting you and you forming a relationship with them. And our past makes me skeptical that you and I can keep this together."

"We were kids back then," he contested. "Let's just pick up where we left off, but know that we're doing it with a more mature outlook. We're obviously meant to be together."

Vanessa kept her hand on his arm, contemplating what he'd said. Maybe they were meant to be together, and fate and destiny had put them back together for that reason. She believed in fate now more than she ever had.

"I'll wait for your divorce," he continued. "And you know that I'll do whatever I can so that May and Emma are comfortable with having a new man around." He stared across at her, right into her eyes. "I'm crazy about you," he whispered. "I've never been one to keep my feelings inside, so there it is. I'm absolutely crazy about you, and I always have been."

She was crazy about him, too. This made everything so much more confusing. "We'll try to make it work after the divorce is final," she said. "We'll give it a chance." All she could do now was throw everything to the wind and hope it came back down softly. "So," she said, and went back to her food, "sometime during the week you'll call me?"

"Of course," he said. "I have to meet up with Brandon this week too." He averted his eyes, and she got the feeling something private was going on between Kyle and Brandon. "And then I have some work to do concerning our Tupperware bowl."

Vanessa tilted her head. "You're not giving up. I knew you

wouldn't."

"Have I ever given up on anything? Someone dug up that bowl and all our stuff, and I'm going to find out who. It's the mystery of the thing now. I'll start with finding out what happened to the old people who lived in the house that the psycho guy lives in now, and if they're still alive, I'll question them. If they're both dead, then I'll question their kids or some old neighbors—anybody who might know something."

"Did it ever occur to you that nature might have unearthed the bowl?" she said. "Maybe it just came up from a storm and got washed away."

"It was too far down." He scraped the last of his vegetables and scooped them onto his fork. "I'm positive that someone dug it up."

Vanessa nodded and finished off her plate. She helped him clean off the table, then gathered her things and stood by his front door. In his eyes she saw the sorrow of their separation, and she truly did not want to leave him behind. He leaned to kiss her, and she wrapped her arms around his neck, holding on.

"I'll miss you," she said when they broke apart. "This morning…it was amazing."

"Many years in the making," he said back.

She laughed and kissed him again, and as she did, something crazy sprung to mind.

"Come with me," she said. "I know it's insane, but living on the edge feels right to me right now. Drive to New York behind me, to my house, and drive home tomorrow morning. The girls won't be home until after school. Stay the night."

"You're serious?"

"It's completely nuts," she replied, shaking her head in beautiful confusion. "But after tonight, we have to stay apart until the divorce is final. Agreed?"

"Agreed."

Vanessa watched as Kyle checked that appliances were off, dropped a few overnight items into a plastic bag, and turned off the lights in his apartment. Whatever had taken hold of her was bordering lunacy, but she had to go with it.

"All set?" she said.

Kyle laughed in response. "What's so funny?"

"In high school, we couldn't stay together. Now, it seems we can't stay apart."

Vanessa shook her head, and before she let herself change her mind about taking Kyle home with her, she was out the door, Kyle following behind.

Chapter Eighteen

Kyle didn't admit to Vanessa, and only a little to himself, that the abundance of pictures of Vanessa's husband in her house rattled him to the bulk of his core. Her house was enormous, a white stately mansion, and when he'd arrived at dusk, the home seemed to take up the full of the horizon. It was nothing he could ever give her, if she expected that from him. Even the money he had stowed away in the bank from the sale of his parents' house would only buy her a modest home at best.

But he sensed that she wasn't after that at all, and even entertained a thought of her being uncomfortable in the mansion, pulled into a lifestyle that perhaps at one time she admired and sought, but now reminded her of everything she hated about men like her husband. Men who loved money more than their wives, men who threw money around so uncaringly that it only had value when other people mentioned its value while salivating over some shiny new car or rare piece of artwork.

As he lay in Vanessa's bed, listening to her rhythmic sleeping breaths, he felt the strain of the last few days. His muscles were sore from shoveling dirt at the pond, his mind was unsettled, wondering what had happened to the Tupperware bowl, and his heart was filled with such a combination of new and old love for Vanessa that his chest seemed to swell just listening to her breathe. How had life landed him here, right beside Vanessa

169

Lawrence?

Vanessa *Greene*, he reminded himself. It was indisputable here, inside her home. With all the pictures of Vincent Greene around the place, it was like lying among ghosts; the ghost of her marriage, the ghost of her former life. He wondered if he was strong enough to break himself out of the guilty thoughts of making love to another man's wife, in the other man's home, right beneath the wedding and honeymoon pictures and pictures of that man's children. His love for Vanessa was intense, but was it enough to combat the guilt? The kind of guilt that only a river of alcohol ever had the power to fully destroy? He slipped in and out of sleep, exhausted but wanting his last few hours with Vanessa spent in clarity, to remember each breath she took as she slept.

At seven o'clock her alarm clock sounded, a loud and incessant buzzing that would have driven him insane if it were his own alarm. Vanessa only stirred, then stuck her arm out from beneath the covers and slapped the alarm button. She spun to face him and he held his breath, hoping she wouldn't gasp in surprise that it was him and not her husband lying beside her, naked, in her bed.

"Morning," she said.

The gold glow of morning framed her face and hair, rendering him momentarily speechless. He could only smile in response.

"You don't look like you slept well," she said, and reached out to smooth his hair.

"Different bed."

"You can't fool me." She sat up and the covers fell, exposing her bare back and the soft curve of her spine. "Something is bothering you."

"Everything in the world bothers me." He sat up, stretched, and kissed her cheek. "I'll go make some breakfast for you before

170

you go to work. Then I'll be out of here and you won't see me until you're ready to." That was the deal they'd struck…no more sex or meetings until the divorce was final, though part of him prayed she'd alter the deal even slightly. "Unless you —"

"Kyle…."

He'd heard his name spoken aloud with that same inflection so many times by women. It meant he was forcing things, so he backed away from Vanessa, both verbally and physically, stepping out of her bed.

"I'll be in the kitchen," he said, wondering where the kitchen even was in this maze of a house. Last night, after his arrival, they'd stayed on the living room couch until lust and foreplay drove them upstairs to Vanessa's bedroom. He hadn't seen much of the home except the passing dark rooms and staircase, and knew it would take some navigating to locate the kitchen.

A few minutes later he found it downstairs, toward the back of the house, a bold yellow kitchen with shiny steel appliances. After preparing an easy meal of scrambled eggs and toast, he sat down at a glass-topped table and waited for Vanessa. She appeared ten minutes later, showered and dressed, wearing a stylish blue dress that accentuated the brightness of her eyes and the cherry blush of her cheeks. The brightness seemed newly born. If he didn't know her, he would have guessed she was a woman who'd just fallen in love.

They spoke as they ate, mostly about her job and the commute, and he assured her that he could find his way back home with little difficulty. The truth was, he'd followed her the entire way to New York and had no idea where the hell he was or how to get home. He drove a 1998 Volkswagen Jetta with no GPS, and didn't own a GPS system. Somebody had told him it was on his cell phone, but he'd never bothered to figure out how to use it. Back in the nineties, all he had to do when he was lost was find the highway, and he hadn't needed any technological guidance to do that, so that's what he was going to do when he left Vanessa's.

Shortly after nine, she glanced at the microwave clock and gasped. "I have to get going," she said. "How did the time get away from me like that?"

"It's okay," he said as she stood. "I'll clean this up and head out after that."

The parting seemed less difficult than the one they'd begun yesterday evening in his apartment. He had two separate encounters to look back on now, and was a bit more confident that Vanessa was falling back in love with him. He questioned why her divorce was taking so long, but what did he know about that sort of thing? It was clear that Vanessa hated her husband and wanted to be with Kyle now, so all he had to do was be patient with time. The divorce would happen, she would push for it to happen soon, and then he could start his life with Vanessa, meet her two girls, and step into an already made family unit.

"I'll call you if I find out anything about the Tupperware bowl," he said, and enclosed Vanessa in a parting embrace. "Other than that, I'll just expect that you'll call me with any news."

"I'll speak to Vincent this week and find out what has to be done," she said, and dipped her head to his shoulder. "Then you and I will figure out where we're going. I promise."

After a long kiss, and some directions on how to lock up the house, she slipped from the kitchen. The front door closed and Kyle glanced around, alone in what felt like another man's home more now than it had earlier. Without Vanessa, it was just a strange house, filled with memories he'd never be privy to; May and Emma's laughter as they grew up and played with toys, countless meals the family ate at the glass table he now looked down at, colds and flus and scrapes and cuts that Vanessa and Vincent had tended to when their girls were young. Who was he to just walk in now, after the children were nearly grown, and assume an easy role as stepdad? But he was going too far with this. There hadn't been talk of marriage, and he and Vanessa had only just begun a new relationship.

He shook his head in a silent reprimand to himself, then started to clean up the breakfast mess, pushing the bag of bread back into some fancy wooden bread box. All the while he tried to cancel his own thoughts, the ones that told him firmly that Vanessa Lawrence had been his since middle school, and that he'd been the first man to love her, so he was doing no wrong by envisioning marriage and pondering life as a stepfather to her children. Even if it was only a fantasy, it still played so beautifully that he would have allowed it even if he hadn't spent the last two days making love to Vanessa. He went back and forth for a while, telling himself that it was all fantasy, then telling himself that it was very true, until what sounded like a scuffle of footsteps sounded behind him as he placed a carton of eggs into the refrigerator.

When he spun around, startled, a teenage girl stood in the doorway of the kitchen. He'd seen pictures of May and knew it was her, though the flesh and blood vision made her almost too real and shocking, especially since he'd just been absorbed in fantasies. He felt his jaw drop, not knowing what to say, and sensing that something bad was going to come out of this unanticipated meeting.

"Most burglars don't put eggs into the refrigerator," May said, and leaned against the doorframe, crossing her arms.

"You must be May," he said. "And no, I'm not a burglar."

They stood looking at one another, not frightened or tense, but scrutinizing, it seemed. Though May was classically beautiful, possessing an old-fashioned appeal beneath a hard but obviously false outer shell, she did not resemble Vanessa as a teenager.

Vanessa had been much bubblier, blonde and brighter. May was dark-haired and emitted a dark vibe. Even her voice was dull and moodless, or maybe that was just the way kids spoke nowadays.

"I'm an old friend of your mother," he said, clarifying. "Kyle Macord."

She didn't look like the name meant anything to her, and he was a little dispirited. Had Vanessa never mentioned her childhood? Not him or Brandon or even Blueberry Pond?

"Where is she?" May asked.

"She just went to work." And then he realized. "Aren't you supposed to be in school?" She let out a faint laugh, steeped in sarcasm, like what he'd just said sounded disciplinary when he'd meant it just as questioning.

"I mean," he continued, "I just thought you were—"

"We were in New York City this weekend, so I didn't get a chance to grab any of my books or homework or anything. I came home to get some stuff, but I'm going back." She stared at him for a few seconds, then turned and left the kitchen.

His body was still, his eyes fixed to where May had just stood, his mind trying to devise a plan. May wasn't supposed to see him yet. Vanessa had been firm on that decision: the kids couldn't meet him until the divorce was final and they had decided what their next move was. He had some damage control to do, but how far could he go without outright lying to May? And if May told Vincent, what kind of problems would that cause in the divorce proceedings?

"May?" he called and stumbled out of the kitchen, trying to catch up with her.

"What do you want?" she said from the foot of the staircase. "To tell me that you and my mother are just old friends when you obviously spent the night with her?"

"Listen," he said, and the awkwardness finally caught up

174

with him. "I realize this isn't the best situation, but I'd appreciate it if you talked to your mother before mentioning any of this to your father."

"Ha!" she said, and slammed her hand down on the railing. "She sleeps with some guy while her kids are away, and I have to lie to my dad about it?"

She was just as difficult as Vanessa had said she was.

"I'm an old friend," he said again.

"Bullshit."

He took a breath to calm himself, then changed gears. The only solution was to jump back into his teenage self and try to see all of this from May's point of view. When he was her age, he wasn't exactly the perfect teenager. He'd been every bit as rebellious as May, every bit as troubled, every bit as bold. All May needed was someone to talk to her as an equal. Someone who didn't push.

"You don't look like your mother," he said. "But there's something about your personality that's the same…I can't figure out what it is, though."

"I'm nothing like my mom."

"Maybe not," he told her, and then it hit him. "But when she was your age — and even a bit now, I think — she was just as fiery as you are."

May's expression softened. "You really knew her when she was my age?"

"No, I knew her since birth, probably. But my earliest memory is when we were four or five." He leaned against the wall. "She didn't get along with her mother when she was sixteen. In fact, she hated her mother."

May's hand dropped off the railing, and her shoulders, tense and lifted, started to release.

"Her mother worked all the time after her parents got

175

divorced, so she was stuck watching her younger sister. I remember one night she was so mad that she threw a laundry basket of clean and folded clothes down her cellar stairs."

"No she didn't."

"Yeah," Kyle said and laughed. "I was there. I'm a witness."

It was probably best not to tell May about her mother's behavior in her teen years, but he sensed this tactic was working. May was rapt with attention, all anger stowed away, at least for the moment. He continued to tell her stories he remembered, things that Vanessa had done that blew his mind back then, like running out of the house when her mother specifically asked her to stay, or threatening to leave her sister — May's Aunt Morgan — alone in the house. Morgan was much younger than Kyle and they didn't hang around with the same people, but he did have memories of Morgan.

May listened to the stories almost hypnotically, like Kyle was telling a fabricated but interesting tale of someone she'd never known. Kyle supposed these were the stories Vanessa would have told May if only the Tupperware bowl had been where they'd left it and Vanessa had retrieved her diary. These stories reflected, through Kyle's memory, how Vanessa had handled her parents' divorce and the months that followed.

"And do you know how she got everything out when she was upset?" he continued. "She wrote everything down in her diary."

"I get it out on paper, too," May said. "Only in a different way."

She didn't elaborate, so Kyle pretended he didn't care. He was curious, but sensed that before May told him her self-remedies, he would have to earn a little more of her trust. She was a teenager, after all, and he remembered not trusting anybody older at that age, especially with his deeper feelings. Only select peers were allowed in — those two peers Vanessa and Brandon.

"Do you tell your boyfriend when you're upset?" Kyle asked her. "Your mother says you're pretty serious with someone."

"Warren." Her eyes sparkled. "Mom hates him. She thinks he's a loser and going nowhere."

"Her mother thought the same way about me."

"You dated my mother in high school?"

"Date isn't really the word." He was certain his eyes were sparkling just as May's were. "We were an inseparable couple. Except, of course, when we separated every few months."

May laughed and sat down on the last stair of the staircase. "Warren and I are like that too. We get into huge fights and break up, but we always end up back together because he's the only one out there who really understands me." She paused and seemed to consider her next words. "I want to be an artist, and he's the only one who gets that."

"You draw." He wasn't shocked at all. "That's how you get everything out."

"Yeah," she replied. "My work is sort of abstract. Everything I draw looks like a puzzle, but it all really comes together if you look at it a certain way. The pieces I did of my parents…they're some of my best work."

Kyle relaxed into a conversation about her artwork, and found it was no longer a strain to talk with her. He didn't have to pretend to be someone he wasn't, didn't have to try to be a cool adult or even flip himself back to adolescence. May wasn't so difficult to understand, just the typical teenager, and as she spoke it was even hard to imagine her fighting with anybody, let alone Vanessa. But such was the mother-daughter relationship, he supposed, and being an outsider he could see what they couldn't. Mother and daughter were exactly alike.

"I have to get back to class," she said after a while. "I parked behind what I assume is your car, so you'll have to wait for me to leave."

Kyle nodded. He spun back to the kitchen, inspected the area and made sure everything was cleaned and appliances were off, then went back to the living room and paused by the staircase. After a few minutes, May came down the stairs with books and notebooks cradled in her arms. When she saw him standing there, she shook her head and rolled her eyes.

"I already saw your phone and shoes and stuff in her room," she said. "You can go upstairs and get your things."

"Thanks," he said, and rushed past her.

After packing up his things, he met with May by the front door, pleased that she would lock up because he barely remembered Vanessa's instructions, and then they were out in the driveway, standing in abundant sunshine.

"I guess…nice to meet you," she said. "I'll see you again?"

"Hopefully," Kyle replied. "Your mother sometimes has a hard time making up her mind."

"Tell me about it."

With a shared laugh they parted ways, and Kyle waited until she backed out of the driveway and disappeared down the road before pulling out himself. He couldn't help but think this was a good start, and was confident that he and May, when and if the time came, would have a pleasant relationship. There'd been an unspoken knowledge between them that he was vying for Vanessa's love in a forever sort of way, and that he was hoping to someday enter the family. May was smart and insightful, just as Vanessa was, and Kyle knew that May read him just as well as Vanessa did. Then again, he was probably easily read by anyone with an ounce of intuition.

It occurred to him then, as he turned off Vanessa's road and onto a busier one, that he hadn't drank in four days. That was a good start. Four days of sobriety could almost equate to a year the way things had been going lately, and he celebrated that monumental four days by turning on his radio and singing along to an old song—Journey's "Don't Stop Believin'"—and steering the car onto street after street, until finally he found the highway back home.

CHAPTER NINETEEN

Brandon told Jean to sleep in, he'd take care of getting the boys off to school. It was Thursday morning, only one more week left in the school year, and the boys were rambunctious. It was this time of year, only rivaled by Christmastime, that the boys were the most poorly behaved. Andrew was usually a quiet kid, but Logan knew how to bring out the sleeping demon, and Brandon dealt with this as he poured milk into cereal bowls.

Shouts and screeches darted back and forth. Logan knocked the spoon from Andrew's hand until Brandon got fed up with it and took both spoons away, threatening to let them go hungry. Each one sat back after that, no longer bickering but still steaming, and Brandon was pleased that he'd halted the arguing. His technique was similar to Jean's, or perhaps he had just picked up her parenting skills over the years.

After getting them both onto the bus and waving goodbye, he headed back inside and cleaned up in the kitchen, not doing the job nearly as well as Jean did it, but still hoping she would wake up to less of a disaster. His 'To Do' list for the day was to let her sleep in, then sit down for an hour on the computer and look for a job. Later that afternoon, he had plans to meet with Kyle in Stratford, at the Volkswagen dealership. He still wasn't sure how to tell Jean he was going some secret place again that afternoon. After coming home Sunday morning, covered in dirt and lost for reasons, he assured her it would never happen again, that it was over. She hadn't been pleased.

The job search proved frustrating, though he did manage to send out three resumes. He was qualified for each job, and though none listed a pay range, he knew by the job descriptions he'd be making less money than he made at Ballas & Monroe. It was only now, as he let his eyes move absently around the room, that he truly considered selling the house. What point was there to struggle to make such a high mortgage when he could be comfortable in a less expensive home? But he'd promised Jean they wouldn't lose the house, so for now, he just had to hope for the best outcome.

After lunch, he walked up behind Jean as she placed their empty lunch dishes into the dishwasher. He grabbed her waist and kissed her earlobe.

"I have to go out for a while," he said into her ear, hoping the news would be less jarring if laced with romance.

Jean spun around, eyes narrowed.

"I'll be home for dinner."

"Wait," she said, following behind as he headed for the front door. "Where are you going?"

He hoped she would have let it go, just assume it was another one of his secret missions, but she didn't seem ready to back down from this one. She was no longer the wife who looked the other way.

"I have to meet with my friend Kyle to discuss something."

"Where to bury the next body?"

"Ha ha," he said, though he wondered if she was joking or not. "Seriously, Jean, you know I can't get into specifics. Believe me, though, Kyle is a good guy. He's not the type to be involved in anything illegal."

In her eyes he saw the pain of his betrayal from him not

telling her the truth when they'd always been honest with each other over the years. If the situation were reversed, would he be so understanding? But he had to get the money from Kyle, had to secure the savings account, though he knew this would raise even more suspicions.

"Just trust me that I'm doing what's best for our family right now." He pulled her close. "Trust me that I would never do anything to hurt another person or get myself into trouble."

"Why won't you tell me?" she whispered against his chest. "What's so secret that you can't tell your wife?"

"It stems from something we did as kids. I told you that." He pulled away, but grasped her hands. "And that part is over — honestly over — but I have one last thing to tie up with Kyle."

He kissed her, trying to ignore the pleading tears in her eyes, and walked out the door.

***

When Brandon arrived at the Volkswagen dealership, Kyle directed him outside the building, moving his hands around as though pretending to show him one of the colorful Volkswagens on the lot. At first Brandon had a difficult time believing Kyle sold cars for a living, but it actually suited him perfectly. Kyle wasn't a pushy person, but had a certain way of swinging people to his way of thinking. He was a go-getter, in a different sense of the term, not ambitious but never one to back down. If something could be done, Kyle would find a way to get it done.

Around the back of the building, Kyle leaned against the wall. He removed an envelope from the inside of his suit jacket and handed it over.

"All there," he said. "Twelve-thousand."

"Thanks," Brandon replied, and stuffed the envelope deep into his pants pocket. "I can't say when I'll pay you back, but you know that I will."

"It's free money," Kyle said. "But if you feel the need to pay me back, then I'll take it and put it back in the bank."

"Thanks." There was no awkwardness with Kyle, another one of his attributes. "So what happened with Vanessa on Sunday?"

Kyle looked up at the sky and smiled. "I think the more appropriate question would be, 'What didn't happen with Vanessa?'"

"You slept with her?"

"Twice."

The news didn't shock Brandon, though he really thought Vanessa would have had better judgement than to sleep with Kyle while she was still married. He sensed something messy was in Vanessa's future, and worried for Kyle. Though Vanessa and Kyle were forever in love, they also had a forever roadblock in front of them and had never been able to keep anything going for more than a month or two at a time. He hoped time had changed this, but he sensed—maybe because he'd been married for so long and knew what it was like to share the bond of marriage and children—that Vanessa was not truly out of her marriage.

"I met May," Kyle said.

"Her daughter?"

Kyle went on to tell him, as they stood in the shade of the building, how Vanessa had asked him to spend the night back at her house in New York, and how the next morning, Kyle had met and bonded with May. From the way it sounded to Brandon, Kyle already had a ring on Vanessa's finger, was down the aisle, and May was already calling him "Dad." This worried Brandon more. Kyle was not seeing this clearly, and he wondered if anyone involved really was.

"I know you care about her and always have," he started. "But you have to wait until she's divorced, and even after that you have to give her some time. There's a bond with her husband that she'll need time to separate from. They have two kids and a long marriage behind them."

"We agreed to wait until the divorce was final before taking things further." He bounced up and down, fidgeting. "I haven't drank in a week," he said. "A full week."

"That's great news."

"Between you and me...." He reached back and tapped his fingers against the wall behind him. "I think if it doesn't work out with Vanessa, I'm going to drink myself into a coffin."

"Don't talk like that." He wasn't sure what to say. Vanessa had always been beside him when Kyle had these scary moments of self-doubt, and she would always know what to say. "You're going to be just fine. You've been fine without her all these years."

"Fine?" Kyle said and laughed. "About a year ago, before I met Ava, I was thinking about ending it all. I just didn't have the courage to do it."

Brandon took a step backward. "You mean...you were suicidal?" He shook his head. "Jesus, Kyle, you really need to talk to someone."

"I do talk to someone. I talk to God. And it's free."

"No, I mean—"

"I know what you mean."

In the distance, auto workers banged and shouted inside the building. Brandon listened to them as cars sped past on the main street. Now that Kyle had admitted to deeper issues, he was not looking forward to giving him some bad news, a piece of information he'd acquired Monday evening. The final blow concerning the lost Tupperware bowl.

"Anyhow," Kyle said, "I've done a good job with not calling her this week. I'm giving her the space she needs, even though I probably should have warned her about me meeting May. I must have picked up the phone twenty times, but she told me not to, and for once, I actually didn't push my way back when a woman pushed me away."

"I was going to call her tonight, but I'll wait too, then." He wanted to settle on a dinner date and time so he could tell Jean when to expect Vanessa. Something inside told him if the two women met, Jean would settle down. "I also had something else to talk to you about."

Once, Brandon had thought of Kyle as clairvoyant, or at least possessing some form of the sixth sense, knowing the good or bad outcomes of a situation without any proof of that situation's trajectory. This moment solidified that for him. Kyle's fidgeting went from slightly irritating to downright unbearable to watch, all within the timeframe of a few seconds.

"My mother called me Monday night," Brandon said, wanting to just get it over with. "We had a conversation about me talking with you and Vanessa again, and I happened to bring up—without mentioning anything about the friendship pact, of course—the old people who used to live by the pond."

"They're dead." Kyle lowered his head.

"You found out?"

"No," Kyle said, staring down at his shoes. "I can just tell where this is going, plus we kind of figured that out when we found out they weren't living in the house anymore. I hadn't had the time this week yet to look into any of that."

"I figured you would have called your mother," Brandon continued, "but because of the circumstances, I don't think your mother would have even known what happened. It's weird that my mother even knows."

Kyle lifted his head and met Brandon's eyes with curiosity. "Their names were Mildred and Tom—"

"McHyde?" Kyle asked. "Something like that?"

"McHardy," Brandon corrected. "Kindest people in the

world, and couldn't have any kids of their own. According to my mother, they thought of all the kids in the neighborhood as their own kids, and that's why they let us hang out at the pond without caring about it."

Kyle scrubbed the back of his neck, starting to fidget again.

"Anyhow, my mother worked on some project with Mildred McHardy's niece. Apparently, a few years ago, maybe just after your mother moved out of the neighborhood, they found… Mildred and Tom both passed away inside the house."

"Both of them? At the same time, you mean?"

"They were in their nineties, and the story is that one passed and the other passed from the shock or just because all they had was each other. Sometimes that happens with old people."

"God." Kyle lowered his head again.

"So…." Brandon started finally. "Mildred and Tom McHardy are the only possible people who could have come across the Tupperware bowl. We've already discussed that the guy who lives there now, when he found out we were after something buried in his yard, would have told us he found our stuff there if he had, rather than have us dig up his property." He sighed. "I guess it's safe to say that what happened to the Tupperware bowl will always be a mystery." He hoped Kyle was finally ready to let it go, though he knew that was not probable.

"Maybe some other neighbor saw —"

"Kyle, we were all the way in the back of the pond, and nobody was there that night. The only people who could have seen us would have been Mr. or Mrs. McHardy. And they're both dead."

Kyle's cheeks drained of color and his body pitched forward. Brandon clapped him on the back, not sure what to do for him and trying to remember that though he now had twelve-thousand dollars in his possession, a temporary fix to his problems, Kyle

186

did not have his cross back. Money was everywhere, if someone was lucky enough to find it or have a friend lend it, but a family heirloom, even one worth a measly few bucks, was irreplaceable.

"My advice?" he said to Kyle. "Try to move on. You don't have any proof that the cross would have saved your father, and you don't have any proof that it can change things for the better for you, either. I mean, you've already gone a week without drinking, and you did it all by yourself, without the cross."

"Yeah," Kyle said and stood to his full height, forever a few inches taller than Brandon. "The problem is, things like this drive me insane. How can I just put it all behind me?"

"You don't really have a choice."

Kyle glanced at the front of the building as though thinking he'd spent too much time outside and probably should get back to work. "Someone must have cleaned out the McHardy's house, right? I bet the Tupperware bowl was right in the basement or attic."

"They were good people," Brandon told him. "They would have returned the contents of the bowl to us or our parents. Even if they hadn't seen us and just came across the bowl, it was obvious whose diary was inside, and my name was engraved on the back of the watch." He was growing tired of Kyle's determination. It was over, and though he felt awful that Kyle hadn't found his cross at a time when he so desperately needed it, there was nothing else to be done at this point. "You should get back to work, and I have to get home to Jean and find a way to hide this money."

"You still didn't tell her?"

"No, but it's okay because she formed her own opinion on what I've been doing out all night, coming home covered in dirt. She thinks I'm murdering people for money and burying the bodies, so this unexpected twelve-thousand dollars? This should clear things right up for her."

Kyle laughed and some color returned to his cheeks. Brandon felt better leaving him this way, rather than having to leave him beneath an umbrella of despair.

"Hey," Kyle said. "I appreciate you listening to me. I know I'm not the easiest person in the world to deal with."

"No, you're not." He clapped him on the back again. "I'll give you a call soon. Thanks again for the money."

He walked beside Kyle to the front of the building, expecting to part ways, but Kyle kept with him until they reached the SUV.

"Want to buy a Passat?" Kyle asked, pointing to the silver car near them on the lot. "It's older, but it's in super shape, and I can get you a good price."

"I might actually put some thought into that." He opened the door of the SUV, then paused as he caught an odd glimmer of triumph in Kyle's eyes, one that didn't entirely fit in with the current situation. "What are you thinking?"

"Could you do me a favor? Could you call your mother and ask if she still talks to Mrs. McHardy's niece? Maybe when the niece cleaned out the house, she saw something. I mean, probably not, because like you said they would have returned our stuff, but if I still have this last question in my mind, I'll never rest."

"You got it."

Kyle thanked him and walked away, then disappeared inside the dealership. It was the least Brandon could do, calling his mother and asking her about Mildred McHardy's niece, though he would have to find a way to word it so his mother didn't find out about the watch. All these years later, he wondered how she would take the news that he'd put the watch in a bowl and buried it by the pond.

He also wondered if this course of action would benefit Kyle. It was bad news after bad news, and though he was just as curious about what happened to their things, he also knew the universe was giving clear signals that their quest was futile. He hopped up into his SUV, quickly studied the silver Passat and decided he liked it, then left the dealership to head back home to Jean.

CHAPTER TWENTY

Vanessa hadn't heard from Kyle all week, and missed him more than she anticipated she would. She'd told him not to call, and he had respected that request, but part of her hoped to hear from him. The week had proved uneventful, just getting May and Emma off to school and then going to work, all the while with the same question in her mind: When would her divorce be final? Monday and Tuesday she thought of ways to bring this up to Vincent, and yesterday, she'd finally concluded the best course of action was to go to his hotel room and sit down for a long discussion.

Thursday evening after work she drove to his hotel, part of her hoping to find him in the company of another woman, another part unable to stomach the thought. As torturous as the vision was, though, at least if he were an adulterer she would be on even ground with him, even if only in her own mind. Vincent would never know she spent the weekend with another man, and if she caught Vincent cheating he would of course look like the devil in the divorce while she was the angel. For that she knew she would suffer a lifetime of guilt, but Kyle was not to enter the picture until the divorce was final, not with her girls and certainly not with Vincent.

The hotel was a fancy stay-a-while place Vincent had found close to the house. She'd been there before to pick up Emma, but had never actually gone inside Vincent's room, though she knew it was number eleven on the bottom floor. The place was tall and luxurious, but Vincent always took the lower rooms even though he could afford the grandest upstairs suites. He was afraid of heights and had been since he was six years old.

It was one of those stories Vincent told over and over to justify his irrational fear of heights to others, because his bigger fear was looking cowardly in front of business acquaintances or within his posh social group. The story went, and Vanessa remembered it verbatim, that when he was six years old, while his family took in the view from atop their friend's apartment in New York City, Vincent's shoes were too big and he stumbled, nearly falling from the high roof. His mother, after hearing the story many times, accused Vincent of making it all up and said that she had no such memory. Over the years after that, however, Vincent held true that he'd tripped and nearly fallen to his death. Vanessa always thought the story was true, but to a lesser degree. There may have been a trip or slip, but no close call with death. Still, as a child the height must have frightened him, so she stood by the story whenever he told it, even rolled her eyes behind his mother's back when she shot it all down.

After parking her car, Vanessa walked down the hallway of the hotel, inhaling the scent of carpet cleaner and fresh coffee, until she reached room eleven. She knocked on Vincent's door and stepped closer to the wood, tilting her head to hear anything inside the room. Only a few seconds passed before Vincent opened the door.

"Vanessa?" He was obviously shocked to see her, but not shocked in such a way that she could conclude he had female company. "Everything okay with the girls?"

"Fine," she said. "May is watching Emma. I just came from work."

He waited for her to elaborate, and when she didn't, making it clear she was there for more than a quick conversation, he stepped aside and let her enter the room. The TV was on, broadcasting the news (Vincent favored the news on TV, sometimes golf or tennis), and Vanessa walked to one of the beds and sat down on the bottom edge.

"Nice place," she said. "I see you keep it clean."

"I have maids," he said and shrugged. "Plus I'm the only one here."

He sat down on the opposite bed, and she crossed her legs. There really wasn't much that could be said in the way of small talk, so she decided to just get it all out. He probably knew why she was there, and wanting to rush the divorce or at least find out why it was stalled was not out of the ordinary as far as questions she should have at this point. He'd been out of the house for two months.

"So…I was wondering what I'm supposed to do next," she said, not looking at him. "Do I sign some papers here or find a lawyer?"

"I don't know," he replied, shocking her.

"You mean you haven't filed anything or talked to anybody?"

"No."

Vincent had always been on top of things like this, not only because he was meticulous and methodical, but because of his family. It was the way the Greenes did things, especially legal things, with a *just get it done quickly so I don't have to deal with it anymore* kind of attitude. They had the money to hand off unpleasantries to other people, lawyers or advisors, and never once had they procrastinated with a legal dealing. Vanessa had assumed things were at least in the works with the divorce, and all she would have to do was sign a paper stating that May and Emma were still hers and she'd receive some kind of alimony

192

from Vincent.

"Have *you* talked to anybody?" he asked.

"No. I just…we talked about the custody, so I thought you had everything going already. I kind of wanted this done quickly so I can get on with my life. There are some changes I'm making, so the sooner—"

"What kind of changes?"

"I just want out of the house already." She stood and paced the floor in front of the television, just now noting that Vincent had muted the sound. "And I hate my job, so I want out of that, too." She paused and faced him. "When things are finalized…I'm moving back to Connecticut."

"What?" He stood, not realizing how close he was to her, and nearly knocked her over. "When I move out of here, I'm going to the city. How the fuck are we supposed to do joint custody if you're moving to Connecticut? Why the hell would you even want to move there?"

"My mother is there," she replied and stood her ground, not moving away from him. "And my sister."

"You hardly talk to your mother," he replied. "And Morgan is never even home."

It was true—Morgan traveled constantly. Her sister had some compulsion for travel that prevented her from staying in the same place for more than a few days at a time, and though she called Connecticut her home base, she was currently in Brazil. Vanessa hadn't spoken to her in a month, at least.

"Just a change," she said and sighed. "I need a change."

"You're out of your mind." He dropped to the bed, then fell silent in thought.

She knew it was all crazy, but if she was moving out of her house in New York, she wanted a full-out change. The only logical choice, now that she'd reconnected with an old friend and an old boyfriend, was to move closer to them, closer to her family, back in Connecticut. There certainly was no way she was moving closer to the city. She wanted to be as far away from that lifestyle as she could get. It all reminded her of Vincent and her old life.

"I have an idea," Vincent said finally. "It's actually something I considered early on."

"Please don't say we'll take them a month at a time, because I can't go that long without seeing them."

"No," he said, and shook his head. "What if…I took May and you took Emma?"

An uncomfortable knot tightened inside Vanessa's chest. She looked at him, unable to vocalize the horror she felt from his solution, then sat down on the bed.

"What?" she whispered.

"I've always been closer to May, and you've always been closer to Emma," he continued. "May loves the city, and Emma would be happier in a more stable, quieter environment."

"We can't break them up."

"We'll get them together for holidays, and maybe one weekend a month."

A searing pain ran from Vanessa's forehead down behind her eyes, ending in her throat. Before she knew what was happening, she was choking back tears. Vincent stood and sat down on the bed, beside her.

"This is why I've been putting it off," he said. "I didn't know you were moving to Connecticut, but I knew joint custody would be a difficult thing for us to work out. Plus, things are working well the way we're doing it now. Why can't we just keep it this way?"

"Because I hate you and I want my life back."

"You don't hate me." He wrapped his arms around her. "You just think you don't love me anymore."

194

"I never loved you," she said. "And you never loved me."

"I've thought about this since our talk at the house," he said. "I think you're just remembering the bad times. Maybe both of us were." His voice was so muffled against her hair she could barely understand his words. "But we had some good times in there. Vacations and dinners out, school functions and those trips you and I would take upstate."

"But you never loved me," she repeated. "You only married me because I was pregnant."

"I told you that I thought you and I could build a life together. And we did. We were happy."

He went on about this supposed happiness for a while, holding her in his arms, reminding her of good times they had together, times when they were obviously in love. By the time he finished the stories, ending on one particularly memorable trip they took when the car broke down on a backroad and they'd ended up making love in the backseat until the tow truck came, she was in such a state of confusion that her breaths were alarmingly shallow.

"We could try counseling," he said. "At least we should try that for the girls."

"You're telling me this now?" she said. "Two months later?"

"I was comfortable with our current arrangement, but I can see now that it's not going to work this way. We need to try something else."

For a while she rested against him, inhaling his cologne, thinking back on all the years they had together, wondering how she'd only picked out and inspected the bad times while totally disregarding the good. Before Vincent had moved out of the house, unable to stand the constant arguing about why he'd really married her and why he was so awful to her, had they really had the horrible marriage she thought they had? She hated

195

him, or maybe she just hated him for that slice of time. Now, alone and together in a setting different from their house, she questioned if she still hated him. She questioned if she'd ever truly hated him at all.

"You've done a lot of bad things to me," she said, still trying to make sense of it all. "And I don't know if I can get past that."

"What bad things?" he said. "I've never beat you or cheated on you or even lied. I was a good father and a good husband."

She supposed that he was.

Over the next twenty minutes, he smoothed over and remedied every argument they'd ever had, every negative issue in their marriage. She asked why he always said she was lucky to have landed him, and he replied that it was a joke and always had been. She asked why his family never took her under their wing into the fashion industry, and he replied that she'd never really asked and they always felt awkward asking her about her goals and future plans. On and on this went, until she was exhausted and had no further questions for him. It was all out, everything she'd kept inside. In front of her now, sitting on a bed in a hotel room, was her husband and the father of her two girls.

"I should go," she whispered.

Vincent leaned to kiss her but she moved away. "Where do we stand?" he asked.

"Just give me some time to think." She stood from the bed. "I'm confused."

"This is for the girls," he whispered. "We should do this for the girls."

"I know," she replied. "I just need a little time."

He nodded and walked her to the door, then embraced her one last time before she sped out of the hotel room and back to her car, in tears.

Chapter Twenty-One

By the time Vanessa got home, Emma was asleep. May was in her bedroom with the door closed, and when Vanessa knocked to let her know she was home, she was met with only a muffled "Okay." All week May had been distant, more distant than usual. When Vanessa had returned from work the last few nights, May sped past her out the door, waiting for Warren or whatever friend she was going out with that night. In the mornings, May didn't eat breakfast, she just left the house in a hurry to get to school. Something was bothering her, something so intense that she didn't even go at Vanessa the same way she usually did, not with the usual hatred and rebellion, not with the antagonistic gleam in her eyes.

After the long talk with Vincent, the last thing Vanessa needed was an argument with May, and she especially did not want to get into whatever huge thing was troubling May that week. She headed for the bathroom to take a shower, hoping that once inside the spray of hot water she could release some of the confusion. Right now, it was all about Vincent and her marriage. There was no room to even think about her relationship with Kyle. Love was pulling in two different directions, and though each of those loves were engulfed in their own unique sea of nostalgia and forever bonds, only one of those loves was the father of her children.

She was about to grab a towel when there was a knock on her bedroom door. May entered tentatively, craning her head from the doorway to locate Vanessa. It was the first time in perhaps a month that Vanessa had seen May in the light of her bedroom. Usually May stayed far away from anything that reminded her of Vanessa.

"Yes?" Vanessa said to her.

"Where were you all this time? I got stuck here so long that Warren went to bed."

"Sorry," Vanessa said, and meant it. She knew she'd been gone too long and that May had to babysit for over five hours. "I was with your father, discussing things." Thinking that was the last of the queries, she grabbed a towel.

"Is that why your eyes are all red?" May asked, coming closer. "You were crying?"

Vanessa wiped her eyes with the back of her hand, though the damage was done. May had seen the result of an evening spent with her father. "You know it's a difficult time."

"So does that mean you guys are finally getting a divorce?"

"I don't know."

She moved away from May, hoping she'd take the hint that she wanted to be alone right now and take a shower. All this time May had spent pulling away, and now she chose to talk, when it was the absolute last thing Vanessa wanted.

"Did you tell him about Kyle?"

Vanessa halted in the doorway of her bathroom.

"What?"

"Your boyfriend Kyle," May said. "Didn't he tell you that I met him Monday morning?"

Her first thought was to lie, but she had no idea what was going on, so she just stood staring at May, who seemed equally as confused.

"I came home Monday morning to get my books and stuff," May continued, clarifying but still shaking her head like she couldn't understand why Vanessa didn't know this already. "He was cleaning up in the kitchen, and we talked for like an hour."

"He didn't...I haven't talked to him." She put the towel back into the closet by the bathroom. "Kyle is just an old friend."

"Please," May said and rolled her eyes. "I know he spent the night with you. I know he was your boyfriend in high school, and that you guys were...really in love."

Something softened in May's eyes, and Vanessa was reminded of the sweet little girl May used to be, light years ago. Even in this moment, as shocked as Vanessa was, she couldn't help but smile in remembrance. May running through the yard, giggling. May jumping rope, missing the rope and tripping. May riding a bike for the first time, straight through the sunshine, straight down the sidewalk with Vincent jogging by her side.

"He also told me that you hated Grandma when you were my age. That you yelled at her and threw things and even threatened to run away."

"Oh...I wasn't all that bad." She couldn't believe Kyle had told May these stories. "And I certainly don't condone treating your mother that way."

May laughed. "Did you really throw a laundry basket down the stairs?"

The laundry basket. Kyle had remembered that incident, though Vanessa would never have recalled it if not hearing about it again, all these years later. She was hit with the blast of that memory, the burning hatred she'd felt toward her mother that day, and how with all her might, she'd hurled a basket of clean laundry down the staircase. Kyle had watched, wide-eyed and open-mouthed. It was no wonder he remembered it, even if she'd blocked it out.

"I was angry," she said. "I had to watch your Aunt Morgan when I wanted to go…never mind."

"Tell me," May said, and sat down on the bed. "Because the person Kyle told me about…I have no idea how that person could be you."

Vanessa sat down beside her and told her what she could remember of the craziness and angst of her adolescence. When she stalled on something she couldn't remember, May filled in the blanks, prompting her with Kyle's tales. Vanessa was a bad teenager, it was all out now. She'd fought with her mother, hung out at Blueberry Pond with two boys, kissed Kyle Macord in the woods, and was even reckless at times. There were still some things she left out, secrets and treasures kept within her own heart, but mostly, over the course of an hour, she told her oldest daughter things she never thought she'd tell her. And that, she realized by the end of their bonding session, was really all it had taken all along.

"So you wrote it all down in your diary?" May said. "That helped you get through the divorce?"

"It helped with everything." Her shoulders shook in a laugh. "I can't believe Kyle told you all of this."

"I liked him," May said and smiled. "He really got me, you know?"

"Kyle is a very unique person," she said, and smiled back. "It really shouldn't surprise me that you got along with him."

"So he'll be by again?"

She was lost on a response and knew May had caught this. Just tonight, within the past hour, she'd understood just how perceptive and intelligent May was and how deep she ran. What a terrific kid she'd raised after all.

"You haven't mentioned Kyle to your father?"

"No," May replied. "Kyle told me not to."

"Okay." She stood, and realizing she'd have to wait for morning to take a shower, grabbed a puffy aqua robe and wrapped it around her. "Honestly, I care about Kyle. I love Kyle in a way I can't even understand. But tonight, your father and I…." For a second, she felt as though she were talking to an adult, a friend, perhaps, and had to remind herself that Vincent was May's father. She still hadn't fully examined her feelings, hadn't made a decision about a divorce, so she couldn't say anything to confirm or deny either man's future presence in her life. "I'm not sure what's going to happen between Kyle and I."

"You mean you're stuck between Kyle and Dad?"

"I don't know if I'd say stuck. At this point it's more…when you're a mom, you think of your children before you think of anyone else. If I still love your father—and I do—then the logical conclusion is to bring our family back together."

Saying it aloud seemed to not only clear it all up, but seal it too, though she now understood that she'd really had her decision made the moment Vincent embraced her in the hotel. If something was still there, and all past arguments were closed up, she owed it to her family to try to make the marriage work. Even if that meant breaking Kyle's heart. Twenty years ago it would have been easy to break Kyle's heart. They would have been even. But now, because of time and circumstances and how hard they'd fallen back in love, breaking Kyle's heart felt like jagged, broken metal tumbling around inside her own heart. And she knew she would carry those broken pieces inside her heart forever.

"Kyle loves you," May said. Her eyes were eager as she sat on the bed, caught up in Vanessa's life and decisions in a way she never had been before. "But I have to be honest. I really, really want you and Dad back together."

Vanessa sat down beside May. She reached out and stroked

201

her hair. "I'm going to give it another try." She sighed. "And because of that, I'll have to tell Kyle that it can't be between us."

May lowered her head. This, Vanessa supposed, was a situation a teenager could relate to, love and loss and a difficult choice between two guys. Thinking back, she would have been just as interested as May if someone else were in this position. But Vanessa was the person inside the dilemma, or now that she'd chosen to stay with her husband, it was no longer a dilemma. She loved Kyle, but it didn't come down to that. And the worst part was that he wouldn't understand, because he'd never been married or had children. He was the type of person who believed love conquered all, and usually it did. The problem was, she loved two men, and one conquered the other by providing the ultimate bond of family.

Kyle may have made her happier. In fact, sitting on the bed and thinking on it, she was certain Kyle would have made her happier. She imagined how it would be with him, living in a small but cozy house, waking up in his arms, not knowing what the day would bring because Kyle was so unpredictable. Then she would come downstairs to find her breakfast made and would leave for the day to her relaxed and much-loved job while Kyle went off to work at the dealership. He would love her children, he would stand by whatever choices she made, and he would be a frantic, back and forth light in her life, shaking things up when necessary, and then letting them back down gently when she needed him to.

But then there were the problems with Kyle that had always been there. He was a recovering alcoholic. He was unpredictable, and that was as much a con as it was a pro. There were emotional outbursts to contend with, and a general awkwardness when he'd fall into a deep state of despair for reasons she would never understand. She would be obligated to lift him up every time this happened, and wondered if she still, closing in on forty, had the stamina and desire to do this. And then there was the overall fear that their relationship may ultimately fizzle itself out, and then she'd have led her children down another road where love ended in an emotional parting.

"I'm going to bed," May said. "Since everyone else went to bed early, I guess I should have an early night, too."

"Thanks for watching Emma all night," Vanessa told her. "I owe you one, okay?"

May nodded and shrugged like it was no big deal, and as she did, Vanessa remembered Vincent's custody solution of breaking up May and Emma. There was no way she would have let that happen. May usually complained about watching Emma, but Vanessa knew how much the two loved each other. It would be impossible for anyone not to love Emma. She was just that kind of kid, and it was precisely Emma's softness and all-around young spirit that seemed to smooth out May's rougher edges. The two balanced each other out, as siblings often do.

"May," she said as May hopped off the bed. "Thanks for not telling your father about Kyle. I think I'll probably have to tell him…but in my own time, okay?"

"Good luck with that," May said, adopting her usual sarcastic drone. "Hopefully Dad won't go and beat Kyle up. I've seen guys in school fight over girls before, and it's not pretty."

With that, she left the bedroom, closing the door behind her. It only now occurred to Vanessa that she'd had a true talk with May, and that the value of that talk was immeasurable. She had to admit that Kyle's involvement had made all the difference in the world. Because of Kyle, she had May back. Because of Kyle, she remembered most of the things that were in her diary, the shadowed memories he brought into the light—and that had been what she'd wanted all along. Those were the memories she'd hoped to use to her advantage, the ones she knew would help her understand where May was coming from.

But how, after everything Kyle had done for her and how much she loved him, was she supposed to tell him that once again, it was not meant to be for them?

CHAPTER TWENTY-TWO

Brandon had the phone number in his hand, but found he couldn't quite dial it up. He'd just gotten off the phone with his mother, had made up some ridiculous lie about wanting to know what happened to the rare bricks that used to line the walkway of the McHardy's cape by Blueberry Pond, and had scribbled down the number of Mrs. McHardy's niece. The bricks weren't really rare—was there such a thing?—but if he wanted the direct cell phone number of Mrs. McHardy's niece, Roseanne Spears, he had to come up with something. Kyle clung to this one last question, and Brandon knew that for all Kyle had done for him, he had to follow through with it. He had to call Roseanne Spears and ask if she recalled a yellow Tupperware bowl in the possession of Mr. and Mrs. McHardy when she'd cleaned out the house after their passing.

Jean was out grabbing groceries for dinner that night, so he had time. Vanessa and her youngest daughter Emma were coming for an outdoor picnic, just an easy and relaxed meal of hot dogs and hamburgers for the kids. Brandon was looking forward to Jean finally meeting Vanessa. He was not, however, looking forward to making the phone call he was now halfway through dialing. Something inside told him that it was a waste of time, and having that confirmed when Roseanne Spears answered her phone and his questions about the Tupperware bowl was beating

205

him up inside. How could he tell Kyle that the last avenue to his lost silver cross had been closed for good?

"Hello?" said a female voice.

"Mrs. Spears?"

"Yes?"

He wasn't sure what to say or how to bring everything up. He sat back in the desk chair and scratched his head.

"My name is Brandon Ballas, and I used to live in the same neighborhood as your aunt, Mrs. McHardy?"

"Okay…." She sounded confused already. "Ballas…I know your mother, right?"

"Yes, that's how I got your phone number. I just had a question for you." He paused and tilted forward in the chair. "When I was younger, I lost something around the pond by your aunt and uncle's house. I was just wondering if you came across it when you cleaned out the house. It was inside a yellow Tupperware bowl. Do you remember seeing anything like that?"

There was a moment's pause, but then she finally said, "No, sorry."

Brandon closed his eyes. This wasn't about the watch anymore, but about Kyle's cross and Vanessa's diary. Trying to find the Tupperware bowl for them was much more of an incentive than trying to find it for himself. Part of him wanted to go out and buy Kyle a new cross, but he knew it wouldn't be the same. And he could never replace the thoughts and memories inside of Vanessa's diary.

"Thanks," he said.

"This was important to you, I gather?"

"Very," he replied. "And just so I'm sure…you didn't come across anything that didn't look as though it belonged to your aunt or uncle, right? Like jewelry or…a book?"

"No," she replied. "They were very clean, straightforward

people, my aunt and uncle. All we really had to clean out was my uncle's crossword puzzle magazines, his TV Guides, and his clothes. My aunt had no jewelry, just her engagement ring and some pearl earrings she wore to church. The house was small. There wasn't much."

"Okay," Brandon said. "I appreciate it. Thanks for taking my call."

He hung up with her, dejected. But then, imagining telling Kyle all of this, trying to jump into Kyle's mind and see where that led him, he came up with one last—very last—scenario. Someone in the neighborhood had seen them. That didn't make sense to him, because if someone had seen them—presumably their own age—and taken their things, they would have returned them or used them against them somehow. Vanessa's diary would have been made public at school, or something of that nature would have transpired. Still, Brandon knew where Kyle would go next, so he spent the next hour exhausting every last angle.

By the time Jean came home, toting bags and bags of groceries, Brandon had phoned anyone he could reach from the old neighborhood. Nobody even knew what he was talking about, and there had even been one awkward conversation with a woman who didn't even remember who he was until he mentioned his house, the biggest one at the top of the street. The whole ordeal had been embarrassing, but at least now he had a sense of closure. The Tupperware bowl was truly gone forever.

***

At six o'clock that evening the doorbell rang, and Logan and Andrew raced to open the door. Brandon followed behind, wondering how from New York Vanessa had made it to the house at precisely six o'clock. Jean was just beside him, nervously patting at her hair, though she had the kind of hair that was never mussed. Still, he was pleased that she was going through so much effort to look presentable for Vanessa, and just to have her over to the house. In the beginning, she'd been against meeting Vanessa at all.

When Logan opened the door, Vanessa stood on the other side smiling, though Brandon could tell that behind the smile something blue was brewing. For the first time since meeting up with her again at Carmella's Restaurant, he noticed a few wrinkles around her eyes, and even some puffiness beneath the rims, as though she'd lost sleep or had been crying. He wondered what was going on now in the constant but forever-doomed romance that was uniquely Vanessa and Kyle's.

"Vanessa!" he said, exaggerating his welcome because he felt that not only she needed it, but that it would benefit Jean as well. "Come on in!"

Vanessa held hands with her daughter Emma, who was very small despite her age. If Brandon hadn't known her true age of ten, he would have thought six or seven. Emma's hair was the same shade of blonde as Vanessa's, a rich lemon-yellow that almost looked fake, and her eyes were just as blue, with the same soft innocence. When Emma saw Logan and Andrew, she rested her head against Vanessa's side.

"It's very nice to meet you," Jean said, extending her hand to Vanessa.

Vanessa shook hands. "It's nice to finally meet you too," she replied. "Brandon has told me so much about you."

"You too," Jean said. "I can't wait to hear all your stories of growing up together."

The women shared a smile, and since the meeting was going well, Brandon decided to give Vanessa a tour of the house while Jean finished up the salads in the kitchen. He walked Vanessa around for a while, Emma still at her side despite Logan's constant badgering to come play in the backyard on the swings, until finally, they made their way to the back patio. Emma seemed to have settled into her surroundings by then, and waved to her mother as she parted with Logan and Andrew to the swing set.

"They look just like you," Vanessa said, sitting down at the outdoor table Jean had already set up with plates, cups, and appetizers. "Especially Andrew. Spitting image."

"Same with Emma," Brandon replied, sitting across from her. He grabbed a carrot stick, swiped it through ranch dressing, and took a bite. "It's weird, isn't it? Almost like someone took an old picture of us and played around just a little."

Vanessa laughed. She watched Emma in the distance, then turned back to Brandon. "Jean is a doll. She's just as I pictured her, and just perfect for you."

"How lucky I am."

They conversed back and forth, about Jean and the boys and Emma, staying a while on the subject of Andrew and Emma's shyness. Andrew's problems didn't seem quite as severe as Emma's, though he wondered if Emma truly had a developmental delay or if that was just her personality. It seemed to him that they threw labels onto children nowadays if they had any kind of differences from other kids. Emma was a loving and shy little girl. He couldn't see how that made her delayed in any way.

"I should go help Jean in the kitchen," Vanessa said and stood. "Would you mind watching Emma?"

"Not at all," he replied. "But later, we really should talk about some things."

"Believe me," she said, "you don't want to know what's been going on."

"Same here. You don't want to know what I found out."

Vanessa shook her head. "Life is just a roller coaster, isn't it?"

"It helps to have certain people along for the ride though, right?"

She smiled, placed her hand on his shoulder, and left the back patio.

***

Dinner was a pleasurable affair. Logan and Andrew got along well with Emma, and surprisingly, none of the kids bickered. Emma's presence softened the boys in a way Brandon hadn't seen before, something like fresh dew against rough blades of grass. He wondered how it would have been if he and Jean had tried for a third baby. How would a little girl fit into their family? Though he was jobless right now, and his financial future floating around in a place he couldn't quite reach, he thought, *Is it too late for another baby?*

"…and him and Kyle fought a lot, but still, deep down, really had a close friendship," Vanessa was saying as the kids ran off to play on the swings again.

"The mysterious Kyle," Jean said.

"The mysterious Kyle," Brandon echoed. "That has sort of a ring to it, don't you think, Vanessa?"

Vanessa playfully rolled her eyes. "Definitely a ring."

The scent of grilled food faded as the sun sank into the horizon, its slow descent making long silhouettes of the swing set and the slide on the grass in the backyard. Brandon listened as Vanessa and Jean conversed back and forth, talking about Vanessa's times with Brandon and Kyle at the pond. When Brandon turned back to Jean, he saw something of revelation in her eyes. It was possible that she'd pieced everything together, knew that he'd been coming home from his long excursions out with Vanessa and Kyle covered in dirt because they'd been at the pond. Maybe now she would let this go. Vanessa's visit, just as he'd suspected, seemed to have cleared a lot up for Jean.

"I'm going to let you two talk while I clean up," Jean said, standing with an empty plate in her hand. "Please, don't worry

210

about helping, Vanessa."

"But—"

Jean waved her away, gathered up plates, and left the patio. Brandon had to wonder what kind of sixth sense Jean had, or maybe she just knew him well enough to know that he needed to talk with Vanessa alone.

"So what's going on?" Vanessa asked.

"A lot," he said, and turned to make sure Jean was back inside the house before telling Vanessa the story of the McHardys and their niece. He had expected her to be upset, but hadn't anticipated such a strong reaction. As he went on, he tried to smooth over the details of his calls to their old neighbors, to make it seem a little less dreary of an outcome. Kyle, of course, would react this way, with wells of tears in his eyes and an overall collapse of his entire frame, but Vanessa was usually sturdier. It all came back, Brandon was certain, to the aura of sorrow he'd noticed around Vanessa when she arrived at the house, and what Vanessa undoubtedly would reveal to him next. Something bad was going on with her and Kyle. Now, just as in high school, he could almost sense the fall coming before either Kyle or Vanessa expressed it to each other. It was like an invisible knife Vanessa carried, and Brandon was the only one who could see it, making its way to Kyle's heart.

"So that's it, then," Vanessa said. "The bowl is just…gone."

"Afraid so." He rubbed his forehead, then glanced back at the boys and Emma, who were now taking turns on the slide. "The McHardy's house was cleaned out and no sign of anything, and nobody in the neighborhood knows anything. I called or emailed everyone I could remember, even people who wouldn't have cared or didn't live close by."

"It got thrown away," Vanessa said, her body slouching in her chair. "There's no other explanation."

"It was probably dug up by accident and got tossed away as junk."

"This is going to kill Kyle," she said. "It's just going to kill him."

"I know. But I'm also concerned about you. The diary was important."

Vanessa wiped her eyes and let out a little laugh. "The funny thing is, I don't even need it anymore. I mean, I would love to read it and see what I wrote down at that age, especially about Kyle, but the original reason I wanted it back…Kyle took care of it for me." She went on to tell him about May and Kyle bonding, how Kyle filled May in on all of Vanessa's emotions and actions during her parents' divorce, which had, in turn, prompted Vanessa and May to bond over their mutual teenage woes. "But before May and I had this talk," she continued, "I had gone to see Vincent about finalizing the divorce."

Here comes the knife, Brandon thought.

"We got everything out," she said. "And I know it's going to take some time, but I think that it's best, for May and Emma—"

"You're going back to your husband." He tipped some wine into his mouth and sat back. "I knew there was that chance."

"We kept it together all those years. There must have been something there, something I'd just forgotten because of all the other stuff, or because he wasn't the perfect doting husband."

"You don't have to sell it to me. I'm married with kids, and I fully understand what kind of bond that is, even though I know that Kyle will be…." Something occurred to him then. "Vanessa," he said, and leaned forward. "Kyle lent me money to get me out of the hole for now."

"Oh God," she said. "That's the secret thing you two had going on this past week?"

He nodded. "I guess he has a lot of money put away from

when his mother sold the house. But here's the thing…he dug us both out, didn't he? I don't need the watch anymore and you don't need the diary, all because of Kyle. And yet, he's the one left here without his cross, and now…without you."

He hadn't meant for it to come out with the punch it had, and before he could soften the blow, Vanessa started crying again. He watched, helpless, as she frantically wiped her eyes with a napkin smudged in ketchup, turning her body away in case Emma was looking in her direction. Brandon reached across the table to comfort her the best he could, rubbing her shoulder until she calmed down.

"I'm sorry," he said. "It's just…how I'm seeing this."

"No, you're right." She dabbed at her eyes until just beneath was dry. "Telling Kyle all of this is going to be the most difficult thing I've ever had to do."

"When are you going to do it?"

Vanessa sucked in a breath and blew it out. "I'm going to drive back down to Connecticut on Monday, his day off."

And just when Brandon thought she'd controlled the tears, they came again, until she sped away inside the house. He hadn't had the time to tell her, and hoped to say it before she left for the night, that she had to be very gentle with Kyle. Kyle was, and perhaps always had been, closer to the edge than Vanessa realized.

Chapter Twenty-Three

Vanessa hadn't called Kyle to tell him she was coming. She was certain that if she had, he would know from the tone of her voice what was ahead, and wanted to let him down as easily as she could, in person. It was a good bet that he'd be at home and alone, though it occurred to her as she drove off the exit ramp how little she really knew of Kyle's life as it was right now. Did he have a lot of friends? Did he socialize at all? It didn't seem like he did. He'd always kept a small circle of friends, two or three at most. Or maybe she just clung to the vision of him in high school and assumed that was him now.

When she pulled into the driveway, Kyle's car was parked just ahead. She turned off her car, tensed her shoulders, and wondered if the surprise attack was really the best way to do this. But, deciding there was really no right or wrong way to break someone's heart, she stepped out of the car and walked to his door.

There was a chance that the moment he saw her, he would know. Kyle had a way with those things, could see hidden emotions like a detective might see hidden clues. He always could, whether with her words or her expressions...he'd always known what she was feeling and what would be the outcome of any situation. She couldn't decide, as she readied herself to ring his bell, if he had superb intuition or some bizarre connection to

214

the universe as a whole, but whatever it was, it was what made Kyle the unique person he was.

When he opened the door, his expression was both of shock and delight, eyes narrowed, sideways smile. She smiled back, rearranging the muscles in her face to hide any evident pain.

"What are you doing here?" he asked. "Not that I'm not happy to see you. I just—"

"Can I come in?"

"Of course."

Inside, the apartment smelled like something fried, maybe a burger or a steak. It was just after noon, close to Vanessa's anticipated arrival time. She'd wanted to make sure Emma had no problems that morning in school before heading out, and had left May instructions to get Emma off the bus as she usually did. Things had been different in the house that weekend, like a dark veil had been yanked away, exposing a brightness beneath. May was still moody, still had the same unamused, slightly bored manner of speaking, but was all-around easier to get along with. She'd even told Vanessa she was considering letting her hair grow out to its original color, a light caramel brown, just between Vanessa's blonde and Vincent's black.

"So you drove all the way from New York," Kyle said, closing the door. "That means you either have something really good to tell me, or really bad."

"Actually, I went to meet Brandon's wife and kids this weekend, so I did have some news from Brandon to tell you." She sat down on the couch. "We didn't invite you because Brandon didn't think Jean was quite up to meeting you yet. He thought having the three of us together would have been like she was in front of a firing range or something like that."

"Firing squad," Kyle said and sat beside her. "So what news? Is it something about the friendship pact?"

"Yes," she said, and turned to grasp his hands. "That niece that cleaned out the McHardy's house? Brandon called her and says she never came across the bowl or any of the contents."

"Okay," he said as though he'd anticipated it. "Then maybe one of the old neighbors—"

"Brandon called everyone." She sighed and squeezed his hands. "Nobody knew anything about it. Nobody who lived there back then, even people who weren't close by, ever saw the Tupperware bowl. I'm sorry."

In his eyes she saw something like a door closing. Even someone like Kyle couldn't come up with a strategy to find the lost bowl now, and she knew that was the last of it. He'd have to let it all go, as difficult as she knew that would be for him.

"What could have happened to it?" he whispered, almost to himself. "Things just don't unearth themselves and disappear."

"Brandon and I think someone dug it up by accident, doing work on the property or just fooling around. They probably just threw it away." She placed her hand on his arm. "But it doesn't matter. Brandon is set for now until he finds a job, and because of the talk you had with May, things with her and I are—"

"She told you we spoke?"

"Well, you didn't tell me." She was still a little upset about this.

"You told me not to call you, and I didn't. I wanted to give you time to sort out your divorce so we could move ahead. May and I got along; I trusted that she wouldn't tell your husband."

"She didn't." She understood now why he hadn't called her about meeting May, and was relieved that she had an answer. All her life, why hadn't she just asked all the questions she had, instead of pondering them until they came out as angry outbursts or tears? "Anyhow," she continued, "my point is that what I found out, from this whole experience, is that finding the bowl really

216

didn't matter. You helped Brandon by loaning him money, and you helped me by talking with May and telling her all about me when I was a teenager, all the things I hadn't remembered. And even though you didn't get your cross back, Brandon says you haven't drank in a week, and I can't help but think that you've stayed away because of our reconnection. So…what I'm trying to tell you is that you didn't need the cross. The power and strength to stop drinking was inside of you all along. I'm not saying you won't still battle it for the rest of—"

He stood from the couch. "That's just the thing, Vanessa. The thing nobody will ever understand. I *will* battle it the rest of my life, because I feel like I killed my father. It doesn't matter whether the cross would have worked or not, because my father *believed* it worked."

"It still wouldn't have mattered if you'd found the cross or not then, because you have it in your mind that you killed your father—which you *didn't*—and nothing will ever change that, cross in hand or not!"

Kyle dropped back to the couch. He held his head in his hands. For a while, it was quiet between them. She wondered how much farther to go, how much more he could take. Maybe it was best to tell him she was going back to her husband another time, when he'd cooled down from this latest blow. Or maybe that would just space it all out, giving it the feel of life piling up and up and up until there was no more light or oxygen, and he'd be left gasping for air. She was here now, and had come here for a specific reason.

"Kyle," she whispered. "You have to move on from this. You have to be strong here."

"When have I ever been strong?" he mumbled back. "When?"

"Right now." She rested a hand to his back. "The reason I came here wasn't just to tell you about the bowl."

"I know."

Of course he knew. He'd probably known the moment he saw her at his front door, just as she suspected he would.

"When I went to talk to Vincent," she continued, "to ask him when the divorce would be final, we ended up…working through some things. It's best for my children if I continue to try to work things out with him."

He may have responded with a faint "Okay" but she couldn't really tell. It felt as though she was drifting downward, settling into a dark and gloomy void, a forever blackness without the soothing light she'd thought she recently found. It was only then, in that moment, that she realized how much she really did love Kyle and what he brought into her life. And she had to let him know exactly how she felt. She owed that to him.

"I love you," she said, and her voice broke. "I love you more than any other man I've ever known. You've determined the course of my entire life." She rested her head on his shoulder. "But I think we both know that you and I can never be together. It's just not meant to be for us, for whatever reason."

They sat in the same position for a while, Vanessa resting on his shoulder, haunted by a decision she'd only just made. Kyle was her one true love, maybe not the father of her children, but time and time again he'd appeared in her life, and she only felt truly happy and alive when he was by her side. Just as she always wished her girls would stay inside the same moment forever, unaffected by the movement of time, she wished she could stay frozen with Kyle the way they were now, breathing in the same air, their bodies forever touching.

She thought back on their years together, from the first time they'd held hands as kids, to the steamy moments they'd spent together last weekend. They connected on every level, she'd found that out during their love making. With Vincent, something had always been missing, not physically or mentally, but emotionally. She was just now coming to realize that to form that perfect triangle, that three-way blend of passionate sex and similar thoughts and identical hearts, was very rare. Vincent hadn't had an identical heart. His heart was not as deep as hers. But Kyle…he ran deeper, matched her perfectly.

Kyle sniffled and raised his head. "I'll still see you, right?"

"We'll try," she replied, sitting up. "Brandon wants us to keep meeting once a month at Carmella's, but I don't know how difficult that will be for you and I."

"We used to do it as kids," he replied. "Stay friends even after…." He rubbed his watery eyes and gave her a sad smile. "If something should change with you and your husband, you know that all you have to do is say the word and—"

"You'll drop the world for me," she finished. "I know."

"I would have asked you to marry me." He reached out and touched a strand of her hair. "I would have loved your kids and made all of you happy."

"I know you would have." She stood and fisted her keys, ready to leave, but something Brandon had warned her of flashed through her mind. "You'll be okay, right? I mean, you won't do anything stupid?"

"I've done stupid things my entire life, so it's a pretty good bet that I'll do them now."

"Seriously."

"I'll be okay, Vanessa."

She wasn't sure if she should believe him, but made up her mind to have Brandon check in on him, make sure he wasn't drinking or burying himself in piles of sad thoughts. It wouldn't surprise her if he went out drinking right after she left, and she didn't want that to happen, but realized there were things that were out of her control. She just had to trust that he'd pull himself through this time, that she'd given him some kind of strength just by talking to him and letting him know that she truly did love him, but had to go back to Vincent for her girls.

"I love you," he said, gazing up at her. He stood from the couch and pulled her into an embrace. "I don't know if I've ever actually told you that."

"I love you too," she whispered into his shoulder.

She held onto him for only a few seconds, then, because it hurt too much to stay in his arms, she let go and walked out the door.

CHAPTER TWENTY-FOUR

Kyle watched out the window as Vanessa's car backed out of his driveway. He'd watched women leave before, but Vanessa leaving was different. Vanessa leaving was a great shatter of the oceans and a horrific splitting of the sky. And the worst part was that he'd known all along, deep down in that intuitive place he had so strongly but hated to acknowledge, that she would eventually leave him and go back to her husband. He always tried to ignore the intuitive feelings, or worse, use them to justify his actions. He'd known Vanessa was going to leave him, and he had tried to force himself into her life to block that final parting. He had a feeling he was going to find the Tupperware bowl, and for that reason, he hadn't yet been able to give up on it, even as every open door had closed. All of these things he knew, and maybe that's why he fought so hard against them. Maybe that's why people saw him as slightly insane.

He went back to the couch and sat, that familiar phantom taste of alcohol on his tongue, that familiar tug inside his chest, that familiar shake in his hands.

"Don't do it," he said aloud. "Don't do it, don't do it, don't do it...." He repeated it over and over, like a mantra, until it blurred into one long sound, "Dondoitdondoitdondoit."

He wanted to drink, and not just to go to the bar and slop down a few my-girl-left-me whiskeys. No, this was the kind of drinking that required darting to the liquor store, buying bottles and bottles of whiskey, coming home and falling onto the living room floor, and drinking and drinking until the world flipped over and fogged into nothingness.

For a while he went back and forth. He could either talk himself up here, or he could talk himself down deeper — and both options were equally enticing. He thought about his church group and the few phone numbers he'd acquired there if he ever needed immediate help from the members, but they really didn't know the extent of his problems. He'd downplayed his drinking, though he knew they were on to him. Saying you only drank a little was the equivalent of saying you were an alcoholic in denial. It was easier, though, to make it seem like he was sane and functioning. Next to suicidal alcoholic, their problems seemed so trivial, just people struggling with the usual tugs and twists of life. He'd known he was the odd man out from the beginning; a drowning man amongst a group of swimmers who'd merely gone adrift.

And that's when the first fantasy hit him. The Gray Walk, as he always thought of it. There was always a way out, a path that did not lead to alcohol but did lead to a forever numbness. The Gray Walk. He could master that walk, steps and steps toward the dark — he could already feel nothingness poking at his skin. But he was a coward, always a coward. He hated blood and physical pain. Maybe if he didn't think as he did it, just let his thoughts run blank as he tied something around his neck and hung from somewhere....

It wasn't just Vanessa, it was everything and had been for years. Still, Vanessa had taken a piece of him with her when she left, and this time it didn't feel like high school; this time he felt the pain as a grown man. And it was so different from the pain of his high school years that he wondered if he was even the same person. Back then it had stung, but there was always a chance she'd come back to him, because she always did. Now, it had a sense of closure that led him straight to The Gray Walk.

The only light he really had left in his life was his mother, and just thinking about her made his heart constrict so painfully that he hoped, in that flash of two seconds, that he was having a heart attack. His mother had never factored into his suicide fantasies, and now, because she had for the first time, he wondered if he was getting closer to actually doing it.

After that he sat back on the couch with his hands on his lap and envisioned different scenarios — pills (did he have enough?), razor blades (too much blood), and ropes (how was a self-hanging actually accomplished?). The scariest thought was that nobody would find him if he did this inside his apartment. His coworkers might wonder where he was, but knowing he was a loner with more than a few problems, they would probably figure he just decided to drink and sleep his days away. His mother wouldn't notice he was missing until he didn't show up on Thursday for their weekly dinner, and that would probably prompt her to come over to his apartment, where she would find him, dead and decaying. He thought about going someplace else, a bridge or highway overpass, but then some poor stranger would have to deal with removing that image from their mind for the rest of their life.

For now, the suicide fantasies would have to remain just fantasies. The earth would have to stay drab and gray, colorless and magicless. He'd been disenchanted with life a long time ago, anyway. He tapped his fingers against the arm of the couch, trying to decide if he should go to the liquor store or just take comfort in his fantasies. Suicide was always a way out, always one way to end all the suffering. It went against everything he'd learned in life through his religion, against all hope and faith of

223

God's true plan, but it was still an option, and thank God he had that option.

Vanessa had told him to be strong. Vanessa had also told him that whether or not he found the Tupperware bowl and the lost silver cross, he would still always believe he killed his father. His father had believed in the cross, whether it was truly magic or not. So maybe, just as it stood for Brandon and Vanessa right now, the lost bowl didn't matter anymore. Maybe it had never mattered. Still, it had brought the three of them back together in a much stronger way than they'd even been in childhood and high school. Brandon and Vanessa were his friends for life, and he'd always have the memory of his weekend with Vanessa. She'd even told him that she loved him, but was going back to her husband because of her children. There was some solace in that. If it weren't for her husband's blood in her children, Kyle would have had the chance to someday marry her. He would have married her as soon as he could get her to say yes to his proposal, because he didn't give up on things; one of his attributes, but also, he knew, one of his downfalls.

His cell phone rang, startling him. Not many people called him, and he knew before looking that it was Brandon, checking in on him. He let it ring five times before finally deciding to pick it up.

"Hello?"

"It's me," Brandon said in a tone that suggested he knew Vanessa had just left. "I'm just seeing if you need me to—"

"Come over?" he said. "Pull the trigger? What?"

"You're okay," Brandon said. "Just…do you need me to come over, or what?"

"No," he said. "Yes…I don't know."

"I'm coming now."

The phone went dead, and Kyle placed it down on the coffee

table. So this was what it felt like to have a friend. Never, in all the times he'd been low, had someone offered to come help him through it. The gesture was so foreign that he wondered what to do when Brandon got to the apartment. Talk about feelings? Listen to old songs? Watch TV?

He sat back and tapped his fingers against the couch arm as he watched the clock on the cable box flash through a half hour. When Brandon arrived, he knocked once, then entered the apartment without waiting for Kyle to come answer the door. He had a frantic, nervous look about him, as though expecting to find Kyle whitening in a puddle of his own blood.

"Hey," he said, and strode to the couch. "I have good news and good news. Which do you want first?"

"Is this a trick question?"

Brandon laughed and sat down beside him. "I got an email this morning from a place called Carey Architects. They got my resume and want to know if I could come in for an interview. Guess where they're located?"

"Another trick question?"

"About five minutes from Blueberry Pond, in the business district they recently set up over there."

Kyle couldn't help but laugh at the coincidence. "That *is* good news," he said and clapped Brandon's shoulder. "Hope it works out for you. I'll say a prayer."

"You and me both." Brandon's face set in a faraway smile. "I'm thinking that if I get this job as project manager—and from the sounds of it, they really think I'm a good fit—I'll move the family down there. Sell the house, sell the SUV, downsize everything. I'll probably take you up on that offer for the Passat. It was a nice-looking car."

"That's really great," Kyle said truthfully. "Not just about the car...about everything."

"I haven't told Jean any of this," he said, and his smile faded. "She wants to keep the house, and I know there's going to be a lot of tears. Plus, the boys love their school and Logan has a lot of friends in the neighborhood. I have some rough stuff ahead, but eventually, I know it's going to be for the best."

For a few moments they sat in silence, Kyle absorbed in Brandon's good news that, in an indirect way, sort of trickled down to him. He was truly happy, and being happy for Brandon seemed to change his own mood.

"You said you had two good things to tell me?"

Brandon smiled. He stood from the couch. "You got a DVD player?"

"I have an old one and it's hooked up, but I haven't used it in a long time. We're not watching porn, are we? Because that's honestly not going to cheer me up right now."

Brandon laughed again. "I'll be right back." He left the apartment, then returned a minute later holding a DVD case. It didn't look like a specific movie, just a blank blue case. "My mother sent this up from Florida," he said, holding up the case. "She had some old videos put onto DVD."

"Dear God," Kyle said, and smiled. "Those aren't —"

"Brandon, Kyle, and Vanessa: The Younger Years," Brandon said. "I know you weren't over to my house that much because —"

"Your mother thought I was a big piece of loser."

"Whatever," Brandon said and waved it off. "But there are a few videos of the three of us."

After messing around with buttons on the remote, the DVD started to play. Brandon fast-forwarded through some videos of his family, mostly family Christmases and one that looked like Brandon's family birthday party. Finally, he stopped on one that looked as though it had been taken outside, at winter.

"Oh my God," Kyle said, and sat forward. He shook his head,

226

almost wanting to shield himself from the humiliation. He was probably in eighth or ninth grade in the video, judging by the fact that his hair was not long yet as it had been in junior and senior year of high school. It was obvious from the videos that he didn't know how to act when a camera was on him, probably because Brandon's family was one of the few he knew who owned a hand-held video recorder at the time. His younger self kept looking at the camera, then would turn back to the snow with Brandon and Vanessa. He wore a puffy blue jacket, one he barely remembered owning.

"We were sled-riding over by Bells Park," Brandon said. "Look at Vanessa."

Vanessa was in the distance, wearing a tall white winter hat that obscured most of her face. Her lemony hair stuck out at strange angles, the bottom strands covered in snow. She turned to the camera, placed a snowy glove to her mouth, and hopped onto a plastic red sled.

"I can't believe this," Kyle said as they watched Vanessa and the red sled disappear down a long hill. "I don't even really remember us doing this."

"There's another one, too."

For a while they watched the videos, finishing up the sled-riding one before skipping to Brandon's fifteenth birthday, then one that was just a fast few minutes of the three of them in Brandon's front yard, running around when they were clearly past the age when they should have been running around like children. When they got together, it seemed, the three of them turned back to this childlike state of existence. Maybe it was the same now. Because they were childhood friends, they would always bring out the young-at-heart spirit they all shared.

"I honestly have no memory of Vanessa playing baseball with us," he said, pointing to the screen.

"I think we were just fooling around," Brandon replied. "I seriously doubt she would have worn a dress like that if we'd planned to play baseball."

"She did wear those crazy dresses all the time, didn't she?"

Brandon nodded and turned off the DVD. "Did you want to come over for dinner sometime this week? If Jean doesn't meet you soon, she's probably going to go crazy with curiosity."

"I'm really no big deal. Just your average, everyday lunatic." He shrugged. "I can come over any day except Thursday."

"Let's make it Friday night dinner then." He popped out the DVD, placed it back in the case, and headed for the door. "And if you need anything before that, you call me immediately, okay?"

"You got it."

"I'm serious," he said as Kyle met him by the door. "I brought over this video to remind you that you have two very close friends."

"I understand."

Brandon nodded, surveyed him for a moment, and left. Kyle counted the seconds until the loneliness returned, and when it did, he dropped onto the couch. For a while he swung back and forth, telling himself that his life was essentially over, then reminding himself that he still had Brandon, Vanessa, and his mother. He wasn't sure which side of himself would win, the pessimist or the optimist, but decided that the only course of action while awaiting each side to battle it out was to take a few sleeping pills and curl up in his bed.

CHAPTER TWENTY-FIVE

Vanessa waited until May was out for the evening and Emma was asleep before opening the door and letting Vincent into the house. He paused in the doorway, glanced around, then stepped inside.

"Emma is asleep?" he whispered.

Vanessa nodded. Both of them agreed it was best that their first meeting back together at the house should be a private thing. That way, if it didn't work out, neither May nor Emma would be confused or upset.

Vanessa had called him Monday night, after she calmed herself from her parting with Kyle. It still felt to her that the scales had tipped in favor of Kyle, and even as Vincent stood in the foyer, debonair in a way Kyle had never been and would never be, she couldn't help but think only of Kyle and what she was leaving behind. The decision she'd made was based solely on the happiness of May and Emma, and though she had to admit that there were feelings between she and Vincent that would always be there, she also knew she would never love Vincent like she loved Kyle.

"Do you want to sit on the couch and have some wine?" she asked. It felt mildly uncomfortable, like bringing a stranger home from a bar or club.

"Or we could just go right upstairs."

"I see you want to just get right back into this."

"It's been two months," he replied. "So, yeah."

Vanessa wasn't sure if sex was the best way to ease back into her marriage. She'd envisioned a night of talking and getting reacquainted with each other, maybe finding a way to move past the problems and make everything brand new. Things had been discussed the night in Vincent's hotel room, but that was only a start. They had to find some way to close up the past and change things around. She wasn't sure if Vincent was the type of man to do that in a way that would satisfy her.

"After you," he said, and gestured toward the staircase.

Upstairs, Vincent closed the bedroom door and glanced around again, as he'd done at the front door. Vanessa sat down on the bed, watching him.

"The same," she said. "Except inside the closet. I rearranged my clothes because yours were gone."

"You left our wedding pictures up. And the pictures of that trip to Nantucket. I guess you couldn't have hated me that much." He continued to walk around, and then, when he seemed satisfied that nothing in the room had changed enough for him to be angry about it, he sat down on the bed beside her. "So, where do we start?"

"I think that first, we should talk a little. Just jumping back into this feels weird. But I understand that it's been a while and that you'll need me tonight."

"All right," he said. "I guess we'll start then with the therapy thing."

For a while, they sat talking quietly about couple's therapy, their options, what day they'd do it, and how it would benefit them. As they spoke, Vanessa still couldn't shake the awkwardness — how much he felt like a stranger. She tried to make the scene erotic, pretend she was sitting in bed with an attractive man she barely knew who wanted to have sex with her, but when that didn't work, she decided on a new strategy — just get right into it. At a pause in the conversation, she reached out and brushed her fingers over his arm.

"I thought you wanted to talk first," he said, and gazed at her hand on his forearm.

"We did talk," she replied and moved closer. "We'll do therapy on Wednesday afternoons, have you move back in soon, and if things go well tonight, we'll tell the girls we're trying to work through things."

"Let's tell Emma the day I move back in," he said, glancing in the direction of Emma's bedroom. "Just so we're sure."

"Okay. Good."

Vincent reached out and cupped her neck, but the awkwardness wasn't going away; it just molded itself around them, itchy and uncomfortable. She considered going downstairs and grabbing a bottle of wine, but before she could make up her mind, Vincent leaned in and kissed her. She kissed back, taking in the strong scent of his cologne and noting how different it was from the way Kyle smelled. Kyle was fresh air and Vincent was cologne. Kyle was glittery and Vincent was sleek. Kyle was a throb in her heart and Vincent was an icy sliver. Kyle was... she reprimanded herself for thinking about Kyle, but couldn't stop, couldn't get into this moment with her husband. With an involuntary shiver, she pulled away from him.

"What?" he said, looking peeved. "What's the problem?"

"I don't know."

He ran a hand through his hair. "We haven't been together for two months. I would think you'd want to get right into this. What's wrong?"

"I don't know," she said again.

She did know what the problem was. Not only was she in

love with another man, but she'd made love to that man right in this very bed, only a week and a half ago. It wasn't fair to Vincent that she'd done that, and it wasn't fair to May that she had to keep that secret from her father indefinitely. Vanessa knew she would have to tell Vincent eventually, but for now it was supposed to be a secret. The problem was, she was just now understanding that secrets as big as this one were torturous to keep, like a constant twisting blade inside an otherwise happy heart. And if she was having difficulty keeping the secret, how did May feel?

Maybe it wasn't enough to decide when they'd do therapy and what the arrangement would be with the girls. Maybe there was still this last thing between them, unknown to Vincent, that Vanessa had to get out. Until she did, she wouldn't be able to get close to him, and she would always feel that twisting blade whenever he was around.

He tried again to kiss her, this time pushing her down to the bed. It was his best attempt at seduction, and she was finally aroused, but her body was still tense. As he moved to lift her dress, she put a hand to his chest.

"I have to tell you something."

"What, Vanessa?" he said. "What the hell is the problem?"

"Okay, first of all, how could you expect to just come over and have sex after two months of living apart and contemplating divorce?" She didn't wait for his response. "And the other thing is…." She sighed and sat up, smoothing the bottom of her dress. "I have something to tell you." There were a few ways he could take this news, and she had to mentally prepare herself for any outcome. "An old friend of mine from high school contacted me recently. An old boyfriend."

Vincent stared straight across at her, not blinking. "I don't like where this is going."

"Vincent, please," she said, knowing exactly how he looked

232

just before a fight. "Let me get this out without arguing, okay? His name is Kyle, and we were very close growing up. You remember how I told you that I used to hang around with two boys growing up? Kyle and Brandon?"

"I remember something about you talking with two boys at a pond," he said, throwing his hands up. "Maybe something about Kyle being your first boyfriend."

"He was my first boyfriend, my first kiss…he's very special to me. And last weekend, because I thought you and I were in the final stages of a divorce…I slept with him."

Vincent's eyes widened in shock, then clouded over in a rage she had never seen before.

"But I broke everything off with him and want to focus on you and I fixing our—"

"Wait a minute," he said, and stood from the bed. "You're telling me that while we were married, you slept with another man?"

"I thought we were getting a divorce." She tucked her legs beneath her, kneeling to face him. "When I went to see you—"

"That's why you came to see me in the hotel? You wanted to know when the divorce was going to be final because you were having sex with this other guy?"

"Shh," she said, and jerked her head toward Emma's room. "She's a light sleeper."

"Unbelievable." He paced the floor, running his fingers through his hair. "Unbelievable! And all these years, I've…do you have any idea how many offers I've had over the years? How many women I've turned down when I was younger and could have had anybody?"

"Vincent, please."

"No." He stopped pacing and met her eyes, his nostrils flaring. "You want to know what?"

"Don't say something you're going to regret," she said. "Please, Vincent."

He threw his head back, laughing. "Truth? You were a whore when I met you, and you're still a whore now."

She gasped. There he was, the old Vincent, stepping back out from whatever screen he'd been hiding behind.

"That's not fair," she said. "I was in my early twenties when we met and a completely different person. I've never cheated on you, all the years we were married, and only slept with Kyle because I was in love with him and thought you and I were done."

"I don't know what I was thinking, trying to fix this up," he continued, ignoring what she'd said as he always did in arguments. "You straight out told me you never loved me, and I still tried to make this work."

"We were going to try to make it work for May and Emma," she said.

"That's been our mistake all along, and now I've wasted my entire life!"

"*You've* wasted your entire life?" she replied. "What about me?"

"Oh yeah, I forgot how fucking awful it's been for you, living in a million dollar house while working an easy job. You married into my money and got comfortable, having my kids so I'd stick around. But you know what? I'm not doing it anymore. I'm done here. You'll get your divorce papers next week, you can sign them, and then go fuck whoever you want to."

She bit her lip. "Just leave," she said, and her voice broke. "Just get out."

"That's what I was going to do. And don't expect this to be easy now. I'm fighting for full custody of my girls."

"What?" She launched off the bed. "You can't...I don't have money and lawyers like your family does. You can't possibly...."

The room went in and out of focus as she tried to catch her breath.

"You want to move my girls to Connecticut or wherever, and I'm not going to let you." He paused, as though he'd just thought of something. "You were going to move in with him, weren't you? He lives in Connecticut, just like you used to, and you were going to bring May and Emma to live with him? Oh my God."

He began pacing again, stopping every few seconds to glare at her. For one horrific second, she even thought he was going to hit her. And in the fragile state she was in, he would have knocked her down easily.

"Vincent, please," she said, trying to remember that he was angry and maybe just lashing out because of that. "I honestly broke it off with Kyle. You can't keep my girls from me. I love them more than anything in the world. And you have absolutely no grounds to take full custody. I'm a good mother."

"A good mother? You think a good mother commits adultery? A good mother leaves her kids alone until seven o'clock at night? And that doesn't even begin on what May has told me. You constantly tell her to babysit, you can't get along with her, the two of you—"

"May and I have been getting along lately. And just because I've had to work doesn't mean I'm not a good mother!"

"You didn't have to work, you *chose* to work."

"Only so I didn't have to rely on you for everything!"

"Whatever," he said. "You'll be hearing from my lawyer." He opened the bedroom door. "And I want you out of my house by the end of this month." He shook his head in disgust, then sped away downstairs and out the front door.

Vanessa dropped to the bed, clutching her heart. It took a full minute to catch her breath, and even when she'd done that, she still felt as though she was suffocating. She listened for a moment, making sure Emma had stayed asleep through the argument, and thankfully, she had. The house was silent, though it still had a shaking feel to it, an aftershock sort of vibration. Could Vincent really take away her girls?

Just the thought of losing her girls left her with such a sense of despair that she could physically feel it, a pressure building all around, taking her air and squeezing her chest. She'd rather die than lose her girls. And if it came down to running away with them, at least with Emma, she would do that. If Vincent actually got close to winning full custody, she would consider running away. How could she not?

She pressed her cheek to her pillow and balled up her body. A corkscrew of pain and chill moved up her spine. This was a sorrow that she'd never felt before, a scenario she'd never once thought she'd have to face. She wasn't sure what she would do next, but whatever it took, she had to fight for custody of her girls. Even though Vincent was rich and had incredible lawyers, even though she'd committed adultery in their marriage, even though the odds did not seem in her favor. She had to fight.

CHAPTER TWENTY-SIX

Brandon read over the email a few times. Starting pay, eighty-thousand a year. Full benefits. Two weeks vacation. One week of sick time. He could hardly believe how quickly he'd landed the job, though he'd known when he left the interview that he clicked with the owners and had the experience they were looking for. He'd showed them his work, pages and pages of drafts and drawings, and they'd been impressed. Not impressed enough to give him the hundred-thousand he wanted. But still, he had a new job at a decent architecture business.

Jean didn't know yet. It was yet another thing he'd kept from her, for her own good, as he kept telling himself. This had been his struggle from the beginning, as much as Jean wanted to be involved and he wanted to involve her. It had been his burden to bear, because he needed to protect his wife and his family like some superhero, keep them from unnecessary stress. But now, because he was going to take a job in his old neighborhood, at a substantial pay-cut, he would have to tell Jean the final outcome of that struggle, what he'd decided days ago.

They were selling the house and moving.

The strange thing about the entire struggle was that now, at the end, it no longer mattered to him that he was losing the house. His greatest fear had been presented to him, and he'd stomped his way through it with a sense of fight that he'd never had before. Of course, he couldn't forget that Kyle loaned him the money that helped ease his mind in the latter half of his battle. Money was important, money was a necessity, but money could not buy him happiness, as cliché as the saying was. He'd learned the difference between fears that were worth losing sleep over, and fears that would pass in their own time. But those were his own personal feelings, and he knew Jean would not feel the same — although the time to discuss it was upon him.

It was Friday afternoon, and the last Brandon heard, Kyle was coming for dinner that evening. Jean was in the kitchen, not quite as frantic as she'd been when Vanessa had come for dinner, but still preparing the food and surroundings with more detail and perfection than she usually did. Brandon held his cell phone as he walked into the kitchen, and when he realized that Logan and Andrew were upstairs playing in their rooms, he sat down at the table.

"I hope Kyle likes Italian food," Jean said, chopping garlic on her favorite wood cutting board. "I'm making a sauce for the spaghetti, and soon I'll start on some meatballs."

"He likes Italian." He tapped his fingers against the table, reminding him of Kyle's nervous habits and fidgeting, then tried to settle himself with a slow intake and expel of air. This was Jean, after all. They were a team, and though he wasn't sure exactly what to expect, he was hoping she'd understand that his decision was in the best interest of the family.

"I have something to talk to you about."

Jean spun around, grasping the knife handle, her eyes narrowed in concern, probably from the tone he'd used. "Okay," she said.

"One of the resumes I sent out was for a place called Carey Architects. They contacted me, and when I went out yesterday to the — well, what I told you was a job fair — I was at an interview

238

with them."

Jean placed the knife down on the counter. "Why did you lie to me?"

"Didn't want you to get your hopes up, but that's not the point here." He stood and walked to her. He was still holding his cell phone like he needed the emailed offer as evidence, or maybe because he couldn't believe it himself and had to keep checking to make sure it was real. "We really hit it off, and they've offered me a position as project manager. I start in two weeks, July eleventh."

"Brandon...." She looked beyond words, her eyes shining with joy. "That's...that's incredible news!"

"I know." He took her hand. "But there are a few things that will need to change for me to accept the position. The pay doesn't even come close to what I needed to make for my bottom-line income. And it's about a half hour from here, twenty-five minutes if I really crank, but with morning traffic on the parkway, I'm looking at a rough commute. So I've made a decision." He squeezed her hand, preparing her. "We're going to put the house on the market and move to my old town, which, coincidentally, is the same town Carey Architects is in."

All her earlier brightness faded, like the end of a brilliant sunset.

"We'll be much more comfortable in a smaller house," he continued. "We'll have a smaller mortgage, and once we get rid of the SUV, we'll have a lower car pay—"

"Wait," she said, just above a whisper. "You're getting rid of the SUV?"

"Kyle can get me a good deal on a car."

"Kyle," she said, and frowned. "Why does it seem like every awful conversation we have lately has his name in it somewhere?"

He guided her to the table and sat her down, trying to explain his plan in greater detail, telling her that everything would work out for the best. As he spoke, she was quiet, her eyes glazed over, not giving him any indicators of her frame of mind.

Finally, he finished with explaining how good the schools were in his old town, and how there were many neighborhoods that not only would fit into their new budget, but were exceptional neighborhoods with cute and cozy homes. Jean's eyes trailed away from him, taking in the kitchen, the cylindrical lights and the frilly curtains, the steel stove, and the little yellow canisters that lined the counter.

"You promised," she whispered.

"Promised what?" he said. "That I'd always take care of you to the best of my ability?"

"That we wouldn't lose the house."

"I know." He wasn't sure where to go next. He'd made his case, and that was really all he could do. "Circumstances changed."

"No, everything is the same." She shook her head. "It's you who changed. Ever since you've been seeing your two old friends again you've been sneaking around and lying to me, and you've been passive when I've tried to discuss money issues and health insurance. You pull money out of thin air without telling me where it came from." Her hands, resting on top of the table, curled into fists. "You made a huge decision about our lives without even asking me about it. You went to a job interview without telling me. This is the first offer you've had—maybe something better is ahead."

"Or maybe this is the best I'm going to get!" He slapped his hand down on the table. "It fits into everything so perfectly. Don't you see?"

"I see all right. What I see is that you're going through some midlife crisis and clinging to your childhood and your childhood friends so tightly that now you want to move your children to a completely different town, just so they can grow up in the neighborhood you grew up in. Have you even thought this through as a rational human being? Or is this just something the impulsive, crazy Kyle would do?"

"You have it all wrong." He tapped a foot against the floor. Jean was off, way off in her assessment. "Listen," he said finally. "I realize this will take a while to get used to, but once you think it through, you'll realize that this is the best direction to go in. It's just a house."

Those were the wrong words.

Jean stood from her chair, squealing the legs against the floor. "Just a house? You and I spent days and weeks deciding on every little detail of this house! We were going to leave it to Logan and Andrew when we died! It was supposed to go on in our name for generations!"

"Jean—"

"It's not about the money, it's about a sentimental attachment that you used to have and you don't seem to have anymore. I don't even know who you are anymore!"

The conversation had shifted, grown ugly. Brandon was thrown. When had this become a discussion about his supposed identity crisis? He listened helplessly as she continued to go off, bringing up things that had happened in the past, but mostly shouting about how he'd changed since he'd been hanging around with Kyle and Vanessa. It was not unlike things his mother had said to him years ago when he was in high school. Kyle was bad news, Kyle had a negative influence on him...and maybe back then all of it was true. But now, as adults, Kyle was perhaps a better human being than Brandon himself. Kyle had problems, but his heart had always been in the right place. It was only now that Brandon understood that perhaps Jean was right about him wanting to emulate Kyle. He envied Kyle and maybe

241

had always wanted to be like him—passionate, persistent, and a touch insane, but in the best possible way.

"I would appreciate if you didn't say things about my friends," he said, and rubbed his forehead. "I've never said anything about your friends, and believe me, I really could have."

And then it went off in another direction: her friends were annoying, his friends were a bad influence; her friends only cared about money, his friends were secretive. It was a release of things he'd wanted to say over the years, but the release was tinged with spite, and when he finished, he had an overall sense of wrongdoing. The things he'd said could not be retracted.

Jean did not show any outward signs of hurt. She stared him down for a few seconds, then walked back to the counter and the garlic with a sort of quiet dignity. He adored this about her, even now, in the middle of their worst fight ever.

"Jean…," he started.

"You ask too much of me lately," she said, and he welcomed the change in direction. "I fully understand and am even grateful that your midlife crisis is this instead of an affair or a red sports car, but you're asking me to change my entire life and accept that you've changed, too."

"But I haven't—"

"When have we ever kept secrets from each other? You tell me another time in our marriage, or even when we were dating, that you kept a secret, and I'll agree that maybe you haven't changed. But as of now, I stand by what I said. I don't know you anymore."

She went back to chopping the garlic. Brandon took a breath and decided that maybe it was best to give a little something up here. This whole disastrous, bit by bit crumbling of his marriage had started with nothing more than a secret kept years ago by three friends. And that secret would always remain intact, though

242

now, with the knowledge that he would never find his watch or Kyle's cross or Vanessa's diary, maybe it was worth saving his marriage to give up just a smidgen of the truth.

"You want to know the real reason Kyle came back into my life? You want to know where I was all those nights? That will fix this for you?"

Jean shrugged. Her back was turned to him as she pulled down a can of tomato paste from the cabinet.

"Back in my old neighborhood, when the three of us were teenagers, we buried something. It was Kyle's idea, and back then, I thought he was nuts for doing it. I thought I was nuts for following through with every crazy thing he came up with. But now as an adult, I realize that you're right in a way, and maybe I always looked up to him because he just lived life as it came to him, rather than planning every minute and worrying about money and everything else like I did. Vanessa told you that he and I used to fight, and that's very true. We fought because he had different views, and maybe a little part of me thought his views were better than mine; the ones I'd been raised on."

Her back was still turned to him. "What did you bury?"

"Let's just say we buried things that we ended up needing in our lives right now." He stood and walked to her. "That's all I can tell you. It's not a secret from you, it's a secret that I'd like to have for myself. I hope you'll understand the difference."

"There's no difference."

"There's a big difference. My friendship with Kyle and Vanessa had a huge impact on my life, not just as a kid and a teenager but now, as an adult. And yes, maybe a part of me wants to move back to my old neighborhood because it feels right. I love living in our beautiful house, but now I need a change, even if that change is to downsize."

"And you expect me to change right along with you? You

expect Logan and Andrew to understand that their father has had an epiphany and wants to move them away from their school and their friends? Think of your family."

"You're all I've been thinking about." Why wasn't she getting this? He was nearly shaking with the effort to try and make her understand. "This is for us. This is for our family."

"Then why are you the only one who's happy about it?"

The fight started up again, back from where it began, about the house and the move, and then it made the grand shift back to her friends and his friends. It went on for so long that Brandon hadn't noticed that upstairs, the playing had ceased. When he finally realized, he spun to the doorway of the kitchen and saw that he had an audience of two.

"Logan," he said and raced to the door. "What's the matter, buddy?"

Logan didn't answer. Andrew looked on the verge of tears. It was the first time, Brandon was certain, that they'd ever witnessed their parents fighting.

He met eyes with Jean. There was an understanding between them that whatever their differences were right now, they were to appear a tight, solid team to their children.

"Mommy and I were just having a discussion about some things," Brandon said. He wasn't sure how much they'd heard.

"Sounded like a big fight going on down here," Logan said, throwing imaginary punches into the air.

"What are you fighting about?" Andrew said, grasping Jean's pants. "Daddy doesn't like your friends?"

"I love Mommy's friends," Brandon said. "It was just a misunderstanding."

Logan shook his head like he didn't believe a word of it, then spun around and stomped out of the kitchen.

"Go play with your brother for a few minutes," Jean told

Andrew. "Daddy and I have to finish our talk."

"No yelling?"

"No yelling," Jean assured.

Andrew followed his brother, and Jean dropped into the kitchen chair. She pressed her eyes closed.

"I don't know what to do from here," Brandon admitted. He sat in the chair beside her. "We've never fought like this, and it scares me."

"I know," she replied.

As Logan and Andrew banged up the stairs, Jean slumped forward. Brandon reached out and rubbed her back, suddenly unsure of how to touch and soothe his wife. What they'd said to each other seemed to take their marriage to a different level, one he was unfamiliar with. Maybe both of them had suffered their grievances in silence over the years because they loved each other too much to argue about them. Maybe that was true love. He just wasn't sure right now.

"Let's get through tonight and then we'll talk more about this tomorrow," he said. "We're obviously in different places and have to find a way to meet in the middle."

"I don't want to lose our house," she said. "Please, let's see if something better comes up. It was your first offer and it came so soon. You'll be in high demand for sure."

Brandon knew what was out there for jobs — he'd been looking constantly. He also knew the reputation of Carey Architects, and was sure that was the place he wanted to be working and the town he wanted to be living in. But he also understood that making Jean happy was his first priority, and if he moved her out of her beloved house, and moved her children away from their friends, he would forever be seen as the man who ruined their lives. For as sure as he'd been before, now he was back to not knowing. There was no meeting in the middle on this one. There

245

was really no way to do it.

"Let me think some more," he said. "But you have to promise to think too. This job and this move mean a lot to me."

He stood from the table and walked out of the kitchen, still absorbing Jean's harsh words, thinking back on what she'd said about Kyle and Vanessa, and how she'd combatted his decision to take a job he really wanted and to move their family.

For the first time ever, he resented his wife.

CHAPTER TWENTY-SEVEN

Kyle had been in such a deep state of unconsciousness that he wasn't sure if the loud banging was inside of his head, inside the apartment, or his own fists banging on heaven's gate. For the past few days, or maybe it had been a week, he'd been popping sleeping pill after sleeping pill, only stumbling out of bed to use the bathroom and eat a few bites of food before sliding back beneath the sheets and blankets.

He'd called out of work, feigning the flu, though he knew how rare it was to be so sick in the summer. Maybe it's something worse then, he'd told his boss. Maybe I should go to the doctor and get checked out. He had no intention of getting out of bed, much less going to a doctor for either a real or made-up disease. He had even tried to squirm his way out of going to dinner last Friday night at Brandon's house, but when he called to cancel, Brandon said Jean had already started on spaghetti and meatballs. It had been a bad idea to go over Brandon's house in the shape he was in. Brandon had accused him of being drunk, even though he swore that he was sober. Brandon's wife Jean barely said a word to him and never met his gaze, and he couldn't really blame her for hating him. He'd made an awful first impression, staggering into the house, then unable to focus or keep his eyes open at the dinner table. He barely remembered the evening at all.

Now he was in bed, as he'd been all day or all week, and the banging continued, even as he let his eyelids flutter open and stay in that position. It was a battle to keep them from falling closed, and for a few seconds, he couldn't even focus on the clock to see what time it was. The only thing he knew for sure was that it was sometime at night and that the banging was most certainly not in his dream or his imagination. There was someone at the door. Someone who was not giving up.

He rolled himself out of bed and slipped on a pair of blue sweatpants. "Coming," he said, and jolted from the sound of his own voice. He hadn't spoken in a while, and now he sounded as though he was talking into a carpet. "I'll be right there!"

He tripped over a remote control in the middle of the living room, then caught himself before he slammed into the front door. When he unlocked the door and creaked it open, his eyes shot open, wide awake. Vanessa Lawrence was at his door.

The first thing he noticed was that she looked the worst he'd ever seen her. Loose strands of hair stuck out like wild hay, reminding him of the home video when Vanessa's hair was messed up from playing in the snow. Tonight, her hair had the appearance of neglect, maybe even frantic tugging or pulling. Her eyes were swollen and lined in red, she wore no makeup, and her cheeks were patched in pink.

"What's the matter?" he said, scratching his head. "You okay?"

Without a response, she fell into his arms. It was all he had in him to hold her up, and he feared that any moment, they'd both go tumbling down into the living room.

"What is it?" he said. His muscles were vibrating from the effort of holding her up. Her body shook in sobs. She was either unable to respond or unwilling, and he wished he was more alert for this. Obviously, she needed a friend right now. "Are May and Emma all right?" he asked.

"I just dropped them off…at my mother's in Stonington," she replied. "I know he'll find them there eventually, but I needed some time and didn't want to…bring them here…if he finds out…."

He was trying to catch everything through her hysterical crying. "Who is 'he'?" he asked. "Vincent?"

She nodded and finally let go of him. "You don't look so good," she said.

"I was asleep."

"At seven o'clock?"

He palmed his forehead, then gestured her to the couch. "Sit down," he said. "I'll make you some coffee. We could both use some."

As he worked in the kitchen, he kept a close eye on her. She was worrying him, rocking back and forth and constantly checking her phone. Whatever was going on had the feeling of something incredibly wrong, perhaps even illegal.

He brought the coffees in and placed them down with her sugars, then dropped onto the couch beside her. "Why did you take May and Emma to your mother's?" he asked as an opening question.

Vanessa checked her phone again, then laid it on the arm of the couch, glancing back once at it before picking up her mug of coffee. She cupped the mug between her hands, shivered, and drank a deep sip before even adding sugar.

"I told Vincent," she said and closed her eyes. "I told him that I slept with you."

"Oh."

His first impulse was to go lock the door. He was in no condition to dodge a punch should Vanessa's husband come barreling through the door, ready to knock him in the jaw for sleeping with his wife. He wasn't programmed for fights as it was, and had avoided them his entire life by a combination of higher brainpower and his own reputation as someone you really didn't want to start trouble with. It also helped that usually, the boys back in school starting the fights could loosely be considered his friends, or were too stupid to know the difference. He fit in comfortably with the other lowlifes in school who wouldn't waste a second before pulling a knife. He never would have started a fight on his own, though even he would admit that sleeping with someone else's wife warranted a knock in the jaw. Vincent was probably on his way.

"Don't worry," she said as his eyes fixed on the door. "He doesn't know your last name or anything about you. And besides, I told him this last week. If he was going to kill you, he would have found you somehow and done it by now. He's certainly out for blood."

With that, it all came together. Vanessa and Vincent were in a war over the girls. And it was all his fault for seducing Vanessa at a time when she was unsure of her future with her husband. He should have known better, and had even been warned by both Brandon and his mother. But as usual, his feelings had taken over and erased any common sense.

"So, you're not supposed to have them? Is that what's going on?"

"Eventually," she replied and bit her lip. "He wants full custody, and I'm not giving that to him."

"And this fight started after you told him about us?"

She went on to explain that Vincent had come over last week expecting a full reconciliation, and Vanessa had guiltily pulled away, then told Vincent about her time with Kyle. After that it spun into a custody battle over the girls, and over the past week had escalated to the point where Vanessa was sure he was going to take them and she'd either never see them again, or he'd make it so she rarely saw them. He was going to paint a picture of her during the divorce that would make her look like all she wanted to do was work and sleep around, that she didn't care about her children. And Vanessa had no defense against that, no money of her own for a good lawyer. Her only option, as she saw it, was to take the girls and run away, but she'd changed her mind and ended up at her mother's house.

"…and then I told my mother I'd be back in a few hours and came here," she finished. "Tell me what to do."

"Okay," he said, trying to keep a calm tone. The truth was, he was terrified and didn't know what to do. From what he knew, taking the girls would equal nothing but more trouble for Vanessa. And now she'd come to him for suggestions and assurances when he'd never taken control of a situation in his entire life. "First, you need to call Vincent and tell him where May and Emma are."

"What?"

"Don't tell him you did this on purpose. Just tell him you decided they needed to spend the weekend with their grandmother or something. Trust me here. If you get caught running away with them — and eventually you will — you'll never see them again."

"You're right," she said at length. "I'll call him and tell him I just took them for a trip."

"Okay," he said. It was actually satisfying to take control. "Now we have to think about getting you a good lawyer."

"But I have no—"

"I have plenty of money." He reached out and swirled a hand around her back. "Let me get you a lawyer."

Vanessa fell into him and spilled the coffee she held loosely in her grip. With her head against his chest, he couldn't help but breathe in the scent of her, the faint perfume that she'd probably dabbed on yesterday, the lingering scent of flowery shampoo in her hair. Gently he smoothed her hair, then took her coffee mug and placed it down on the coffee table.

"I should go," she whispered. "I should call Vincent and then go back to May and Emma."

"May hasn't suspected anything?"

"May knows everything, even if she pretends she doesn't. But I think even she knows that what Vincent was going to do is wrong. She went along with me."

Vanessa pulled away, but kept her eyes locked on his. The strength of her eyes. God, even in this moment he was enchanted.

"I made a stupid mistake by choosing him over you," she said.

"You were doing what was best for your family."

"Don't do that," she said and stood. "Don't make it seem like I'm such a perfect woman. You, out of everybody in the world, should know better."

He stood to face her. "And you should know that I'm not perfect, either. Not that anyone would ever question that."

She nodded as though she understood. "Have you been drinking this week? Is that why you were in bed and you look so out of it?"

"I haven't drank since the night I went to my mother's house and looked at all those old pictures. I've been taking handfuls of sleeping pills, though, to get me through the rough patch I've landed myself in right now. The world, as I've known it for the past few days, has been my bed."

"That's not good for you."

Again, she locked her eyes on his. Now that he took a good, deep look, he saw something else there, something other than the anxiety. Maybe he was the only person in the world who could see it, but he somehow knew she had more going on right now than the custody battle.

He reached down and grabbed her hands, holding both of them in his own. "You have something to tell me," he said. "There's something else on your mind."

Vanessa squeezed his hands. "How do you always know?"

"Most people talk with their eyes, and I can read that—it's what makes me a good salesman." Vanessa let out a soft chuckle. "So what is it?"

She didn't reply at first, and he sensed a hesitancy. Then, as if in response to something she had not yet said, he felt a shooting surge of happiness that he'd never felt in his life.

"I probably shouldn't say anything," she whispered. "It's probably just stress, but...I'm late for my period."

Kyle felt a physical shift, as though some invisible force had just pushed away that forever wall of darkness to make room for something bright and colorful and beautiful. He'd been waiting his entire adult life to hear the words Vanessa had just spoken.

"I was...I was careful," he replied. He hadn't used a condom the first time they'd slept together. There hadn't been time for that. But he had been careful, not knowing if she was on birth control, and not really wanting to ask for details in the heat of passion. Still, he'd been careful.

"I'm very fertile," Vanessa said. "I've found that out over the years."

"And you and Vincent—"

"We never slept together that night he came over. You're the only man I've been with for over two months."

He nodded and realized how tightly he was holding her hands. "God," he whispered.

"I'll wait a few more days, and if I don't get it, I'll take a test and call you."

"And you'll want to keep the—"

"Of course," she said, and smiled. "I mean, I'm in my late thirties, so I'll have to discuss the risk factors with my doctor. But of course I'm keeping the baby. It's yours." She kissed his cheek and rested her forehead against his. "And even if I'm not pregnant, when my divorce is over...I'll ask you to drop the world for me. Will you still do that?"

"What do you think?" he said.

She embraced him, and left just as abruptly as she'd come. He stared at the door for a few seconds, wondering if perhaps he was still in his bed and this was all a dream. Just to be sure, he went to the window and watched her car pull out of the driveway. He placed his hand against the glass pane and felt the realness of warmth sink into his palm. Definitely not a dream.

Just a week ago he was contemplating ways to end it all. Now there was a possibility that he'd finally be a father. And Vanessa Lawrence was the mother. He couldn't let himself fall into visions of what would have been if he had killed himself last week. And if it weren't for Brandon coming over that day, he may have done it. He would never have known that Vanessa might be carrying his baby. He never would have been able to help her in her moment of need, never would hear the words that she wanted him back.

For the first time in years, he was happy to be alive.

CHAPTER TWENTY-EIGHT

Vanessa folded her favorite blue blouse and placed it on top of the other clothes in a cardboard box. She'd lived in the house for many years, and there was so much to pack that she really wasn't sure where to start. She'd wanted to keep the packing a secret until she could sit Emma down and explain what was going on, but Vincent wanted her out of the house by the first of July and that was approaching quickly. The only positive light was that Emma was out of school for summer vacation and might not feel the sting of changing schools so harshly now. Although, Vanessa still was not entirely sure where Emma would be going to school in the fall.

She was assuming, of course, that she'd win joint custody of the girls. Now that she'd gone to see Kyle and he'd offered to get her a lawyer, she was confident that between having a good divorce lawyer and the girls' own desire to be with her, she would keep them most of the time. From what May told her, Vincent was starting to cool down, and maybe it wouldn't even come down to a long and drawn-out court battle for the girls. Maybe he would see reason and give her joint custody, though it would be difficult to figure out the living arrangements.

Vanessa was either going to live with her mother or with Kyle, both in Connecticut, even if just temporarily. Vincent had already put a down payment on an apartment in the city. They

255

would both be far away from their starting point, and May was so stressed about this that her long and beautiful hair was actually starting to fall out. May had friends here and a boyfriend. She wasn't ready to give all that up, and Vanessa, for the first time, actually understood and identified with the pain of leaving friends and a boyfriend behind.

Though it was late in the evening, Emma was still awake. The schedule, no matter how hard Vanessa tried, changed in the summertime. Emma stayed up a little later, slept a little later, and was downstairs now, at ten o'clock, watching television. May was out with Warren, and even though she'd promised to come home early and help Vanessa pack, she hadn't yet come back. Vanessa wasn't angry, especially since May and Warren's days together were numbered. She tried to remember how she would have felt at that age if her mother told her she was moving away from Kyle, and was surprisingly able to conjure a feeling akin to notification that the end of the world was on top of her.

"Mommy?" Emma said from the doorway. She was rubbing her eyes.

"Past your bedtime," Vanessa said to her. "You want to brush your teeth in my bathroom tonight?"

Emma surveyed the cardboard box on the bed. "Is that my stuff in there?" she asked.

"No, sweetie." Vanessa closed up the box and placed it on the floor, beside a second box. She didn't want Emma to be overwhelmed, but at the same time, Emma deserved an explanation. "Come here," she said and sat down on the bed.

"Bigger boxes have better things in them," Emma said, crawling up on the bed.

"That's not always true. Small boxes can have diamonds or jewelry in them."

Emma's eyes grew larger.

256

"Or gold, right? Like pirate gold?"

"Yes, like pirate gold." She brushed back Emma's hair and tucked it behind her ear. "How would you like to go on an adventure?"

"Like the other night?"

"No." She shook her head. "That was just a long trip to Grandma's house. I mean, an adventure like you've never taken before."

Emma replied with an eager nod. If only she knew what was really going on, saw the battlefield all around her, all the damage. But that was the best part of childhood, a built-in protection from the truth. There was always that parental shield, a silver shelter that Vanessa tried to keep Emma inside of, safe. Vanessa couldn't give Emma much, but she could protect her with everything she had.

"I'm really looking forward to this new adventure," Vanessa continued. "And it starts with packing all our stuff up, like all our stuff is playing hide-and-seek, and then we open it all up in a different place. We'll like the new place, and our stuff will like the new place, too."

Emma's shoulders slouched. "The new place isn't Grandma's house, is it? Because it smells like fish there and makes my belly hurt."

"Maybe Grandma's house, I'm not sure yet," Vanessa replied. "But if it is, then only for a little while. Or maybe we'll stay with somebody else." She hadn't asked Kyle yet, but knew he would say yes…and besides, she would prefer living with Kyle. Emma was right, the little house by the water smelled awful, like rotten fish and low tide. Kyle's place would be better for now, closer to New York than Stonington. He had an extra room, and though small, it would probably fit May and Emma for now. "I have a friend we might stay with. He's one of the greatest people in the

257

whole wide world. He's like a superhero."

"How is he like a superhero?"

Vanessa smiled. "Because he always manages to save the day."

"Really?"

"I promise, cuckoo bird."

"Cluck cluck," Emma said and laughed. Her head turned as the door opened and closed downstairs. May had come home early after all. "May's home!"

Emma jumped off the bed and raced to the stairs. The move didn't seem to be bothering her, at least not now, with the early terms Vanessa had given her. That gave Vanessa a sense of hope. She continued to pack as May put Emma to bed, and at eleven o'clock, had a second wind of energy as she started on another box of clothes. May entered the room, looking just as wide awake.

"I'm almost done in here," Vanessa said, assuming she was coming to help. "And I have to talk to your father about the kitchen stuff, so we could do the living room or—"

"I have to talk to you about something."

May closed the bedroom door and sat down on Vanessa's bed. Vanessa was not sure how much more she could take, but her new rule was never shut May out or disregard her feelings. She sat down beside her.

"I don't want to move with Dad to New York City," she said.

"You might not have a choice in that."

"Just hear me out," May said. "I don't really want to move to Connecticut, either. I mean, both you and Dad will be so far away from here." She paused and took a breath. "I'm going into my senior year. Do you really expect me to leave now after I've gone through all these years with my friends?"

"Again, it's not a choice. I really have no alternative. I can't afford to live around here on my own. I've all but quit my job as it is now, and it's going to take me a while to find the job I want in my field."

"I have a plan," May said. She'd pretty much ignored Vanessa's words, which, in that moment, reminded Vanessa of Vincent. "It will make things easier for you and Dad when you decide who gets me."

"I'm listening."

"Just for my last year of high school, I want to move in with Warren."

Vanessa stood from the bed. "Absolutely not."

"Just listen," May continued. "Not move in with Warren as in just me and him, but with him and his mother. She loves me like a daughter and has no problem with me living there until I leave for college. Warren and I will have separate rooms, and I promise I'll spend every weekend with you and Dad. I'll drive to Connecticut on Fridays and stay over till Saturday night, then I'll go to Dad's place in the city and stay over there till Sunday night."

Vanessa was surprised when she actually began to contemplate this arrangement. It would keep May happy, staying here with her friends and graduating with them next spring, and it would also keep the custody battle contained to just Emma. She would still see May every weekend and Vincent would get to see her too.

"I'll be moving out for college in a year anyway," May said as her closing argument.

"Have you talked to your father about this?"

"He hasn't been my favorite person lately." She shrugged. "It's confusing. I went from hating you to hating him. During that New York trip, he didn't want to deal with Emma at all, and I got stuck doing everything."

"Lovely."

She always tried not to bad-mouth Vincent in front of her girls. May had to form her own adult opinions of her father, just as she'd had to after her parents got divorced. Although, now that she thought about it, her father might have been worse than Vincent. Her own father, after the divorce, had married a free-spirited redhead and moved to California to bask in the sunshine. The woman hated that he had a past, so her father rarely spoke to Vanessa or her sister after he moved away. Occasionally she would get a handwritten letter, but other than that, he had disappeared from her life.

"So?" May said.

"I'll think about it."

She sat back down on the bed, beside May, trying to give herself the same positive spin on the situation that she'd given Emma earlier: This was going to be a great adventure. Still, their family of four was splitting up, living in different places, and life would never be the same. Vanessa had tried so hard to freeze her moments with her children for this very reason. Life and circumstances always changed.

"Between you and me," May said, "I don't think Dad really wants full custody of Emma."

Vanessa kept her mouth shut.

"He might have taken me, but she's too much for him to handle on his own. You know, special needs and all that."

"I still want to make sure he gets to see her, even if he doesn't want full custody. I assume he'll probably cool down and back off. That is, until he finds out that I'm probably going to live with Kyle."

"He took you back?"

A pleasant warmth grew in Vanessa's body, spreading through her limbs and even into her fingertips. "Can you keep a secret?" she asked.

"Not really. But I will in this case."

Vanessa wasn't sure how May was going to take the news, but she had to tell somebody. It had been tingling through her all day, all the joy she felt at having a third baby. May was going to find out soon enough anyhow.

"I'm pregnant."

May's jaw dropped. "You're what?"

"I'm pregnant. I took two pregnancy tests this afternoon and both came out positive."

"Oh my God." May placed her hand over her mouth. "Is it... Dad's baby?"

Vanessa shook her head. She tried to look sad for May that the baby wasn't an answer to May's last-minute prayer to keep the family together, but found that she was unable to do that.

"Does Kyle know?" May asked.

"Sort of. I told him I was late, but I haven't told him about the positive tests yet. I'm trying to figure out just how to say it. He's wanted to be a father for a long time and had pretty much given up hope."

"So this was planned?"

"Maybe somewhere it was planned," Vanessa replied. "But no, Kyle and I didn't plan it."

"Then I have something in common with my new sister or brother already." May smiled. "We were both accidents."

Vanessa wrapped her arm around May and pulled her close. "You're the best thing that's ever happened to me," she said softly. "So in that way, you weren't an accident at all."

***

At two a.m., when Vanessa had depleted most of her energy and sank onto the couch next to a slumbering May, she began to think about how she would tell Kyle the news. She knew how terrible it was to keep him waiting, and that he was probably pacing the living room with his phone in his hand, anticipating her call. But she'd had to close up everything in her own life first, before moving into a new life with him. With tonight's finality, she could concentrate on figuring out just what to say when she called Kyle, though after fifteen minutes of different scenarios, one of which included an email with an enclosed picture of a stork, she finally decided that the best way to do this was to just call Kyle and tell him without any theatrics. He could fill in his own theatrics.

He always did.

CHAPTER TWENTY-NINE

Summer had closed in completely. The air was scented with cut grass and barbecues, people were coming out of their houses more and wearing less, and swimming pools were shedding their winter covers. Dogs barked as joggers sped past Brandon's house, and trees bloomed full and healthy. In the distance, Brandon could hear the shouts and splashes of children playing in the water. He could smell the sweet budding flowers, feel the warmth of summer on his skin.

Late morning, he sat in a lawn chair in his backyard, the sun hanging over him like a charged and fiery polka dot. If Brandon weren't so miserable, he would have enjoyed the sunlight and the extra boost of energy it had given him and the boys. But today, he just watched Logan and Andrew run around the grassy backyard, thick beads of sweat growing on his forehead, a determined crankiness settling into his planned demeanor for the day.

Other than the normal conversation required to run a household, he hadn't really spoken to Jean in the past few days. Kyle's lackluster first impression had made everything so much worse, and after an argument about Kyle Friday night after he'd left, Brandon had resolved himself to the fact that his marriage, as he knew it, had changed. He was on a totally different page from the one Jean was on, and that realization had exposed a

263

latent truth beneath their happy marriage. Jean wanted to live her life in luxury, doused in gifts, painted in gold, surrounded by comforts. They'd shared the same dream since college, but now Brandon's dream had changed.

Jean was a good woman. She was a superb mother and wife, and had sacrificed a career to stay at home and be a mom. And Brandon understood that. He could not condemn her for being who she was, especially when they'd met and connected with the same attitude and goals. Raising a family and living a life of luxury was their shared dream, and they'd lived it. But when life changed, they hadn't been able to change along with it. And he wondered if what was left smoldering would be strong enough to blaze up and rise again and form something new, something stable and secure. He wondered if they could put it all back together.

The fight after Kyle had left was another one that could fit into the category Worst Fight Ever. Jean had no experience with recovering alcoholics, and assumed Kyle was a terrible person with a personality similar to a common criminal. Or a bum. Kyle had certainly looked like an alcoholic bum, walking into the house with a pronounced lean, his face unshaven, his eyes heavy and unfocussed. Brandon even theorized that if Kyle had showed up at his door a month or two ago, he probably wouldn't have let him inside, around his family. By that acknowledgement, Jean was not so different from Brandon.

Brandon thought about all of this as he sat back in the lawn chair, watching Logan and Andrew bounce around from the swing set to the slide, then toss around a baseball, then blow bubbles. They did all this in about five minutes. It was the type of energy he hadn't had in years, except, he recalled, the night at Blueberry Pond when he'd run through the woods to escape the massive man who owned the house by the pond. That had been a night he would never forget, not only because he'd feared impending death, but because of his youth revival, fleeing a scene, then bonding again with Kyle and Vanessa.

The backdoor opened and Jean stepped out, holding an iced tea. She sat down on her own lawn chair, placed her flip-flops on the bottom edge, and laid back with her beverage.

"Do we still have a sprinkler somewhere?" he asked her. They always tried to have some kind of water toy for the boys to cool off. Jean had a fear of pools, so they'd never purchased one.

"Somewhere," she replied.

"Somewhere," he echoed. "And thanks for bringing me an iced tea." He pointed to her drink.

"You know where the refrigerator is."

"Dad!" Andrew called. "Watch me!"

Brandon left Jean's glare and turned to watch Andrew on the slide. "I give it a ten!" he said. Andrew always wanted to be judged on his sliding style. Sometimes he'd go backwards, sometimes on his stomach. It wasn't a long drop, so Brandon let him do whatever he wanted.

He watched and judged for a while, until Andrew got bored with constant tens and ran after Logan, who was migrating toward the side of the house.

"Stay where we can see you!" Jean called, but was ignored.

"I guess it will probably be in the nineties by this afternoon," Brandon said to change the subject. "I'll try to find that sprinkler in the garage."

"Like you know where anything is," she said, and sipped her iced tea. "Last year, when you were working all the time, I took care of everything."

"Then I find it hard to believe you don't know where the sprinkler is."

"It's in the garage!"

265

He wasn't sure if it was the heat, but the fighting was exhausting, and he had to keep wiping a splash of sweat from his forehead as Jean shouted about this and that, the merry-go-round argument of the past month.

"He's not always like that!" Brandon said, defending Kyle as she went on. "I admit he's had some drinking problems in the past, but that wasn't the case that night! Vanessa broke up with him, and he took some—"

Car brakes squealed from the front of the house, drowning out his shout. Jean bolted off the lawn chair so fast that her flip-flop caught in the plastic lining.

"Dad!" Logan shouted through the neighborhood. "Daaaaaad!"

Without hesitation, without even taking time to think, Brandon cut through the side yard and ran out toward the street. He made it to the curb before his knees buckled and he nearly fell onto the pavement from the sight before him.

"Andrew!" Jean cried, and sped past Brandon into the street. "Oh my God!"

The neighbor's car, a red sedan, was sideways in the street. Amy Garrish, an older woman with white-blonde hair who lived down the street, was gripping the steering wheel, her body visibly shaking. But Brandon only had a second to register this. His eyes shot to Andrew, who was just inches from the stopped car.

"It just missed him, Dad!" Logan said. "Just missed him!"

Brandon sped into the road and scooped up Andrew. He brushed back his hair, frantically inspecting him as Jean did the same, checking his arms and face.

"What happened?" Jean asked.

"He ran out and didn't see the car!" Logan said. "It swerved and just missed him!"

The next minutes went by in a dizzying blur. Brandon tried

266

to calm down both Jean and Amy Garrish, all the while stroking Andrew's hair and holding onto his hand. Thankfully, there hadn't been a hit or even any damage. Amy had seen Andrew speed out into the road and stopped the car just in time. Everybody was just shaken up.

Inside the house, Jean locked the doors and announced that everyone was staying inside for the rest of the day. Andrew was quiet, so Logan, fueled by nervous energy, led him to the playroom. Within minutes Andrew had bounced back and was playing with his toys. It wasn't until Jean settled into the armchair in the living room that she completely broke down. Brandon sped to her side.

"It's okay," he said. He dropped to his knees in front of her and wrapped his arms around her waist. "He's okay."

"But he might not have been," Jean said. "And we weren't paying attention because we were—"

"He's okay," Brandon said again.

Jean's soft sobs filled the room. Everything had happened so fast. Brandon had just been outside in the sunshine, judging Andrew's sliding technique, and now he was comforting his wife after Andrew's close call with death or serious injury. It was one of those moments in his fatherhood he knew he would never forget. The sound of the brakes, the scream from Logan, the car sideways in the road. It had just happened so damn fast.

"I'm sorry," Jean whispered. "I don't want to do this anymore."

He wasn't sure if she meant she didn't want to fight with him anymore, or she didn't want to be in the marriage anymore. Everything seemed in slow motion, so out of his control. "I love you," he said.

"I love you too," she told him. "And I don't want to fight anymore."

He slid into the chair beside her and bundled her up in his arms. They cuddled there until she finally stopped crying. Until it felt like it had before.

"We have to figure out what we're going to do," Brandon whispered after a while. "But whatever we decide, we stick together."

"Agreed," she said.

An hour later, everyone had settled down. Brandon made an iced tea for himself, then another one for Jean, and brought them to the downstairs playroom where both Logan and Andrew were playing a video game. Jean had a firm rule about spending more time outside in the fresh air than inside with video games, but today that rule did not apply. She watched over Logan and Andrew with a mother's fierceness, and when Brandon placed her iced tea down on the little plastic play table, she barely registered it.

"Here's what I'm thinking," he said, sitting back in an uncomfortable plastic chair. "We compromise. I take the job, and we'll stay in the house as long as we can keep the mortgage up."

"If I go to work in the fall, that added salary will bring us up to where we can afford the mortgage. We'll have to cut back a bit, that's all."

Brandon thought about this. If she made at least thirty-thousand, that would make up the difference to his bottom-line income needed to keep the house and pay their current expenses. He still didn't want her to have to work, but understood how badly she wanted to contribute, how badly she wanted to get back to her career. It was true, the boys were old enough now.

"Okay," he said. "We'll do that."

Jean smiled at him and went back to watching the boys play their video game. She reached over and placed her hand on his. "Thank you," she whispered.

Brandon didn't reply. The compromise would work for now, and when the time came that things changed again, they'd have to find other ways to compromise. They still had some issues to work out, but he figured these issues were no worse than what every married couple had to work through. The key to a happy marriage, he supposed, was being able to compromise differences. And it was those very differences that made a marriage work. Too many similarities and the marriage would be uneventful. Too many differences and the marriage would struggle. But a middle ground, where he and Jean stood now, seemed to be just perfect.

CHAPTER THIRTY

As soon as Kyle walked into his apartment, he turned on the CD player, dumped two full shopping bags onto the couch, and kicked off his shoes. He'd stopped at *JC Penney* after work, a store he never usually went into unless accompanied by a female, and had purchased two red throw pillows for his couch. He'd also bought new sheets for his bed and two pillowcases in a crazy pattern that looked like orange and red starbursts. It was probably for kids, he realized, but the colors had spoken to him.

It was a hot day, probably the first one to reach the nineties. He contemplated finally putting the air conditioner into the window in his bedroom, but that required a physical effort that he just did not want to summon this afternoon. His body was still recovering from a week of sleeping pills and the resulting never-ending loop of slumber. It was like just waking up from a coma, one where the world was different and explorable, but he was still too out of it and drowsy to fully enjoy it.

The music helped. It had been a long time since he'd used music as therapy. The beat of the drums lifted his spirit, and he used it as a backdrop to his decorating spree, removing the pillows from the shopping bag and positioning them on the couch. Vanessa had been right, all the place needed was a touch of flair and color. Just a little bit of red and the room seemed to pop to life. Just a little bit of music and the room jumped with liveliness. He was just moving his body to the beat when his house phone rang.

"Please be Vanessa," he said out loud. She hadn't called as she said she would, and he had pretty much given up hope. He turned down the stereo, picked up the phone, and said, "Hello?"

"Hi," Vanessa said. "You busy?"

"Just listening to The Red Hot Chili Peppers," he replied. "And waiting for you to call."

"When did you start listening to The Red Hot Chili Peppers?"

"The nineties, I guess." He sat down on the couch and rested his arm on one of the new red pillows. "Are May and Emma home and okay?"

"They're fine," she replied. "I brought them back from my mother's like you said to, and just told Vincent I took them for a quick trip to her house. Emma hates it there."

She paused and seemed to know that although he truly did care what was going on with the girls, what he really wanted was to find out if she'd taken a pregnancy test.

"I've looked into some good divorce lawyers," he said. "So whenever you're ready, we'll pick one and get everything started."

"That's good. May told me that Vincent will probably back down from full custody of Emma. It doesn't seem like he wants to handle her by himself, which doesn't surprise me. He always favored May and blamed me for Emma's supposed developmental delay. Anyhow...."

Her voice trailed off and Kyle sat forward. He held his breath.

"I've taken a pregnancy test," she said. "Actually, I've taken two."

"And?"

"It seems that Kyle Macord is going to be a father."

Kyle's head fell into his hands. "Thank you, God," he

whispered. He took a moment to absorb the news, holding the phone loosely in one hand, hoping Vanessa would understand his silence. It was a kind of joy he'd never felt in his life, and he wanted to remember it, carry it with him always.

"Kyle?" she said after a while. "You okay?"

"Never better," he replied, coming back to the phone.

"Me too," she said. "But we should wait to tell anyone. That's what people usually do. I'm going to make a doctor's appointment and get my prenatal vitamins, so after that we'll talk about telling people."

"Can I tell my mother?"

She paused. "Yes, you can tell her," she said. "I told May, so I guess we each get to tell one person. Agreed?"

"Yes," he replied. "Oh my God, Vanessa."

She let out a nervous laugh. "Tell me about it."

They spoke a little about if it was a boy or a girl, how Vanessa was feeling about a pregnancy in her late thirties, and how people would take the news. Both of them couldn't wait to tell Brandon, but knew it was best to wait until Vanessa saw a doctor.

"I had something else to talk to you about," she said, and sounded hesitant. "I was wondering if you would mind having two new roommates for a little while."

"Two?"

"Emma and I. May is going to stay with Warren, and she'll be down on the weekends. It's kind of a long story, but for now, I have no place to live, other than with my mother. Emma hates it there, so I thought—"

"That's not a problem at all," he said, and stood. "I can set up the spare room for her, and I'll just tell my landlord that you'll be staying here. There's a duck pond down the street that we can walk to with her. She'll love it."

"You can't see it, but I'm smiling."

Kyle laughed. He paced the room, a new energy pumping through his limbs as he thought about cleaning out the spare room for Emma.

"So, if all goes well with the divorce, then we'll decide what to do from there. I guess we'll need more space for the baby when she comes."

"She?"

"Just used to having girls, I guess." She laughed.

"Ah," Kyle said, and closed his eyes. He sat for a moment, drifting, thinking ahead. "It's a boy," he said to her. "We're having a boy."

"A Kyle premonition?" she said back.

"Maybe," he said. "If you believe in that stuff."

"I believe more now than I ever have," she replied. "Anyhow, I'll call you back later with details. You probably want to call your mother."

"Actually, I think I'll just go right over and see her. I want to see the look on her face." He thought about his father just then, and how his father would have loved to be a grandfather. His eyes tingled just a little around the corners, but he didn't want Vanessa to know he was struggling. Now was a time to be happy. "Talk to you soon," he said.

He hung up with her, turned off the stereo, slipped his shoes back on, and left the apartment.

CHAPTER THIRTY-ONE

Kyle pulled into the driveway of Aunt Bev's house and turned off the car engine. He was still shaking, something he'd been doing uncontrollably since Vanessa had given him the news, and the thought of telling his mother only made the shaking worse. It was a nervous, excited sort of shaking, and even if he tried to hold his hand still, it wouldn't stop. Thinking his mother might assume he was drunk, he squeezed his hands into fists and stepped out of the car.

His visit was not expected, so he knocked on the door and stepped back, arranging his face into a blankness his mother wouldn't be able to read, but not an expression that would cause her to think something was wrong. Beside him on the walkway, his mother or Aunt Bev had planted a row of marigolds, and their starburst pattern reminded him of his new pillowcases. He laughed out loud but fell silent when his mother opened the door.

"Kyle," she said, looking surprised. "What's the matter?"

"Can't a son come and visit his mother once in a while?" He stepped past her into the house. "You got a hot date hidden in here or something?"

"A hot...what's the matter with you?"

"Where's Aunt Bev?"

His mother closed the front door. "She just went to the grocery store. She'll be back soon. What's going on?"

"I was in the area." He dropped onto the couch. "No, that's a lie. I wasn't in the area."

"Kyle, if you don't tell me what's going on this very inst—"

"Okay, okay," he said and laughed. "I have some good news to tell you. Sit down." Although he'd just told her it was good news, she seemed more frightened than she had when she'd first seen him on her doorstep. With a blush of fear in her cheeks, she sat down in the armchair across from him.

"You're going to be a grandmother."

She stared straight across at him, unblinking. "You're buying a dog?"

"No, Mom." He shook his head. "I'm going to be a father. I'm having a baby." Her eyes widened, and he couldn't tell if she was overjoyed or in massive shock.

"Oh my goodness," she said finally. "That's…that's wonderful! But…you're not married."

"Really?" he said sarcastically. "Don't worry, I plan on marrying her. She's moving in soon with her daughter, and then we'll probably buy a small—"

"With her daughter?" She tilted her head. "Ava doesn't have children."

"Mom, I told you a million times. Ava and I broke up weeks ago. The mother is Vanessa Lawrence."

All the color drained from his mother's cheeks.

"Come on," he said. "She sat on my lap when she was sixteen, and you're going to hold that against her? She's an adult now. And she's the mother of your future grandchild."

"You got Vanessa Lawrence pregnant? Are you insane?"

"Why do people always ask me that?" He stood, no longer able to stay still, and started to move around the room, taking in the old pictures and all of Aunt Bev's ugly giraffe figurines.

"I'm in love with Vanessa. I've always been in love with her."

He paused to look at his mother, battling a sudden but intense surge of anger. "This is the happiest moment of my entire life, and you have to ruin it just because of something Vanessa did when she was a teenager?"

"Vanessa Lawrence is nothing but trouble." Her fists shook, but she remained sitting. "She's a horrible, horrible girl who has nothing but sex on her mind. She hates her own parents, and—" She squeezed her eyes closed and exhaled loudly, like someone who was on the verge of giving up a piece of secret information. "Sit down, Kyle."

Kyle's blood pulsed in his ears. How could his mother hate Vanessa for something so stupid? Something from when they were kids? He sat down on the couch again and raised his feet up onto the coffee table, crossing his arms on his chest.

"I am a woman who lives by the rules God has handed down to me," his mother said softly. "I do not believe in sex before marriage, but I've looked the other way when you've gone through your relationships. It was none of my business. I had to believe that I raised you correctly."

His anger with her was beginning to ebb. "You did raise me correctly, Mom. I live by those rules too. I just don't believe that sex is a bad thing. If you love someone, then why shouldn't you show that?"

"Kyle, this is not a moral discussion about you and your beliefs, it's about me, so let me continue. I've looked the other way when you've been in relationships as an adult, but as an adolescent, of course I had to step in when I believed a girl was no good for you or she was going to bring you down the wrong path. I was pleased when you and Vanessa stopped seeing each other in your last year of high school."

"Let me interrupt," he said and sat forward, angry again. "You hated her because of one incident, but to be honest, there

276

were girls who were much, much worse than she was."

"Oh really?" Her face contorted in disgust. "There were girls who said they wanted their first time with sex to be with you, in the woods by a pond? That's what the other girls said? Because that was the most disgusting thing I've ever—"

"Wait a second." Something sounded way too specific about this piece of information. "You think Vanessa said that about me? Where would you have heard that?"

His mother lowered her head. "I read her diary."

"You what?" He nearly fell off the couch. "Mom—"

"I'm a terrible woman, I know." Her voice was low, confessional. "And I've asked God's forgiveness many times for what I did. It was so long ago, but now I'm finally being punished. The girl is carrying my grandchild."

Kyle did not have time to address the sin involved, or the fact that his mother felt her future grandchild was some kind of punishment. All he could think of was that somehow, his mother had gotten hold of a diary that had been buried years ago and was supposedly lost forever.

"Mom," he said carefully. "How did you get Vanessa's diary?"

She hesitated, her eyes focused on the ceiling as she thought back. "It was inside of my good Tupperware bowl," she said finally. "I don't know, Kyle. It was so long ago. I remember that I read the diary, but I—"

"You had to have dug up the Tupperware bowl, then. It was by Blueberry Pond."

"No, our old neighbor, Mr. McHardy, dug it up. I remember that." She rubbed her head as she thought. "It was around the year you and Brandon and Vanessa got out of high school. I was at a bake sale at church and could not stop complaining about how I'd somehow lost my good Tupperware bowl. I used to

277

bring all my baked goods to church in it. It was a good bowl."

"I get that," he said. "Think really hard and tell me what happened next."

"Mrs. McHardy was at the bake sale and heard me complaining. She said she knew where the bowl was, that she saw you kids bury it one night. She thought maybe you buried a dead animal in it or something, but that it was by the pond, by a…I think she said it was by a tall tree she had a particular fondness for. Yes, that's it! I guess the tree brought a lot of nice shade onto her backyard. I think I told her that I couldn't recall a dead animal, so I had her husband dig up the bowl for me. It was my good bowl."

"I know," Kyle said. "I'm sorry about that. But why…. God, Mom, why didn't you tell me you found Vanessa's diary and Brandon's watch? It had his name on it, so you knew it was—"

"Brandon's mother hated you," she said, sticking her finger out at him. "If she found out that Brandon's expensive watch had ended up in my possession, she would have thought you stole it. Brandon was in college, so I just pretended I never saw the watch. It was ugly and flashy anyhow. But Vanessa's diary…I just flipped it open to see whose it was. I swear that was my initial intent. And then I saw your name a million times. Kyle sex, Kyle virginity, Kyle pond…all this awful stuff about my own son! And to top it off, she wrote about how she hated her own parents. She isn't a good girl, Kyle, just as I'd always suspected when you went through high school together. She's just not a decent girl."

Kyle rested his body against the back cushion of the couch. If he wasn't in such a state of shock, he probably would have let out a long and solid breath of relief. The bowl had been discovered and dug up, and now he had a sense of closure. Almost.

"Dad's cross was in there." He scratched his head. "But that doesn't make sense to me. Why didn't you give him the cross when he asked for it?"

"That cross was your father's?"

And then it hit him. The cross must have been a secret. Only the men in the family knew about it. His mother had never known of its importance.

"Yes, the cross was his." He joined his hands and eased them to his forehead. "He asked for it back just before he died. I thought it was buried." He went on to explain the friendship pact, how it had been his idea, and how they'd all put their most valued possessions inside of the Tupperware bowl.

"Why in the world would you have done something like that?" his mother said when he finished.

"I don't know." He stood up again, his body pumped with so much adrenalin there was no way he could keep still. "I just thought it was a way for us all to stay together. And I'm glad we did it. Because of that pact, Brandon ended up getting the money he needed while he was in-between jobs, and Vanessa and I reconnected. Because of that pact, I'm the happiest I've ever been in my life." He stopped in front of his mother. "So I guess in that way, I can't be mad at you for never telling me you found our stuff."

"I might have mentioned it, Kyle," she said. "Or you might have seen the bowl around, and you just don't remember. You weren't very focused during that period of time."

Kyle understood. The months and even years after high school he was drinking a lot, experimenting with different drugs, and job-hopping to keep some semi-sense of responsibility in his life. It was all a ball of fog, and there was always a chance he'd been high when his mother mentioned the bowl. Or maybe she didn't tell him. There was no way he'd ever know. For now, he'd just have to believe she thought she was doing the right thing by keeping Brandon's watch and not telling his family.

"What did you think when you saw all that stuff in the bowl?" he asked.

"Probably that these were things you were all hiding from your parents. Maybe you forgot about them or where you'd put them. I don't know."

He nodded again and tried to sit down on the couch. Slowly, his body was recovering.

Until he thought of something else.

"Mom," he said, sitting forward. "Do you...you don't still have our things, do you?"

"I don't remember throwing them away." Her gaze shifted upward, toward the ceiling. "If I still had them, they would be with all the old pictures, in the back of my closet."

"Can you look?"

She was already standing. "I'll be right back."

CHAPTER THIRTY-TWO

One month later

Vanessa arrived at Carmella's Restaurant before Kyle or Brandon. She'd dropped Emma off with her mother in Stonington, then driven back to Carmella's for the first get-together with Brandon in a month. He'd been so busy with his new job that this was the first chance they'd all had to get together as planned for a monthly dinner. Vanessa had been busy as well, moving out of the house in New York and in with Kyle.

She and Vincent had sat down, without lawyers, to discuss custody arrangements. With May's input and in the interest of getting the divorce over with quickly, it was decided that Vanessa and Vincent would have joint custody of both children, though May would stay with her boyfriend Warren on weekdays to attend school in the fall and finish her senior year, and she would stay with each parent on weekends and holidays. Emma would stay with Vanessa, with bi-weekly visits to New York City. The divorce was in a waiting period, not yet finalized, but Vanessa hoped it would all be over soon. In her mind, the marriage had really been over years ago.

She'd been to the doctor and her pregnancy was going well. Because it was Kyle's first time with fatherhood, she couldn't wait for his reaction when he heard the heartbeat for the first time or when he saw a clear ultrasound. The doctor had taken one ultrasound picture, but Vanessa was still so early into the pregnancy that the baby only appeared as a grayish ball inside a black oval. Still, Kyle looked at the picture constantly.

Vanessa had no doubt that he'd be a great father. Right away, he'd bonded with Emma. The first day they moved in, Kyle proclaimed it "Emma Day," and had taken Emma anywhere she wanted to go — the duck pond by his apartment, out for ice cream, then back home to watch television, Emma's favorite pastime. He'd decorated her new room in Disney Princess decor, similar to her old bedroom but a little overdone on the pink. At night, he would stand in the doorway while Vanessa tucked Emma into bed, then he'd wave goodnight to Emma. He was not trying to stand in for Vincent, though Vanessa thought that already he was doing a better job.

Vanessa sat down at the back table at Carmella's, opened the menu, and ordered a pitcher of lemon water for when Kyle and Brandon arrived. Kyle was doing well with not drinking, though he'd had one difficult night when he felt overwhelmed by all the positive changes in his life. Vanessa had sat him down and talked about him going for help, something a little more geared toward his specific problem than the church group he was currently attending. She also wanted him in some kind of therapy, but so far, he'd refused.

"Hey," Kyle said from behind her. He kissed her cheek and sat down. "Brandon's not here yet?"

"No." She shook her head. "But every time I think about telling him about the baby, I get all wound up in nerves." They'd decided they would tell him tonight, even though they thought it best to wait until the first trimester was over before telling people. It was just too hard to keep it a secret, especially from their best friend. "What do you have there?" she asked, pointing to a yellow plastic bag he was holding by the handles.

"Just some things I have to show you and Brandon. I wanted to wait until the three of us were together." He set the bag down on the chair beside him.

A few minutes later Brandon walked in, looking rushed. He shook his bangs back and pulled out a chair.

"I am so sorry," he said. "This job is taking all my time, and Logan had a soccer thing, Andrew has some summer program—"

"It's okay," Vanessa said, cutting him off. "We all knew it would be difficult to meet up. The important thing is that you made it."

He settled in and they ordered Carmella's Famous Bruschetta Plate, then talked a bit about where they were now. Vanessa explained how the divorce was nearly finalized and that Emma was functioning well in her new environment. May, out of school for the summer, was currently bouncing back and forth between Kyle's apartment and Vincent's apartment, while spending some nights at Warren's house, trying to get settled there.

"So you're doing okay with not having May around?" Brandon asked, sipping some water. "The transition has been little by little, right?"

"It still hurts when I lie down at night and she's not right near me," she replied. "Sometimes I almost break down, but Kyle is right there to cheer me up."

"Are you and Kyle...you know, sleeping in the same bed?" The waitress set down the bruschetta plate and walked away. "Was that confusing for Emma?"

"Vanessa stayed out in the living room for about a week," Kyle replied. "Then we kind of explained to Emma that we were...." He looked at Vanessa and smiled. "Liking each other enough to share a bed."

Vanessa reached out and grabbed Kyle's hand. She rested

their joined hands on the table top. Now seemed like a good time to tell Brandon they were expecting.

"We have to tell you our good news," she said.

"You're getting married." Brandon crunched into a piece of bruschetta, smiling as olive oil dripped off the charred bread.

"Eventually," Kyle said. "Vanessa just doesn't want to take a second trip down the aisle with a fat stomach, so we're waiting until next year, probably June."

"Nice way to tell him," Vanessa said, and shook her head.

Brandon's eyes widened. "Get out," he said. "You're pregnant?"

"Almost two months," she confirmed. "And God help us, there will be a little Kyle running around in the world."

"Ha!" Brandon said. He stood and reached across the table to shake Kyle's hand, then leaned forward to hug Vanessa. "Unbelievable news," he said in her ear. "So happy for my old friends."

After that they finished appetizers, still catching up over the last month. Brandon's job was going well, though he hated the commute. The architecture firm he was working for had some solid clients, and though they'd struggled a bit with the down economy as Brandon's business had, they still had enough jobs to secure Brandon's future paychecks. Jean had taken a job as teacher's aide in the fall with the hopes of advancing into full placement as a teacher. Their budget was tight, but with the extra money Kyle had loaned them, they would probably be secure in the house until Jean got a full and permanent teaching position.

As their entrees arrived, Kyle began to fidget. Vanessa was used to this and placed her hand on his knee. She wasn't sure what was bothering him, but the technique had worked before, so she let her hand stay there until he stopped moving his leg. He started on his chicken, but was only a few bites in when he rested his fork against his plate and drummed his fingers on the tabletop.

"What's wrong?" she whispered.

"I have to do something now," he said. "I can't sit here any longer without doing it."

Brandon glanced up from his plate of baked ziti. "What's the matter?"

Kyle reached over to the yellow bag on the seat beside him. "Let me ask you something," he said, addressing both of them. "If you could change the outcome of that night we tried to dig up the Tupperware bowl, and make it so the bowl was really there with all our stuff still in it, would you change it? Or would you leave it just as it is now?"

Vanessa looked to Brandon.

"Another one of his crazy questions," Brandon said.

"Just answer it," Kyle returned.

Vanessa thought about it. If they had retrieved their things that night at the pond, she would have probably separated from Kyle and Brandon again. She would have stayed in touch, because at that point they were obviously close again, but it wouldn't be as it was now. She wouldn't be carrying Kyle's baby, and the most in love she'd ever been in her life.

"It wouldn't have mattered," Brandon said. "So no, I wouldn't change it. I would leave it just as it is now."

"Even though that meant not getting your watch back?"

Brandon nodded. Kyle turned to Vanessa.

"What do you think?" she said.

Kyle smiled. He started to fidget again, so much that Vanessa had to look around to make sure nobody was watching him and thought he was having a fit or something. Slowly, he pulled open the bag and stuck his hand in. He reached out to Brandon, holding something shiny.

285

"Look familiar?" he said.

Vanessa gasped as Kyle handed a gold watch to Brandon. It was obviously an expensive watch, one with diamonds on the face that looked like a duplicate of the one Brandon had buried at the pond so many years ago.

"Kyle," Brandon said. "You didn't have to buy me a new —"

"Flip it over."

Brandon inspected the watch. He flipped it over and drew back in the chair. "Holy shit," he said and Kyle laughed. "It's not…it can't be."

"It's the one," Kyle confirmed. "And remarkably it doesn't even have a scratch."

Vanessa turned to him, shocked. "How —?"

But before she could get anything out, Kyle reached into the bag and pulled out a small magenta book.

"This is impossible," she whispered. "You had these things all along?"

"Sort of," Kyle replied, and forced the diary into her shaky hand. "My mother actually had them; I just didn't know."

As Vanessa sat in a foggy state of shock, Kyle told them some crazy story of his mother at church, something about a bake sale, and something about Mr. McHardy digging up the Tupperware bowl for Kyle's mother.

Vanessa held her diary to her chest. She closed her eyes, not able to inspect it just yet. A piece of her childhood had found its way back to her, even when she thought it was gone forever. It was a strange feeling, like holding onto a ghost.

"Did you know that our song was 'I Died in Your Arms'?" Kyle asked.

"'I Just Died in Your Arms'," she corrected. "You read this?"

"No, no." He waved his hands. "The song is written on the back cover, around our names."

Pulling the diary forward, Vanessa saw, in her own slanted handwriting, the words:

Vanessa + Kyle 4-21-87 to Forever.

Beneath that was the song title, "I Just Died in Your Arms," and that was all the proof she needed that in her hands was her beloved diary. Quickly she opened to the first page and followed the words down, only half-reading them in her haste. It was something about school that day, wearing an orange dress with a black belt and feeling way too Halloween-ish, and then it went into a rant about Kyle and how mad she was that he was supposed to come over that past weekend but went to the Oyster Festival instead. She couldn't help but laugh.

"I can't wait to read this," she said, and leaned to hug him.

"The pages are a little yellowed," Kyle said when they broke apart. "And it smells like my mother's closet. But just like Brandon's watch, it stood the test of time pretty well." He knocked his hand against the back of the diary. "I told you guys our stuff was still out there somewhere."

"Wait a second," Brandon said. He was still gazing down at his watch like he couldn't believe he was holding it, but his head shot up to address Kyle. "Did you get your cross back?"

"Oh my God," Vanessa said. "Yes! Kyle, did you get your cross back?"

Kyle stuck his closed hand into the center of the table. Slowly, he opened his palm. There was his little silver cross, shining under the overhead lights of Carmella's. Somehow, this little cross struck Vanessa as so much more important than her diary or Brandon's watch. Somehow, the little cross seemed like the catalyst, the tiny but crucial item that had in so many ways completely changed her life and the lives of her two closest friends. In a way, she supposed the cross really was magic.

"You didn't need it," Brandon told Kyle. "I told you that you didn't."

"I don't think my father needed it either," he said, and closed his fingers over the cross. "With all the years of drinking and the stress he was under, I think he would have passed even if he had the cross. And even if that wasn't the case, that's how I'm going to look at it now."

Vanessa wrapped her arm around his shoulder.

"He's okay," Brandon said.

Kyle nodded. "I'm okay," he said.

After that they all went back to their items. Brandon ran his finger along the inscription on his watch, and Vanessa flipped the pages of her diary until she landed on the page with little hearts, each one enclosing Kyle's attributes. FUNNY, one of the hearts said. SMART, another one said. CUTE, said another. She looked up at him and smiled. Twenty-three years later, he was still funny, smart, and cute.

"So," Brandon said, placing the watch beside his dish of ziti. "I guess it's safe to assume that with living together and a baby on the way, that's the end of the Kyle and Vanessa on-again, off-again relationship?"

Vanessa set her diary down on the table. "I think we're where we are supposed to be, where we were meant to be in the end," she said. "It took us a while to get here, but that's the end of it, yes."

She placed her hand on the diary, and Kyle's hand fell on top of hers, squeezing in agreement.

EPILOGUE

Kyle knelt in front of his father's grave. It was a golden autumn afternoon, the air crisp, the wind blowing curly dead leaves around the bases of tombstones. He turned his face toward the sun, let the warmth sink into his cheeks, and thought about his father. He thought about heaven and God, then felt the assurance of a reply to his open questions: Was his father up there watching? Did his father know he had a grandson on the way? Did his father forgive him for not giving him the cross when he'd asked for it? The answer to each of those questions was a resounding yes. Kyle felt it in his heart, felt it as though the cemetery was shaking just beneath him with the strength of the answer.

Using a gardener's shovel, he dug a small hole just in front of his father's headstone. When the hole was deep enough, he reached into the pocket of his jeans and extracted the little silver cross. He knelt down again, pressed the cross between his palms, and whispered a few words to his father: an apology for burying the cross when he was sixteen, a thank you for being a great father over the years, and a congratulations for becoming a new grandfather. He knew when the time came, his father would be watching down when Vanessa gave birth. He knew he would see it all.

He placed the cross into the hole, tucked the dirt in around it,

289

and dragged the little mound of dirt over to cover it. He patted it all down, kissed his palm, and rested it on the ground, just above his father. With a sense of restored balance and peace, Kyle stood and left the graveyard.

That evening, Kyle watched from the doorway as Vanessa tucked Emma into bed. They had a nightly routine, one he had comfortably fit into, and one he truly loved being a part of. Vanessa would call Emma a cuckoo bird, Emma would cluck, and he would smile when Vanessa turned back to look at him. Then she would kiss Emma, and he would wave from the doorway and turn off the light. He fit so well into the routine, it was almost like he'd always been a part of it.

"Where do you want to start?" Vanessa whispered, closing the door of Emma's little room.

"I don't want you lifting anything heavy," he replied. "So you can sit down in the living room and wrap up the glasses and stuff while I pull everything out of the cabinets."

"I can't believe I have to pack up and move again," Vanessa said, and stomped to the living room.

They'd bought a small house, only a few streets over from Kyle's apartment so he would still be close to work. Vanessa had fallen in love with the house the moment she saw it, stating — though Kyle had to really use his imagination to see it — that the house resembled the little white cape beside Blueberry Pond. There were three bedrooms, the perfect size for their family, and the finished basement was big enough to put a bed down there for when May came to visit.

Vanessa was working from home, writing a fashion blog as well as some fashion articles here and there. This arrangement worked well for Kyle. He just kissed her goodbye in the morning, then went off to work. His routine hadn't changed, it only had the added bonus of a family waiting for him back at the apartment

290

each day.

It wasn't long before Vanessa grew tired of packing. They headed to bed, and he folded her up in his arms, hoping she wasn't too tired for their private nightly ritual of Vanessa reading him exactly one page from her magenta diary before closing it up and hiding it back in her nightstand.

"We were on a good part," he said, prodding. "You didn't want to go on some camping trip because you'd be away from me for a week, and you were fighting with your mother about it."

"I hadn't even remembered that," she said, and laughed. "But I know I did end up going on the trip."

"So let's see what happened while you were away from me for that week."

She pulled the diary out of her nightstand, rested it open on her lap, and began to read. Kyle listened with rapt attention, as he did each night. She often paused as she read, and Kyle was sure she was skipping over something private, even now, after all these years. He also knew that tonight, when she fell asleep, he would sneak out of bed to read what she had skipped. He'd done this every night since she started reading him the diary.

But of course tonight, like every other night, he would go back to bed without reading the diary, leaving it safe and secure in her nightstand.

THE END

BOOK CLUB/READER QUESTIONS

What item from your teen years would you have put in the Tupperware bowl? Why might you have needed that item later in life?

Throughout the story, Jean looks the other way or tries to understand Brandon's "secret." Would you have been patient with a spouse or partner in the same situation?

Was Jean right or wrong in wanting to keep the house? Was she merely protecting what she loved or was she materialistic?

What drove Kyle to never give up on the Tupperware bowl? Was he "psychic" or just determined? Did his quest to find the bowl and his friendship with Brandon and Vanessa save him from alcoholism and possibly suicide? How did his faith help guide him and the story?

Did Kyle really kill his father by not giving him the silver cross? Was the cross magic?

Did Brandon's fear of being poor stem from his wealthy upbringing? How had his feelings changed by the end of the story? How did his friendship with Kyle influence that change?

Was May a normal teenager or was she troubled? How must she have felt while going through her parents' divorce and taking care of her sister?

Vanessa sees Vincent as the bad guy, but was Vincent as bad as she thought? Were both to blame for the failed marriage?

At the root of the story is a childhood friendship. Do you have any friendships from childhood that remind you of Kyle, Vanessa, and Brandon's friendship? Do you think you could bring those old friendships back to life? Why or why not?

Would you have kept some of the secrets in your diary still hidden, over twenty years after you'd written them? What might some of Vanessa's secrets have been? What secrets would you never reveal?

Did it really matter if the three had found the Tupperware bowl or not?

Over the course of the story, Kyle and Vanessa struggle with their romance. Do you feel they ended up where they were supposed to in the end? Do you feel they would have stayed together if they had married young? How would all of their lives be different if Kyle and Vanessa had never split up in senior year of high school?

ABOUT THE AUTHOR

Carla Trueheart is a New England-based writer who holds certificates in poetry, romance writing, copyediting, forensic science writing, historical fiction writing, and writing for young adults. She has studied writing at Gotham Writers' Workshop and The Writers Studio and is currently working toward completion of her BA in Creative Writing and English through Southern New Hampshire University. She has worked as submissions editor for various online publications, and her poetry and short stories have been featured in *The Litchfield Literary Review*. Her first novel, *The Ritual of the Four*, was a finalist in the 2016 International Book Awards.

Carla currently works as a novelist with World Castle Publishing and as a professional book reviewer. In her spare time, she enjoys cooking, listening to music, reading, and collecting candles. You can contact her through her website: www.carlatrueheart.com. She loves connecting with her readers!